# Ben Palmer? It couldn't be.

In complete disbelief, she saw him coming toward her, picking up speed as the tree she was hoisting began to fall. Six feet and a couple of inches of darkly gorgeous but self-righteous, self-satisfied male who despised and distrusted her... What was he doing here? As though her life wasn't already fraught with more problems than she could deal with. He—

She lost her balance completely as he tried but failed to help.

"Corie?" he asked.

She wanted to say something clever, sound flippant, as though it didn't matter that he was the man she hated and he considered her an incorrigible criminal. "No, I'm the Druid that came with the tree. Of *course*, it's me."

She felt his sigh against her forehead. "I know it's you. I want to know if you're okay."

"No, I'm not okay. I have twelve feet of tree on me and six feet of hateful man."

Dear Reader,

I love November. It's a time for giving thanks, a preparation for the holiday season, a time for family. And that's what Manning Family Reunion is all about. Jack, from *In My Dreams*, is determined to put his family back together after most of a lifetime of separation.

*To Love and Protect* is Corie's story. She was four years old when the Manning kids were separated, and her life took a much different path from Jack's. She's small in stature but big in courage and resourcefulness—with an interesting tendency toward flaunting the rules when necessary.

Ben, Jack's adopted brother, is all heart. But as a police officer, he has great respect for the rules and serious concerns about Jack's devotion to his newly discovered sister. Particularly when she presents a threat to their family, and Jack is away on his honeymoon. It's Ben to the rescue—or is it?

Happy holiday season!

*Muriel*

# HEARTWARMING

## *To Love and Protect*

---

*Muriel Jensen*

**H HARLEQUIN**® HEARTWARMING™

Recycling programs
for this product may
not exist in your area.

ISBN-13: 978-0-373-36749-8

To Love and Protect

Printed in U.S.A.

**Muriel Jensen** lives with her husband, Ron, in a simple old Victorian looking down on the Columbia River in Astoria, Oregon. They share the space with a loudmouthed husky mix and two eccentric tabbies. They have three children, eight grandchildren and five great-grandchildren. Their neighborhood is charmed, populated with the kindest and most fun-to-be-around people.

### Select Books by Muriel Jensen

### Harlequin Heartwarming

*Always Florence*
*In My Dreams*

### Harlequin Superromance

*All Summer Long*
"Home, Hearth and Hayley"
*Man with a Mission*
*Man with a Message*
*Man with a Miracle*
*Man in a Million*
*The Man She Married*
*The Man under the Mistletoe*

### Harlequin American Romance

*Daddy to Be Determined*
*Jackpot Baby*
*That Summer in Maine*
*His Baby*
*His Wife*
*His Family*
*His Wedding*

Visit the Author Profile page
at Harlequin.com for more titles.

In loving memory of Wayne McVey, who was a wonderful friend to Ron and me, who loved Starbucks, and onion rings, casinos and dinner at Dooger's. And to Diane McVey, who soldiers on without him. Love you both!

# CHAPTER ONE

"I'M GOING TO wring her pretty ballerina neck," Ben Palmer told himself as he drove from the airport in McAllen, Texas, to Querida, where his quarry lived. He studied the side of the road for the break in the dry brush he remembered from a couple of weeks ago when he and his brother, Jack, had been here together in search of Jack's sister. He was glad Elizabeth Corazon Manning Ochoa wasn't *his* sister—the little thief! As if her full name wasn't enough to deal with, her given name was the Spanish word for *heart*. It should have been whatever the Spanish word was for *trouble*. "There it is."

He turned right onto the narrow, bumpy lane, watching for the Rio Road sign. High weeds lined the path that led to the impoverished little two-block-long downtown. The side with city hall, the post office and the library, all built in traditional Spanish style with arches and red-tiled roofs, looked tidy and well-kept in contrast to the stores and services opposite them and the run-down bed-and-breakfast at the very end. Fall flowers lined the street on the city hall side but the commercial businesses looked as though they struggled to stay alive.

He slowed as he passed the Grill, the café where Corie waitressed. It was the only structure on the block that looked even mildly prosperous. He noticed that her black Ford truck was not in the parking lot. She must have the day off.

Remembering the directions to her home from the last visit, he turned onto Hidalgo Road just beyond downtown.

Two minutes later he pulled the SUV to a stop across from the little house she rented and saw immediately that her truck wasn't there, either. Maybe she was at Teresa McGinnis's foster home.

He drove to the property and pulled up to the chain-link fence. A crowd of children played in the front yard. Behind them stood the large hacienda-style home, its faded pink stone a picture of Old West glory.

He knew Corie spent much of her free time helping Teresa, who'd brought her here when she was twelve. He could see the backyard where Corie usually parked but the only vehicle there today was Teresa's old dark blue Safari van. He hoped she knew where Corie was.

He parked then took a moment to stretch after climbing out of his rental car. The temperature was in the low seventies in this eastern reach of the Rio Grande Valley and he soaked up the sunshine while his usually active muscles protested the long confinement on the plane. When he'd left Oregon this morning it had been thirty-seven degrees. He told himself to relax but he was wound tighter than a spool of cable.

He pushed open the gate and walked up to the house, ignored by all the children but two boys he guessed to be about nine and ten. The younger one was short, sturdily built and appeared to be Hispanic, while the older, taller boy had shaggy, carrot-red hair and blue eyes. He was scrawny but smiling. The boys flanked Ben as he strode up the walk to the house.

"Who are you?" the older boy asked as he ran alongside Ben to keep up. He offered his hand. "I'm Soren."

Ben stopped to shake hands. "Hi, Soren. I'm Ben."

Soren indicated his friend. "This is Carlos."

The boy shook Ben's hand but didn't smile. He pointed to three little boys playing with a tether ball. "Those are my brothers."

"Hi, Carlos. Good to meet you." Ben started toward the house. "Excuse me, guys. I came to see Teresa."

Both boys stopped. Soren's smile faded. "Are you from Corpus Christi?"

Ben stopped, too. "No. I'm from Oregon. Why? Are you expecting someone from Corpus Christi?" Cyrus Tyree of Corpus Christi, Teresa's landlord, was part of the reason Ben was here.

"No, but somebody came from there and he made Teresa cry," Soren said. He and Carlos exchanged an angry look. "We're going to have to go."

"Go?"

"Live somewhere else. We don't want to. We want to stay right here."

Suddenly they were surrounded by the other kids, girls and boys who looked younger than Soren and Carlos. One little girl held a large purse over her arm. Ben guessed they'd overheard the conversation about leaving. They ran along with Ben and his two new friends as they climbed the step to the broken-down veranda. He wished the kids would go back to their play. He liked kids as a rule. Many of his friends had them and he found them amazing. But this trip was about saving Jack's sister, himself, Jack and his new bride from jail. He didn't have time for the distraction of soulful eyes and needy little faces.

"Do we have to go *now*?" a little boy asked. He stood with the group of three Carlos had identified as his brothers. They looked remarkably alike.

Before Ben could reply, a pudgy little girl about eight in glossy black braids said authoritatively, "I think it's against the law to make us go. Families get to stay together."

"Oh, yeah?" Soren turned on her. "Where's *your* dad?"

The little girl folded her arms, the question apparently compromising her confidence. She answered more quietly, "He's coming to get me."

"When, Rosie? You've been here six months. Families don't always get to stay together."

One of the little boys said, "Maybe he died. Our mom died."

"He's not dead!" Rosie's voice cracked, her eyes a heartbreaking mixture of anger and sorrow. "He's coming for me."

Ben stood in the middle of the turbulent

little group. He stretched both arms out, prepared to explain that he needed time to talk to Teresa. But the children crowded around him as though his open arms offered shelter. He was speechless for an instant.

"Ah, well…when families don't get to stay together," he heard himself say, "you can sometimes make your own family with friends. That happened to my brother, Jack. His mom had to go away for a long time, so he came to live with my parents and me. He's part of our family now."

"That's being adopted," Rosie said knowledgeably. "But my dad's coming to get me, so I don't want to get another family. I want to stay with Teresa until he comes."

"The man said Teresa can't stay here." Carlos's voice was gentle. If Soren was the leader of this group, Carlos was its chaplain. "We…"

The front door opened and Teresa stood there, a plump toddler in her arms. Roberto, Ben remembered, seemed permanently attached to her. As he had the last time Ben was here, the baby reached for him.

"Hey. You remember me." He laughed and took the little guy from Teresa, flattered and distracted by his wide smile and eager reach.

"We're staying right here for now," Teresa

told the children firmly. "And I don't want anyone talking about going away until we know what's going to happen." She focused on one child, then the next, until she'd looked into each of their faces with the determination in hers. It was a matter of presence. As a cop, Ben knew all about that. You had to believe you were invincible so that whoever you were trying to convince believed it, too. She was good.

The kids looked at each other with clear suspicion, but they didn't seem quite as worried anymore. Soren and Carlos, older and possibly more experienced in such situations, simply walked away, more in the spirit of doing as she asked rather than believing what she said.

Teresa refocused on Ben. She was average in height, in her forties, had short, rough-cut dark hair, wore little makeup and was blessed with good bone structure. The strong, caring woman inside showed through in her dark eyes and her warm smile, making her attractive.

"Ben," she said, offering her free hand. "How are you? Corie tells me Jack got married and you and she stood up for him and his bride when you took her back with you for Thanksgiving."

"He did." Ben smiled at the memory of that morning while Roberto chewed on the collar of his shirt. "He was so happy that Corie was there. I don't know if anyone else will ever understand how he's longed to put his family back together."

Teresa nodded. "I think I do. I deal with broken families on a daily basis. Would you like to come inside? You look angry under that smile and that worries me. Your being here has to have something to do with Corie."

"Thank you. It does. Do you know where she is?" He didn't want to bring up what he thought Corie had done. He was pretty sure Teresa didn't know Corie had stolen Delia Tyree's jewelry in the first place, much less sabotaged the return of the jewelry he and Jack had orchestrated. "Her truck isn't at the restaurant or her home."

"She went to get a tree," Teresa said.

"A tree?"

"A Christmas tree."

He frowned. "It's still November."

"It's November 28 and this is a house filled with children. They've talked of nothing but Christmas since Halloween." She laughed at his confusion then turned her head toward the back of the house and the sound of an engine.

"There she is now, Ben. What did you want to see her about?"

"I just want to talk to her." He followed Teresa through the house to the kitchen and the back door.

She stopped there and smiled inquisitively as she reclaimed the toddler. "Something that couldn't be done by phone? Or email?"

The real answer to that was complicated, so he took the simple approach. "Yes," he said.

"Okay. Well, if we can clear a path through the children, and you help us unload the tree, we'll find a quiet place for you to talk."

Every child who'd been playing in the front yard was now part of a shouting, excited crowd gathered at the back of Corie's truck. From where Ben stood, it looked as though Jack's sister had brought back a sequoia. Part of the tree stuck out past the lowered tailgate, a red flag attached, and the main body, branches swept upward, spilled over the sides. The children squealed in excitement.

Wondering how Corie intended to get the giant thing out, he started around Teresa to lend a hand. The tree had been loaded top-first onto a tarp, he noticed, so that its weight would be coming right at her. Corie made a broad gesture with both arms and shouted orders he couldn't hear over the din of the children's voices. They all backed out of the way.

She pushed up the long sleeves of her plain blue T-shirt and stood still for a moment, studying the tree. It occurred to him later that he should have acted then, but he was momentarily paralyzed by the sight of her small, shapely body and what seemed like a foot and a half of glossy black hair shifting sinuously, seductively, over her shoulder, thin bangs above a dark, thoughtful stare. Then she firmed her expressive mouth and reached for the tree.

She pulled hard and the tree slid toward her. As he hurried forward, hoping he wasn't going to have to explain to Jack why he'd allowed his long-lost little sister to be crushed by a Christmas tree, he saw that Corie was using the tarp to move the tree. He gave her points for smarts, but strode toward her as she leaned it against the tailgate, suspecting she was still in danger. Was she really going to try to lift it?

Of course, she was. She leaned into the tree, wrapped her arms around it about a third of the way up from the bottom and pulled.

He shouted her name and picked up his pace. As she tried to hold the tree upright, presumably so the children could see it better, she turned toward the sound of his voice. Both her arms were lost in the tree, which was much more than twice her height. Her eyes and mouth widened in complete surprise when she saw him.

She lost control of the tree.

AT THE SOUND of that male voice, Corie Ochoa's hard-to-muster Christmas spirit seized and cramped. Ben Palmer? It couldn't be.

In complete disbelief, she saw him coming toward her, picking up speed, six feet and a couple of inches of darkly gorgeous but self-righteous, self-satisfied male who disliked and distrusted her. What was he doing here? He...

And then she remembered she was holding a tree. A big one. She felt the weight of it push against her as that momentary distraction caused her to lose her grip. The weight of the tipping tree drove her backward and she struggled futilely to disentangle her arms.

She heard the children screaming as she and the tree went down. Just before she hit the grass, a steely grip on her arm yanked her sideways, pulling her body away from the trunk and probably her arm out of its socket. A branch thwacked her in the face.

*Dislocated arm beats crushed sternum*, she thought as she landed on her back on the lawn, buried beneath twelve feet of Leyland Spruce. And something else. Curiously the branches weren't crushing her as much as she'd expected. Then she realized she was not alone in her bowery tomb. Ben Palmer was lying on top of her.

"Great," she said, pushing on him. "You're just what I need right now. Who sent you? The Grinch? The Ghost of Christmas Past?"

He didn't reply.

She pushed again but the tree was heavy and so was he. "Ben! Would you please move?" she demanded. She wasn't sure how he'd accomplish that, but she *was* sure he was as uncomfortable being body to body with her as she was with him.

He groaned.

"Ben?" she asked worriedly, then said his name louder when his reply was another groan. "Are you hurt?"

"Corie?" Teresa lay on her stomach, looking at Corie through the lacy pattern of needles and branches. "Are you all right? You got smacked by a branch and I think the trunk might have hit Ben hard."

"I'm okay. I just can't move," Corie replied. "Call 9-1-1."

"No." The single word came firmly if a little quietly from Ben, followed by a small gasp of pain. "No. Just...give me a minute."

Relieved to hear his voice, though the words he spoke usually annoyed her, she said, "I don't have a minute, Ben. You weigh a ton. I think my stomach is coming out my ears."

"I believe that's physically impossible. But there seems to be a lot coming out of your mouth."

There. Annoying. "Hey!" she complained.

"Relax. Maybe we can roll out of here." He sighed and wrapped his arms around her. "You're sure you're okay?"

"Apart from the fact that I have twelve feet of tree on me and six feet of hateful man?"

He muttered something unintelligible then it felt as though he tried to boost himself off her and couldn't. He tried again. No luck. It alarmed her that she was very aware of every muscle in his body pressed into every soft surface of hers.

"Don't panic," he said. "I can't lift up, so we're going sideways. Okay?"

"Please hurry. Before we start growing moss."

"Keep your hands tucked in," he said sharply.

He cupped the back of her head in one of his hands, tucked her face into the hollow of his shoulder and, with a leg wrapped around hers, rolled them sideways.

Teresa and the older children pulled on them. Sweaty little hands grabbed her arm. Ben pushed her away from him. Suddenly she was on her knees, the sun on her face.

She reached toward Ben, who lay on his back, his chest moving comfortingly up and down, a broken branch of the tree still covering him. Corie dragged it away and she and Teresa pulled him clear.

Teresa put her hands to Ben's face and looked him over feature by feature. "Oh, Ben. Can you see? Does your head hurt?"

His thick, blunt eyelashes rose up then down. "I'm fine." He rolled over and stood carefully. When he straightened, he wobbled.

Corie put his arm around her shoulders and wrapped hers around his waist. "Easy. Don't fall," she pleaded, "or we'll never get you up."

"We could put him in the wheelbarrow," Soren suggested helpfully, hovering around them. "Want me to get it?"

Ben smiled and Corie heard a low laugh escape him. "No, thanks. I can make it."

With Teresa on his other side, they started

for the house. "Just go slowly," she instructed as though he were one of the children. "Let us share your weight. Boys, run and open the door and make sure the couch is clear."

Let them share his weight. He felt like Gulliver being led away by the Lilliputians.

Ben let them lead him to the sofa but refused to lie down. As soon as he was seated Teresa headed for the kitchen. Ben ran a hand over his face to clear blurry eyes and looked up at Corie. "You're sure you're okay? There's a bruise near your cheekbone."

"I just carried you across the yard, didn't I?"

He saw a hint of humor in her expression. He couldn't stop an answering smile—until he remembered why he was here. But before he could raise the subject, Teresa returned with two wet washcloths. She placed one unceremoniously on his upturned face and the other she put against Corie's cheek.

"That bruise might be from Ben's shoulder," she said, "when he went down on top of you. I'm sure the trunk missed you, but you got a branch in the face. I think you're okay but... Ben? Are *you*? The trunk smacked right into you."

"Yeah." He held the cold cloth to his face one more minute then took it down. His back prickled and he shifted uncomfortably. "Apart from having needles down my shirt."

"I'll get you another shirt and wash that one for you. How're you doing, Corie? Want a glass of water? A cup of tea?"

"I'm fine, thanks."

Nine little bodies crowded around them as Teresa left the room again. Rosie held Roberto.

"Everything's okay," Corie told them. "I'm fine. Ben's fine. You can go play."

Carlos frowned and pointed outside. "But the tree."

"We might have to leave hauling it in until tomorrow. I have to go to work pretty soon. We'll get it up, don't worry."

Ben thought they looked more disappointed than worried.

"Why don't you go keep an eye on it," he told the children. "I'm coming out in a minute and I'd like you to help me bring it into the house. Does anybody know where the Christmas tree stand is?"

"I do." Soren took off, Carlos and the other children right behind him.

The moment they were out of earshot, Corie sat beside him. "We'll take care of the tree. Why are you here, anyway?" she asked sharply.

With a quick glance around to make sure no one had lingered, he replied quietly, "I want to talk to you about the jewelry you stole from Tyree. But I'd rather do it in private."

She made a sound of disgust and stood. To think she'd saved his life. Well, actually, he'd gotten into trouble trying to save hers. Still— same old Ben. Suspicious. Judgmental. "Yeah, well, I don't want to talk about it at all."

"You don't have a choice."

"Everyone has a choice. You know what happened. You were there." It was such an injustice that Jack had come in search of her after all those years on the very day she'd chosen to break into Cyrus Tyree's house and steal the jewelry that could secure the future of Teresa's foster home.

He stood beside her, a good head taller than she was. She looked right into his face so he wouldn't think he could intimidate her with his size.

"I was, but something seems to have changed along the way," he said. "I put the jewelry into a priority-mail box and sent it to Tyree. But, according to the news report on national television, what was delivered was not what I sent. Mrs. Tyree held up a handful of Mardi Gras beads for the camera. Not the diamonds, emeralds and gold that you stole and that I packed up and mailed back." He folded his arms, biceps rounded under the thin cotton of his shirt. "How'd you do that?"

She felt such dislike for him at that moment she didn't trust herself to remain in his presence. She started to walk away but he made the mistake of stopping her again.

BEN DODGED FISTS, fingernails, even feet as he caught her to him when she rounded on him like a cornered coyote.

"What about the security footage Tyree claims to have from that night?" He grabbed a flailing fist. "I'm guessing it's just a matter of time before someone recognizes you then— by extension—Jack and Sarah and me." He freed her hand and turned her so that her back was against him. He asked angrily in her ear, "You want to talk about *that*? Your war-hero brother's reputation ruined because he tried to help his thieving little sister? Not to mention Sarah's reputation and mine."

And that was how Teresa found them; Corie flailing in his arms, her legs bicycling the air a foot off the floor.

Her expression changed as she approached them, a red sweatshirt in her hand. The warm, sweet-natured woman was now the wild coyote pup's mother.

"Put her down," she said.

He did.

To his complete surprise Corie explained. "I started it." She combed her fingers through her tangled hair and spared him a quick, dark glance. "We'll put the tree in the stand, then I have to get to work and he's going back to Oregon."

"I'm not going back to Oregon," he corrected.

"Don't you have a job? Aren't you Beggar's Bay's most vigilant and disagreeable cop?"

He smiled blandly at her. "I am, but I'm on leave. Built-up vacation time."

Teresa looked from one to the other, her expression grave. "What is this about?"

Unwilling to rat out Corie, Ben said nothing.

Corie waved both hands in a gesture that suggested it was difficult to explain. "It's nothing for you to worry about."

Teresa clearly didn't believe her but finally handed Ben the shirt and said wryly, "That's good, because I'm overextended on worry at the moment. Give me your shirt, Ben, and I'll throw it in the wash. This one was Soren's dad's."

Ben yanked his shirt off. The sleeve's hem caught on his watch and Teresa reached up to help him then winced at something on his back.

Corie, looking away from a formidable six-pack of abs, walked around him to see what had caused such a reaction. A large bruise, already livid, ran from the middle of his back at an angle across his left shoulder.

Teresa touched it gingerly. "You pulled Corie away from the trunk, but it must have glanced off you. Does it hurt?"

He flexed the shoulder and hesitated just an instant. "Not much."

She came around him to offer help with the sweatshirt then gasped again at the still livid scar Corie hadn't noticed since she'd been trying hard not to look at his bare chest. It was on his left shoulder, an inch long and bright red.

He pulled on the sweatshirt. "I got shot," he said when his head reappeared. "I'm fine. The bullet hit muscle. I had surgery. No big deal."

Still angry, Corie had to admit that it was a desecration of such a perfect torso. She remembered what it had been like to have her body covered by his under the tree. She ignored the heat flushing her cheeks and reminded herself that she hated him despite his perfect chest and shoulders.

Soren and Carlos joined them breathlessly with a rusty stand that was far too small for the tree.

"That'll never do," Teresa said. "Corie, do you have time to go to Wolf's Hardware for a bigger one before you go to work?"

Happy for an excuse to leave, Corie ran out to her truck.

BEN HAD THE most willing team he'd ever worked with. The biggest problem was that most of them were under four and half feet tall and had no sense of self-preservation. Teresa and the kids each grabbed a handful of tarp and helped him pull the tree as far as the back door.

"Okay, drop it," he ordered, turning to see that everyone had complied.

Teresa smiled. "Usually, I have to do this by myself. Of course, I buy a six-foot tree, but this is Corie. She wants this Christmas to be special." She didn't explain, though the strain of the eviction threat showed in her face.

He put himself into the spirit Corie and Teresa were trying to create for the children.

He'd flown out from Oregon to talk to Corie, but that was going to take a little longer than he'd imagined. So, if he had to wait for her, he may as well make himself useful.

He looked for Soren and Carlos. "Can you guys help Teresa clear a path for us inside?"

As the boys were shepherded indoors, he was left with the other seven children. They came closer and stared at him. The small girl in blue-striped shirt and shorts, tiny feet in too big flip-flops, that purse still over her arm, asked, "Are you Santa?"

Two of Carlos's brothers scorned the question. "Santa's fat!"

"He brings presents, not trees."

The youngest boy stuck up for her and pointed at Ben. "He wears a red shirt."

Ah. The loaner shirt had prompted the question.

"I'm Ben," he said. "I'm a...friend of Corie's." Inaccurate but a good way to explain his presence to the children.

"So are we." The little girl smiled that they had something in common. "She said Santa's gonna come to see us. For sure, this time."

Another girl maybe a year older in a similar striped shirt and shorts took a step forward. "He doesn't always come," she said as though it were a tough truth she'd accepted. "Sometimes he doesn't have toys left."

A third girl in the same uniform made a face. "Our mom doesn't have a lot of money. She's working so she can come and get us. Sometimes you have to help Santa pay for stuff."

"You don't have to *buy* presents," Carlos's younger brother Rigo said. "The elves make them."

"They have to buy the stuff to make them *with*."

"No, they don't. It's magic."

"There's no magic," Rosie said in her know-it-all voice. "Santa comes if you're good but not if you're bad."

Ben prayed for Teresa's return, but she was busy. He was it.

"I think Santa loves all kids," he said. "And if you do something wrong, he understands that we all mess up sometimes, and he gives you another chance."

The middle girl in stripes asked hopefully, "You think so?"

"I do," he replied with confidence.

Immersed in his deep discussion with the children, he missed Corie's return and was surprised to find her standing behind Rosie when he glanced up. She held a Christmas tree stand in a very large box. Her midnight eyes looked into his.

"He's right," she said to the children without looking away from him. "Everybody gets another chance."

He heard Teresa say, "Okay. We've cleared a path." Ben was aware of the children climbing over the tree and going inside but he didn't move, still ensnared by Corie's gaze.

"Interesting that you know about the second-chance thing." She spoke under her breath as she passed the stand to Teresa. "And yet you don't apply it."

"That," he said, tearing his gaze away, "is because *I'm* not Santa." He took a large step over the top branches, grabbed the tarp and yanked the tree inside.

# CHAPTER TWO

CORIE WATCHED BEN assemble the outsize Christmas tree stand with all the boys helping. She was impressed that he somehow maintained a sense of humor she hadn't known he had. He fitted the trunk into the stand with the tree still on the ground, then righted it and asked her to help hold it while Teresa gave centering directions.

When it was in place, they all stood back to admire it.

"Wow," Rosie said on a reverent gasp. Even without decoration, it was magnificent.

"Holy s—!" Soren exclaimed.

Teresa frowned at him. "Soren Peterson."

"Sorry." He turned to Ben. "I'll bet *you* swear."

"Sometimes," Ben admitted. "But never at Christmastime. And *never* around little kids."

"Yeah," Rosie said. "Even if Santa gives second chances, you've used yours all up. You won't get *anything*."

Soren glowered at her. "Neither will you, 'cause you're always *mean*." He stalked away. Corie went to follow him, but Teresa caught her arm. "You go to work. I'll talk to him." She turned to Ben. "You'll be back tomorrow to help decorate? We need someone tall for our ladder."

Ben opened his mouth to tell her he was here only to talk to Corie, but the children told him they were going to have hot chocolate and cookies and he *had* to come. The youngest Stripe Sister, as he'd designated them, held his hand.

"Sure," he said. "Thank you."

As Teresa followed Soren, Corie touched Rosie's dark head. "It would be nice if you wouldn't always mention people's bad points, Rosie. Usually they know when they're wrong. Your job as a friend is to tell them they'll do better next time."

Rosie, who seemed to consider herself the world's moral monitor, looked at her as though she were crazy. "But he said a bad word. He does it *all* the time."

"He needs a friend," Corie added. "Try to point out the nice things about him instead of the bad." She gave Rosie a quick hug. "I have to go to work. I'll see you tomorrow." She cast a general wave in the direction of the children and they chorused a goodbye.

Shouldering a large, colorful straw satchel, Corie ran out the door. Ben followed, stopping her when she would have climbed into her truck. She rummaged in her bag and looked up at him impatiently. "What? I'm going to be late."

"I'm here to talk to you," he said firmly, "and I'm not leaving until I do."

She yanked open the driver's-side door and put her bag on the seat for easier access. "So, talk," she said, but he got the distinct impression she wasn't listening. That was confirmed when she dumped out the contents of her bag and growled when whatever she'd been looking for wasn't there. She said the word that had gotten Soren in trouble.

Still ignoring him, she walked around the truck, patting her pockets. Too short to see into the truck bed, she put a foot on a tire and climbed up. Hands braced on the side, she leaned in, scanned front to back then leaped down again.

As she dusted off her hands, she noticed him and seemed surprised he was still there. She looked cross, but then, she usually did with him.

"Lost your keys?" he asked.

"I'm sure I've just misplaced them." She glanced at her watch.

He pulled open the passenger's-side door of his rented Navigator. "Need a ride to work?"

Her chin dropped onto her chest when she accepted that she did. With impressive precision, she swept the contents of her purse off the driver's seat and into her bag, slammed her door closed and walked, arms folded, to where he stood.

"I do," she said, "but I'd rather walk if you're going to badger me the whole way."

"There'd be no badgering required if you just answer my questions."

She considered him a moment then climbed in. "Okay, but I'm almost late for work. I'll answer your questions after." She buckled her seat belt.

"What time is your shift over?"

"We close at nine. Cleanup takes a little while."

"All right."

When he pulled up in front of the café five minutes later she jumped out with a very reluctant, "Thank you." She was about to close the door then stopped and sighed heavily. "If you come just before nine, I'll get your dinner."

He had to pretend not to be surprised. "Thank you. That would be nice."

"Then you're going back to Oregon?"

"Depends on how our conversation goes."

She seemed to want to say more but simply closed the door and hurried inside.

That was a baby step forward, he thought, but it *was* forward.

CORIE PUT HER purse in the small back room that served as the supply storage and employees' lounge, and tied on a white, ruffle-trimmed half apron while her personal history raced across her mind.

She'd been four years old when she and Jack and their younger sister, Cassidy, had been separated. She had only vague memories of her life until that day, impressions of a woman's slurred voice, of eating peanut butter on bread in their bedrooms because there was shouting in the living room. She remembered Jack—dark hair, dark eyes, always there.

Then Roscoe Brauer, her mother's boyfriend, had been shot, and she and Jack and Cassie had spent a couple of nights with Ben's family, the Palmers. When their mother went to jail Cassie had been sent to her father, who lived in Maine, and Corie went to Texas where her father lived.

She remembered the big change her new life had been, her stepmother and two stepsisters, who'd made it clear from the beginning that she wasn't welcome. Missing Jack and two-year-old Cassidy had hurt with a physical pain.

Her father, Miguel Ochoa, had explained that her mother, Charlene Manning, had been a singer in small clubs. She'd gotten caught up with friends who partied with drugs. Jack's father, a drug dealer, died in the crash of a light plane when Jack was three. Miguel had also pushed drugs, but left her mother when even he thought she wasn't sober long enough to be in a relationship. Cassidy's father, a counselor, had tried to help her get her life on track, but that hadn't lasted long either. She had died in jail.

Talk about baggage.

"Who's that?" Polly Benedict asked, peering through the blinds that covered the café's window. She was twenty-two, had a boyfriend who was always off with the rodeo and lamented Corie's lack of a romantic relationship. "He's *gorgeous*!"

Corie walked past her on her way to the

kitchen. She glanced up at the clock and saw that she was two minutes early.

Polly, several inches taller than Corie, fresh-faced and curvaceous, and unfailingly cheerful, stopped her progress and pinched her cheek.

"Look at you! You're smiling. My goodness, how long has it been since I've seen your teeth? Is he responsible for that smile?"

She didn't feel like smiling, but customers hated a moody waitress.

"He's my brother's brother. That's all. He's… visiting for a few days."

Polly frowned over the "brother's brother" explanation. "You've explained that to me before, but it's so weird. How many people have a brother whose brother isn't their brother?"

Corie hooked her arm in Polly's and led her toward the kitchen. "I know, but putting it that way only makes it worse. So, what's going on tonight? What's the special?"

The bell rang. "Order up, Pol," Hector called as they walked into the kitchen. With a parting grin for Corie, Polly detoured to the window to pick up her order.

"Corazon!" Wiping his hands on a kitchen rag, Hector glanced up at the clock. "I thought you were going to be late. You're always ten minutes early. Did I hear you talking about your brother's brother who isn't *your* brother? I thought they lived in Washington."

"Oregon," she corrected. "I promised him dinner if he comes before closing."

Hector was not very tall but his apron covered a generous middle. He was laid-back and kind, unless someone criticized his food or mistreated an employee. He'd given Corie a job based on nothing more than Teresa's recommendation, and Corie would be forever grateful. His restaurant was a favorite hangout for families and young people on a date. People came from around the county.

Hector whisked an egg and cream mixture. "Good. What's he doing here? I mean, since he's not your brother. And you said he didn't like you."

Corie was tired of things she couldn't explain. "He came to talk." She looked in all the pots to see what was on the menu tonight.

"His phone doesn't work?" Hector was smart and her reply had been lame.

"He's a cop, Hector. I used to be a thief. He thinks that Jack and I reconnecting means trouble for Jack."

Hector frowned. "You want me to set him straight?"

She shook her head, smiling. "I'm going to do that."

"By buying him dinner? Or was the plan that I give him dinner?"

She grinned as she passed him. "I'm buying him dinner."

"Didn't I see you go by earlier with a big tree in the back of your truck? That must have set you back. Christmas trees are a fortune this year."

"It's for Teresa and the kids."

"I know. You're so good to her, but someday you have to fly the nest a second time and concentrate on *you*."

The bell rang over the front door, announcing customers. She began to fill water glasses.

"I'm doing just fine."

IT WAS AN average Saturday night. They did enough business to run out of the special, but not enough that Corie and Polly couldn't keep up. Families came and left while one couple had spent the past two hours gazing into each other's eyes while their *enchiladas de queso* grew cold.

Sukie Cunningham sat with her Kindle at a table at the back of the room. She was blonde and blue-eyed, a plump thirtysomething who had a taste for clothing from the junior department. She was administrative assistant to the deputy mayor, Robert Pimental. It was clear she'd been hired by Pimental for her curvaceous proportions and her too tight, too short clothing rather than her competence. Still, her pleasant personality and her look of wide-eyed innocence made her impossible to dislike.

Polly picked up a coffeepot, ready to do the refill rounds. "Do you think she has any idea Pimental is never going to leave his wife and marry her?" she asked Corie under her voice.

"I'm sure she doesn't." It was rumored that Sukie did more for her employer than misschedule his appointments and lose his messages.

"What is it about that man that appeals to her?"

"Power, I suppose. She thinks he can change her life. Her parents were poor and she waited tables here for a while before you came. But she forgot to put up orders, got them confused and dropped a tray of pies. She was always apologetic, but Hector was losing money. He finally had to fire her. Then Pimental hired her and eventually set her up in a little rental house on the other side of town."

"She's very loyal to him."

Corie nodded but thought about the change she'd seen in Sukie recently—a loss of innocence in her eyes, a smile that didn't come as easily as it used to. "She has been. I'm not sure what's going on with them now. Maybe she's catching a glimpse of the real him."

Polly nodded. "Yeah. Crooked, mean, scary."

"Yeah."

Polly headed toward Sukie with the coffee.

BEN ARRIVED JUST before nine. He wore dark slacks and a dark cotton shirt. Corie had to stare for a minute. He'd combed his hair and actually dressed for dinner. In Querida. Good breeding was an impressive thing.

She led him to a table at the back. "Hector makes mean fajitas, wonderful *camarónes*— that's shrimp if you're not familiar with the word. All kinds of quesadillas, beef—"

He stopped her. "*Camarones* sounds wonderful."

"Sautéed with lemon butter, done in salsa chipotle or á la *diablo*?"

"*Diablo?* Devil?"

"Yes. Pretty hot. Or we can go easy on the red chili."

"I can take it," he said. "*Diablo*. As it comes."

"Something to drink? We have beer and wine."

"Coffee's good."

She placed his order and brought his coffee. "Did you get a room at the B and B?"

"Yes. The owner seems suspicious of me, though. Mrs...?"

"McMinn."

"That's it. I don't know what she thinks I'm doing here, but she seems convinced I'm up to no good."

"Ah. That's because I'm sure word is out now that you're here to see me. She's from Manzanita, a little town up the road where my family lived. We didn't have a very good reputation. My father was a nice man, but hung around with people who weren't, and Juanita was a dragon. My stepmother," she explained. "She was unpleasant to everyone except her two daughters from a previous marriage."

"But that's them. How did you come by this reputation?"

She rested the coffeepot on the table. "One Easter when I was eleven, Juanita made dresses for her girls but not for me. Her girls were sweet and obedient. I wasn't. Actually, they were scared and I wasn't. I saw a dress in the window at a thrift shop, but I didn't have any money. So, I stole it." She arched an eyebrow. "Mrs. McMinn ran the shop at the time. She caught me and called the police. Juvenile Court made me pay it back. I think you're considered suspect if you have anything to do with me."

She couldn't tell what he thought of that, but he finally nodded and said, "All right. Good to know."

When Ben was finished, Corie took away his plate and put a dessert bowl containing custard with a sweet-smelling brown sauce in its place.

"Flan," she said, "with caramel espresso sauce." And walked away again, saying over her shoulder, "Best custard you'll ever have."

CORIE WAS CLEARING tables when Robert Pimental arrived just before closing. He stopped inside the door for a moment, supposedly to scan the room for Sukie but Corie suspected it was to pose there. He had visions of himself as an important figure who was generally irresistible to women. Sukie waved madly to get his attention.

He strode toward her table, about five-seven of portly arrogance. He'd come into office with his friend the mayor several years ago. The mayor had ALS and had been allowed to have a deputy for the times when the job was hard for him. The illness had sidelined the mayor a year ago and left Pimental to do pretty much as he liked in this town of two thousand.

Publicly, he'd made a few changes to earn favor with his constituents—removed parking meters, spruced up the park and playground, and created a committee to attract business to Querida.

Privately he was a philanderer with a Jaguar and an extravagant lifestyle, unusual for a small-town politician without a large inheritance.

Before Corie knew about his behavior in private, she'd gone to him for help in fighting Cyrus Tyree's efforts to evict Teresa. She'd found him in an empty hallway, on his way to a meeting. Pimental had appeared willing to help until it became clear that he expected payment in return—and not in cash. When she'd turned to leave, he'd caught her arm to show her how generous she would have to be in return for his cooperation.

She'd swung her purse at him, forgetting that it contained a small coffee can in which she kept her tips. The loaded purse had left a visible scar above his right eye.

He'd been infuriated by her rejection—and her coffee can of tips—and had her arrested for assault. Fortunately for her, a delivery person had seen everything and volunteered to testify for her. Pimental had dropped the charges but there was venom in his eyes every time he looked at her.

As now. He stopped her as he made his way toward Sukie. "Coffee," he said to Corie. "Decaf. And coconut cream pie."

They were out of coconut cream. She couldn't help but be happy about that.

BEN SAVORED THE last bite of flan and pulled his coffee cup toward him. A large man in kitchen whites approached his table.

"You're Ben," he said, offering his hand. There was an undercurrent of accusation in the statement.

Ben shook his hand and tried to stand in the narrow booth. "I am." The man gestured him back down.

"I'm Hector, Corie's boss."

"Ah. Wonderful dinner. Those were the best shrimp I've ever had."

"Thank you." Hector squeezed into the opposite side of the booth. "Why are you here?" he asked bluntly.

Surprised by that question, Ben replied politely, "Family business."

"But you're not her family. Your brother is her brother, but you're not…her brother."

Ben laughed as Hector struggled with the family connections. "You must have her confidence if you know the Palmer-Manning family structure."

"Manning?"

"Manning was their mother's name and since their fathers came and went rapidly, their mother thought it was easier for all of them if they went by her name. Jack was adopted by my family, so he's now a Palmer."

Hector nodded, then tried to lean toward him but his girth was too firmly wedged into the booth to allow that. "She's my friend," he said, "and one of the best waitresses I've ever had." He bobbed his head from side to side. "There are some not-so-good stories from when she was a kid. She had a tough life."

Ben agreed with that but had to add, "She was arrested for assault just last year."

Hector hooked a thumb in the direction of the man who'd arrived a short time ago. "Against him. She was defending herself from…you know."

The man in question was now nuzzling a

blonde, who seemed pleased by his attention. "That's Pimental?"

"Yes."

He didn't seem particularly impressive or scary, though Ben had been a cop long enough to never trust appearances.

"Why is he allowed to remain in office if he behaves like that with women?"

Hector made a scornful sound. "The charges were dropped. The case never went to trial, but the point is, what happened wasn't her fault. Don't give her trouble about things she can't do anything about."

"I'm not here to give her trouble. I'm here to find out the truth..." He doubted Corie had confided in her boss about stealing the jewels. "About some personal things."

Hector measured him with a look. "All right. See that you don't or I'll have to give you trouble. And don't think I can't."

"Understood."

"Good."

As Hector shifted out of the booth, angry words came from Pimental, who was now standing at the cash register with Sukie.

Ben leaned sideways to see what was going on.

"I got this," Hector said and started toward

Pimental and Corie, who stood behind the counter.

Ben wandered over anyway. Corie was handing back Pimental's credit card. "I'm sorry," she said. "It was declined. Do you want to use another one?"

Pimental pushed it back at her. "I said, run it again."

"And I said," she replied, "I ran it twice. It was declined. Twice."

"That's impossible."

She turned the credit card processing terminal toward him. The word DECLINED was clearly visible on the small screen. "I'm sorry."

"I'll just bet you are," Pimental said darkly.

Corie smiled blandly. "Is it possible your wife overdrew it and neglected to tell you?"

Ben had to admire her complete disregard for discretion considering the man was here with another woman. Pimental's face flushed dark red.

"Oh, for heaven's sake." Sukie stepped between Pimental and the counter and handed Corie several bills, hitting her with a mildly disapproving glance for the reference to Mrs. Pimental. "I'm sure it's a mistake, but I'll just pay until it's sorted out."

Corie made change and handed it to Sukie.

Sukie gave her back a five-dollar tip. She smiled at Hector. "It was a lovely dinner, Hector. Good night. Come on, Bobby." She looped her arm in Pimental's and led him away.

He held Sukie back long enough to snatch the money out of Corie's hand. "Personal comments are poor service," he accused. "You don't deserve a tip."

As his customers walked out the door, Hector looked reluctantly amused. "Not nice to mention Mrs. Pimental."

Corie conceded that with a nod. "I know. But it's not like he tries to hide his infidelity or that Sukie doesn't know she exists."

"True. But you're out five bucks."

She grinned. "It was worth it."

He reached into the till to pull out a ten-dollar bill and handed it to her. "Yes, it was. I enjoyed it, too. Let's lock up."

## CHAPTER THREE

CORIE AND POLLY filled the dishwasher while Ben helped Hector turn chairs upside down on the tables to mop the floor. Hector told him how he'd gotten into the business, shown him pictures of his three boys and three girls and his wife, and said his daughters loved Corie because she helped them update their clothes to look new and fashionable. "When you're a girl in school, that's important," he said. "And Corie has this gift with design."

Ben had taken it all in. This flair for fashion was something he hadn't known about her. He wondered if Jack did.

In the car on the way home he asked her about it.

"I've always perked up my clothes by adding trim or parts of other pieces."

"Hector said his girls love what you do."

She smiled at that. "They're appreciative because they don't have a lot of money and there's a certain satisfaction in dressing up something to make it look new again. Or even better."

"Jack never mentioned you designed clothing."

She shrugged. "It never came up. A couple of years ago I went to New York and got a job with a designer just starting out. I got good, practical experience, but he had a bad season and ran out of capital. My style wasn't thrilling to more traditional designers, so when I couldn't find another job in the field, I thought rather than waitress in New York, where living was so expensive, I may as well come home and work here so I can save to go back, and I could help Teresa while I was at it."

Ben pulled up in front of her house. "I hope you get to work in design again," he said sincerely. He'd like knowing she was happily settled somewhere because it would make Jack happy. "Meanwhile," he went on in the sudden quiet, "will you make me a cup of coffee and tell me the truth about the jewelry?"

She let out an exaggerated breath. "Come on in."

In the dim light over the doorway he saw that the run-down little white house with red trim had probably once been a cozy home but was now badly in need of paint and a few

homey touches. There was a little bit of lawn
in front that someone was trying to maintain,
but it was crowding out the short walkway
and weeds were growing through the simple
picket fence that surrounded it.

A look of weariness had suddenly replaced
the anger he'd grown used to seeing in Corie's
eyes, and she looked as though she belonged
in this sad little place.

Ben steeled himself against softness. Corie
was pretty and fascinatingly fearless, but if
she did have the jewels, she could be a danger to Jack and his brother had been through
enough. Though she'd originally stolen the
jewelry to sell it and buy the house and property Teresa rented to free her from the constant threat of eviction, the act was illegal.

Jack was on his honeymoon in the Cali-
fornia wine country right now, and his parents were partying with his bride's family in
Branson, Missouri. It was up to Ben to make
sure the film of Corie's appearance on the
Tyree property—and what would look like
his, Jack's and Sarah's complicity in the jewel
theft—somehow disappeared. He only hoped
he wasn't too late.

He followed her inside the small living
room. He and Jack and Sarah had spent the

night on this floor the last time he was here. They'd felt it necessary to stay close until they had Corie safely on the plane with them, back to Oregon. Jack had insisted she go home with them to meet their family. After the theft and Jack's sudden appearance in her life, she'd been emotional and trying hard to keep her distance. Afraid she'd run off, Jack, Ben and Sarah had stayed the night with Corie.

He remembered the set of natural wicker furniture more appropriate to a patio than a living room; it looked feminine and had probably been more affordable than upholstered pieces. The cushions were a blue-and-white pattern, and mismatched coffee table and end tables and an old rocker made up the rest of the furnishings. A few floral prints on the walls brightened the space.

She dropped her purse on the sofa. "I'll get that coffee. Make yourself comfortable."

He sat on the rocker and looked out the window behind the wicker sofa at the dark, quiet street. Most of the homes in the neighborhood were a lot like hers, some a little nicer, some a lot less cared for. He knew this part of Texas was populated with low-income workers and probably a few illegals looking for a better life, with family on both sides of the border.

That was probably why some members of the town government of Querida managed to operate the way they did, perpetrating crimes they continued to get away with. Everyone had secrets. No one wanted to talk.

He thought if he could deal with being here, he might be able to do something about it. But this part of Texas was dusty and hot, and he missed the rivers and forests of home. His plan was to quit the force and open an investigative services business in Beggar's Bay. He'd even half convinced Grady Nelson, his partner on the force, to join him part-time until he got the business under way.

Corie returned with a steaming mug and placed it on a small table beside him.

"Thank you," he said as she went to sit on the sofa. She pulled out the pins and rubber band that held her hair up for work and made a sound of relief when it fell free in a rippled sheet. She massaged her scalp with her fingertips.

"How come you don't wilt in the heat?" he asked. "You wrestled a tree, worked a busy shift and did verbal battle with Pimental." He sipped the coffee then rested the mug on one knee. "And you still have the energy to make my life difficult."

She met his grin with her own. "I'm part cactus. I almost froze to death in Beggar's Bay. Fortunately, Sarah lent me a sweater she'd borrowed from your mom when she moved in with you and Jack after the fire in her apartment."

He nodded. "The red one."

She seemed surprised that he remembered the color. He'd noticed it because the red had been dramatic with her dark features.

"About the jewelry..." he said, impatient with himself for letting her see that he'd been aware of her. He didn't trust her but he'd have to be unconscious not to notice that she was beautiful. And a different woman when she was around those children. He took another sip of coffee. "Where is the jewelry?"

CORIE WISHED BEN PALMER would just go home. Life was difficult enough around here, trying to keep Teresa and the kids in their home and herself out of Pimental's way. She didn't need the annoyance of her brother's brother. He reminded her of her childhood and everyone who dismissed her out of hand because she was that Ochoa brat from that awful family. He was clearly convinced that she was as bad as her legend.

"I believe you sent the jewelry back to the Tyrees," she said, her tone deliberately airy because he looked so grave and she enjoyed refusing to take him seriously. "In a priority-mail box. Your partner, Grady, mailed it from Seattle when he went to visit his girlfriend, so no one would know that you and Jack were involved."

"I never told you Grady mailed it."

"Jack did. After making a point of explaining to me that I couldn't possibly move forward in my life with such a crime behind me."

He took exception to the subtle criticism of their brother in her reply and the suggestion that Jack was somehow unsympathetic. "Jack remembers the sweet little sister he lost all those years ago. He seems to be convinced that you're the same person, and now his name could be compromised because Tyree has your burglary on tape. You might have a little more respect for all Jack's been through to find you, and the fact that he risked himself that night to get you out of there."

She'd regretted her cavalier response the moment the words were out of her mouth. But Ben made her prickly—like the cactus she claimed to be.

"I could never explain to you," she said,

"how important Jack is to me. I would never deliberately hurt him."

"Right." It was clear he didn't believe her. She couldn't imagine what she'd have to do to prove it. "So where is the jewelry?"

"You mailed it to Tyree," she repeated.

"I'm sure you saw the interview with him on the evening news where Mrs. Tyree held up all the junk beads that arrived in the box." He leaned back again, accusing gaze steady. "How'd you make the switch? And where's the jewelry now?"

"I did see the news." She folded her legs up on the love seat. Used to having her honesty called into question, she wasn't sure why it was so particularly annoying when he did it. But it was. She held back the angry words on the tip of her tongue. "It's interesting to me," she said calmly, "that you're convinced I somehow switched the jewelry for Mardi Gras junk. When would I have done that? I never saw the jewelry again after we got to your parents' house. You took it from me, remember?"

She couldn't tell whether or not she'd shaken his conviction of her guilt. His steady gaze gave very little away. He said nothing and waited for her to go on.

"And, you know, it makes me wonder what kind of cop you are," she continued, unable to hold back her annoyance, "that it hasn't occurred to you that Tyree did get the jewelry back, but because he'd probably already filed a claim with his insurance company and gotten paid, he decided to pretend that it was junk in that box. By going on television and flashing the dime-store beads, Mrs. Tyree can have her jewelry and he can keep the insurance money.

"He's got *somebody* on security footage as having robbed him," she continued, "so he's golden with the insurance company. And you were careful to make sure you and Jack and Sarah weren't implicated by mailing the package without a return address and from some distance from where you live. You can't come out now and tell the authorities that you sent the jewelry back because then they'd know you helped me in the first place."

He rolled his eyes. "Come on, Corie. Really? You want me to believe this is simple insurance fraud?"

"Why not?" She sat a little straighter. "Tyree is a smart-mouthed lawyer who defends the shady, and is one of Pimental's cronies. I can't suggest to anyone that he's scamming the insurance company because that would suggest

I *knew* the jewelry had been returned. The obvious conclusion would be that *I* sent it back. How could I have done that unless I'd stolen it in the first place? And I can't separate you and Jack and Sarah from that night because you were there and are probably on film. See? Pays to mind your own business."

"There's no such thing as that when family's involved. I know." He forestalled her protest with a raised hand. "I'm not your family, Jack is. But he's *my* family, so...what we now have is a big mess."

"I'm used to messes," she said. "Just go home and let me deal with this one."

"And how are you going to do that with the surveillance tape out there? I'm surprised the Corpus Christi police haven't arrested you already."

"I was scared to death of that at first, but I got to thinking about it. It was so dark, there were so many bushes and trees, I don't think there's any way they could identify us. My truck is black and was in the bushes. We all stayed in the bushes when we ran to the house. That tape helped Tyree with the insurance company, but I can't imagine it did the police any good."

"I'd like to know that for sure."

"So would I, but I don't see how you can."

"Then you underestimate me." He pushed to his feet.

Corie wasn't sure whether to be relieved that he was going or nervous about that "underestimate me" remark.

She stood, too. "What are you going to do?"

"Not sure. I have to see the tape. I guess I have to make friends with someone who can help with that, so I'm going to be around for a few days. And I promised Teresa that I'd help decorate the tree tomorrow. Shall I pick you up?"

She felt depressed and then resigned. "Sure."

She followed him to the door and caught his arm when he would have stepped out. It was warm and muscled. He stopped instantly, looking down at her hand then up into her eyes. His were watchful, waiting.

"Yes?" he asked.

"You should think about this twice. Please."

"Corie," he said with a patience that surprised her. "We've just been through all this. After I find out what's on the tape, maybe I'll have time to prove your theory about Tyree defrauding the insurance company. In case you *are* spotted on it."

She arched an eyebrow in surprise. "You believe me?"

"No." He answered without hesitation. "But it's a place to start."

She wondered if he worked at being hateful or if it just came naturally. "Ben, you don't know what you're dealing with. You're naive where Querida and Pimental and his cronies are concerned."

"What?" He seemed as amused as he was offended. "Naive? I'm a cop. A cop who remains *naive* after nine years on the force isn't doing his job."

"You know what I mean. This little Texas town is filled with secrets. If anything happens to you, I'm sure *I'd* have to answer to Jack, just as you claim you'd have to if anything happened to me."

She realized she was holding his arm and dropped her hand, suddenly self-conscious. Her fingertips still felt the soft light hair, warm sinew and the thrum of a steady pulse. Her own pulse, a little erratic, seemed to accelerate and steal her breath.

She stared at the shoulder muscle moving under his shirt as he put a hand on *her* arm.

"Then doesn't that suggest," he asked, "that we should work on this together to prevent

Jack from getting angry at either of us? That is, if you *are* innocent and not afraid of exposure."

"If we tried to do anything together," she noted, "one of us wouldn't survive. I'm thinking, *you*."

"Well…see, now, rather than discourage me that simply challenges me. You think I'm not capable of being tougher than you are?"

"Oh, I know you're tough," she said, adding with complete conviction, "You're just not as cussed as I am."

He laughed softly. "Well, that may be true."

THAT WAS HEAVY STUFF, he thought. She seemed completely convinced she had an iron interior. Of course, she couldn't see into her own eyes. But he imagined that when she met her gaze in a mirror while putting on makeup or brushing her teeth, she did it fiercely, needing to convince herself of her invincibility.

When he looked into her eyes, he saw the cactus she claimed to be.

He took out his cell phone. "Give me your number and I'll give you mine. You can call me anytime if you need to." They recorded each other's information then she held open the door for him.

"What time shall I pick you up in the morning? Does the Grill serve breakfast?"

"Yes, Abelia cooks. That's Hector's wife. They open at seven."

"Is that too early?"

"The kids will be up at six and waiting for you."

"All right. I'll pick you up just before seven."

She closed the door behind him as he walked out to his car. He thought about what she'd said. All those children with the big, questioning eyes. And they'd mistaken him for Santa.

Mercy.

# CHAPTER FOUR

BEN LOOKED FRESH and capable as he hauled the twelve-foot ladder Hector had loaned them out of the shed behind the restaurant. Corie, who hadn't slept well at all, knew she looked a little like a refugee from a zombie walk. She picked up the back end of the ladder and helped him carry it to her truck.

They'd had a quiet breakfast at the Grill and then driven to Teresa's to discover that her ladder wasn't tall enough to reach the top of the Christmas tree and that she didn't have enough ornaments. Corie had made a quick call to Hector, who'd agreed to lend them his ladder, but the matter of more ornaments had necessitated a craft project. Teresa and the children had been left in charge of resolving that problem.

"Where'd you find your keys?" Ben asked as he placed the ladder on the tarp that remained in her truck.

She walked around to open the driver's-side

door, smiling ruefully at him when they were both in the cab. "Bianca had them. She loves to put things in her purse."

"Ah. The youngest Stripe. I noticed the purse. She doesn't look big enough to carry it."

"She's tougher than she appears."

Corie loved the way he identified the children. The Flores girls were the Stripe Sisters. The Santiago brothers, the Army.

"I should have thought about that but I was stressed and late for work. Karina, the middle sister, found them and gave them to me." She pulled away from the front of the restaurant, executed a wide U-turn then headed for Teresa's.

"Is a U-turn legal in Querida?" he asked, his elbow resting on his open window. She noticed he was holding on to the roof of the truck.

"Not sure," she replied. "Why? You going to arrest me? You're not even on duty. Especially not here."

"A cop's always on duty," he corrected. "Depends on the danger of the situation to the public as to whether or not he steps in."

"Am I scaring you?" she teased. "I thought you were fearless."

"That's our brother, Jack. And you did almost

take out that trash box in front of Hector's, then the mailbox across the street while executing the turn." He grinned at her. "That would have gotten you a pricey traffic ticket in Beggar's Bay. Don't know what the law is in Querida."

"I do it all the time and I've never gotten a ticket."

"Let's hope your luck continues. Nice of Hector to send pastries back for the kids."

"They'll love them with their hot chocolate. So will I."

"I noticed your sweet tooth. You had three pieces of cake at Jack and Sarah's wedding, as I recall."

She was a little embarrassed that he'd noticed that. She'd been nervous. For the woman whose mother had gone to jail, whose father had been a drug dealer and whose stepmother disliked her, the Palmer-Reed family harmony had been alien territory. Their happiness in each other's company had been so thick she'd been afraid someone would notice she felt out of place. She tended to overeat when she was nervous. "It's not very polite to point it out."

He laughed lightly. "It's not like it's an evil quality or anything. It's just nice to know you have a weakness. I'm guessing you've spent most of your life pretending you don't have any."

She ignored that and kept driving. He was spot-on, actually. She hated that about him.

FOR THE FIRST fifteen minutes of tree decorating, Ben thought he would go insane. Kids were everywhere. It was just the same ten kids, with Roberto safely tucked away in a playpen to protect him from being trampled, but the noise level and general activity made it seem as though they'd doubled, or even tripled, in number.

He thought it remarkable that the women didn't seem to notice. They directed the wrapping of lights around the bottom branches and let the older children climb Teresa's short ladder to help with the upper branches. Teresa hovered around them as Corie occupied the younger ones, who were stretching out the colorful paper chains they'd made.

Ben watched the happy, laughing faces. Only Rosie was looking on with a strange detachment that finally caught Corie's attention. The lights were now halfway up the tree and the smaller children were placing ornaments on the branches they could reach. As Ben opened the large boxes of decorations, he heard Corie try to encourage Rosie's participation.

"I think you should put up that pretty purple chain you made," she said, catching Rosie's hand and leading her toward the tree.

Rosie resisted. "I want to save it," she said, "for *our* tree when my dad comes to get me."

"He might not come in time for Christmas." Corie knelt beside her.

Rosie met her gaze with firm, dark eyes. "He's coming."

Putting an arm around her, Corie squeezed her close. "Okay. Why don't we put it on our tree and, when he comes, you can still take it home with you for *your* tree?"

Appearing reluctant to accept the compromise, Rosie sighed. The child reminded him of Corie. Her own imperfect family made it hard for her to give or to accept love when it was offered from someone else. She finally went with Corie to the big box that had held the chains the children had made, pulled out the remaining bright purple one and looked for the right spot on the tree.

Rosie pointed over her head. With the two ladders occupied, Corie stood on tiptoe to see if she could reach. She was at least a foot short.

Ben went to help. Moving Corie aside with a teasing, "Out of my way, short stuff," he lifted Rosie onto his shoulders. She squealed in surprise then giggled when she found herself high enough to place the chain a third of the way from the top.

"How does that look?" Rosie asked of the room in general.

"It's beautiful." Corie stood back to admire it and Teresa nodded.

"Good job," Ben agreed, lowering Rosie to her feet.

By the time they broke for pastries and cocoa, Ben concluded that all he could do in such a situation was abandon the need to control and simply embrace the chaos. Teresa had a little directorial control, but, for the most part, let the children experience the thrill of decorating by themselves.

They all sat around the large kitchen table, Corie and Teresa making sure there was an equitable distribution of treats. Ben leaned against the counter with a cup of coffee, listening in on the conversations.

Rosie and the Stripe Sisters talked about what they would do when their parents came for them. There were small, homey plans that involved doing their chores and cleaning their rooms. Lupe, the oldest sister, intended to plant flowers.

"What if we live in an apartment?" Karina asked.

"You can have flowers in an apartment," Rosie said. "In a pot instead of in the ground."

"But that's not a garden," Lupe protested.

"Sometimes you can't have a garden," Rosie said. "Sometimes you can only have a pot."

The girls nodded seriously. Ben thought about how sage an observation that was.

"I'm gonna learn to play football. Catch, Peterson." Carlos pretended to throw a pass. Soren, across the table, reached a skinny arm up to catch the imaginary ball. The two boys laughed.

"We don't have a football," Rigo, the next oldest Santiago brother, pointed out.

"That's okay, I do." Soren picked up his cocoa. "When your family comes, you can have my football." He shrugged.

Ben suspected the boy didn't believe that would happen.

"Maybe Santa will bring us one," the youngest Santiago brother said hopefully.

Miguel, brother number three, chimed in with, "You'd have to be good for that to happen, Tonio."

The boys laughed. "We'd better take Soren's football."

Corie came with the coffeepot to top up Ben's mug. "You doing all right?" she asked. "These guys can be hard on the nerves when they're excited. You got your strength training in for the day by lifting them all up to hang their paper chains. It's fun for them to go beyond their reach."

He had to agree with that. "It's fun for all of us. What brought each of them here?"

She put the pot back on the warmer and came to lean beside him. "The Flores girls'— or Stripe Sisters, as you call them—mother is a widow and lost her job. She's being retrained at a place in Florida that teaches food service skills and hotel management. Teresa got her into the program—it's run by friends of hers. The Santiago Army's dad was injured on the job in an oil field and, when he recovered, he went for retraining, too."

"The kids have been here through all that?"

"Eight months for the Flores girls, six for the Santiago boys."

"What about Rosie?"

"Teresa's been in touch with her father, who is a US citizen living in Mexico. Her mom was in poor health and died at home and the neighbors brought Rosie here so her father, who remained in Mexico, could come for her and take her home without having to deal with the system."

"Her parents were divorced?"

"I think so. Not sure. He doesn't think he can support her but has been looking for a solution."

Ben said in annoyance, "Like a job?"

Corie hitched a shoulder. "Teresa tries not to make judgments. Soren was the son of a border guard who died in the line of duty. He'd been a friend of Teresa's, so she took Soren in. He's sort of happy here."

"Sort of? Shouldn't a kid be definitely happy?"

"Ideally. It's just not in the cards for some."

He thought he heard a personal note in her voice. "Like you?"

Her eyes narrowed. "I was happy when I was really little. I remember Jack taking good care of me. I didn't even realize how bad our mother was until they sent Cassie and me back to our fathers. That part of my life was okay until my father died. Then it was awful. Until Teresa found me when I was twelve."

Ben sighed, realizing how much strength was around the table—and standing beside him. "Lots of sad stories."

"Yes. Well. It's a foster home. This is often sad-story central." She straightened from the counter. "It's too bad you'll be going home soon. The kids really like you."

"I have some things to do first." He toasted her with his mug. "You'll have to deal with me a little—"

The sound of the doorbell rang through the house. Teresa, arbitrating a dispute between Soren and Rosie, looked up.

Corie stayed her with a hand. "I'll get it." She set her cup down and crossed the living room to pull the door open.

Gil Bigelow, Querida's chief of police, stood there in his dark blue uniform, his brimmed hat at a testy angle over light blue eyes. His craggy face was etched in stern lines. He was another good friend of Robert Pimental's and one of Corie's least favorite people. When Pimental had had her arrested for assault, Bigelow hadn't even listened to her side of the story. If it hadn't been for that passing delivery person, she'd probably be doing time today.

Bigelow's hands rested lightly on his creaky leather belt overloaded with tools of the job. Teresa came up beside Corie.

"Good morning, Chief," she said. "What is it?"

He firmed his stance. "I'm here to tell you that you have to be out of here in five days. According to Mr. Tyree, you've ignored all his efforts to encourage you to abide by the rules of your renter's agreement. You argued with the assistant he sent. Therefore—"

"That isn't true, Gil Bigelow, and you know it." Angry color filled Teresa's cheeks. "I *am* behind in the rent, but I've told him over and over again about the leaky ceiling, the bad plumbing in the kitchen and the wide cracks in the veranda. Those are his responsibilities as my landlord and he's done nothing about them."

"Now, Teresa, there's no point in getting hysterical. The law is the law. He has the right—"

"I am not hysterical. I'm loud because you don't hear me otherwise."

Corie struggled to remain calm. "He's done nothing but harass Teresa since he inherited the house from his father. He—"

"Pardon me." Corie was completely surprised by the sound of a male voice behind her. A hand on her upper arm moved her aside as Ben stepped between her and Teresa. All the children, she noticed, had clustered around them, Rosie holding Roberto.

Ben extended his hand to Bigelow, his

manner courteous but somehow charged, as though a current ran beneath the calm. The chief seemed to recognize it. "Good morning, Chief," Ben said. "I'm Ben Palmer. I'm visiting for a few days. What's this about eviction?"

Bigelow sized up the intruder then widened his stance, as though taking up more room somehow expanded his position. *"This,"* he said, his voice lowering a pitch, "is none of your business, Mr. Palmer. It's between Ms. McGinnis and me."

Ben continued to smile. "I'm sure you don't want to violate the law, Chief. As a police officer, myself, I know that only a county sheriff or one of his deputies can enforce an eviction order, and then, only at the end of the court process."

Anger and offended male ego lit Bigelow's eyes. He cleared his throat. "Where you from, Palmer?" he asked.

"Oregon."

"Well, this is Texas."

"Right. But unless Texas has seceded, this law applies to you. It's a federal law. It applies everywhere in the United States. You can't make her leave."

The chief took what he likely thought was an intimidating step toward Ben.

Ben stood firm and watched him approach, his manner still polite.

"I want her," the chief said, a furious tremor in his voice, "and the children out of here in five days."

Ben shook his head. "The landlord has to file an eviction notice. That would be a five-day notice for nonpayment of rent, which isn't the case here—at least not without good cause. A ten-day notice for a breach of the lease, which isn't the case, either. So, a thirty-day notice would be required. Still, the tenant could contest it. A formal eviction notice has to be filed first before a court case can proceed. At the very least, Ms. McGinnis can remain here for the next two months."

Ben's manner changed, the smile gone as he took a step toward the chief. "You're the one who has to leave. You have no right to be here, therefore, you're trespassing."

"I," Bigelow said, "am a representative of the law."

"Without legitimate reason for the eviction you're trying to serve, without the required paperwork and, apparently, without a working knowledge of the law you claim to represent."

Corie's heart pounded as the men stared at

each other. Bigelow was clearly on the brink of violence, Ben waiting for it.

Expecting the chief to lay a hand on Ben at any second, Corie was surprised when he inhaled a breath and seemed to think better of it. Wisely so, she thought. Ben was a good fifteen years younger and considerably more fit.

"We'll see about this, Palmer," the chief said. Then he turned, strode toward his up-accessorized police car, got in and sped away.

Teresa threw her arms around Ben's neck. "How do you know all that?" she asked.

"We had a situation at an apartment building at home. My partner and I were called in to keep the peace until everything was done properly. I learned a lot."

Corie was astonished by what had just happened. Ben had defended them against one of Querida's bullies. He'd stood up to the police chief's intimidation tactics on her behalf. Well, not *her* behalf. He'd stood up for Teresa and the children, but their problem was as important to her as any of her own, so he might as well have defended her.

"We don't have to go?" Rosie asked. "Ben made it so we don't have to go, right?"

Soren laughed and patted Ben's arm. "Ben

scared the police chief," he said. "We can stay for two more months."

Corie ushered the children back while Teresa pulled herself together. The past year had been a nightmare with Tyree's repeated threats to evict her. She held on to Ben the way Corie wanted to—as though he were a strong hand-hold in a hurricane. And it had been so long since either of them had anyone to hold on to in tough times except each other.

Corie sat the children at the table again, gave them each another pastry half, knowing she was taking the coward's way out to soothe their nerves but accepting that it was expedient. She made more cocoa, turned up the Christmas carols and got a discussion going about what they should make for Teresa's present.

BEN LOOKED DOWN into Teresa's tear-filled eyes and felt an eerie change take place inside him.

She hugged him fiercely again. "Thank you, thank you!" she whispered thickly. "I'm so glad you were here."

He patted her shoulder, feeling his whole world go south on him. To be honest, he had to admit that it had begun when he and Jack and Sarah had followed Corie on her path to theft and vengeance.

"We've held him off for now," he said, watching her pull tissues out of her pocket and dab at her nose. "But this is just going to continue unless we settle this once and for all."

She looked up at him doubtfully. "Tyree doesn't care about our situation. His father was a good man, but all Cyrus cares about is getting me out. I hate it when the children are worried. I wish they could just go to school and come home and play and be happy."

"Are their parents really coming back? Any of them?"

"Absolutely," she said, her eyes suddenly dry, her customary confidence returning. "They're not bad people. They've just had bad things happen to them. I started this place so that when parents are ready to take their children back, they don't have to wait forever for the court to do its thing. They can just reclaim their children and make a home again. They'll be back. I know Joel Santiago and Amelia Flores thought they'd be finished with school by Christmas."

"All right," he heard himself say, "then we'll do everything we can to see that you stay."

"How will we do that?"

"Leave it to me."

"*You'd* have to stay around for a while."

Yeah. He was getting that.

He'd never been a selfish person—he'd been raised better than that. But his life so far, apart from his job, had been about doing what he wanted to do. He was enthused and excited about his plans to start an investigative agency. He was willing to work hard and had a fairly good business head. He could make a success of Palmer Private Investigations.

But he wasn't going to be able to launch his business until he had Teresa and Corie and the children on a safer footing and he'd resigned from the Beggar's Bay police force. And then there was the jewelry... He had no illusions that he could single-handedly solve either issue. He needed an ally in the cause, but he was going to do his best to brighten up the children's world and give them the stability they deserved.

Teresa hooked her arm in his and tugged him back into the house. "Thanks, Ben, for caring about us."

"I'm glad I was here."

"And for agreeing to stay."

He was about to deny that he had done that,

but it would have been pointless. He hadn't said the words but in his heart he'd made the promise.

And it was all Corie's fault.

## CHAPTER FIVE

BEN WENT TO town in the afternoon while the children made more ornaments for the tree. On an errand to buy more lights, he decided to make a detour to the local newspaper office.

Querida was too small to support a daily newspaper, but the *Weekly Standard* had its office in an unpretentious storefront in a strip mall on the other side of town.

The editor, a tall, slender man Ben guessed to be in his forties, seemed to be a one-person operation, except for a receptionist. He introduced himself as Will Fennerty.

Ben asked him if he could take a look at all the articles that had run that year on the Querida government, particularly Robert Pimental, the chief of police and Cyrus Tyree.

"I can," he replied. "Fortunately for you, there's no such thing as a weekend off in the life of a small town editor/publisher."

Will provided copies in twenty minutes. He leaned across a battered counter toward Ben and asked if he was from the attorney general's office.

Ben laughed and asked if the Querida town government required such attention.

The man nodded. "It absolutely does, but with just myself doing the reporting, I don't have the staff to follow up on all my investigations. And if I don't spend half my time selling advertising, I won't survive anyway. I'd suggest if you're going to look into things, find out how a deputy mayor in this tiny town can support a palatial home on Ocean Drive in Corpus Christi."

"Doesn't Pimental have to live in Querida to work in its government?" Ben asked.

"He has a modest little place here, too."

"Maybe his wife has money?"

"She was a car salesman's daughter from Dallas."

"So, his job here is funding the Corpus Christi lifestyle?"

"I think so."

Ben remembered that elegant Ocean Drive neighborhood because that was where Tyree lived. He, Jack and Sarah had trailed Corie there the night of the robbery.

"And nobody's noticed? I mean, what's a

town this size doing with a deputy mayor, anyway?"

Will shrugged. "The mayor had ALS. When he was voted in he brought along Pimental, who had a car agency in Manzanita. The two of them were childhood friends. Since the mayor's illness has become completely debilitating, Pimental's been pretty much on his own."

Ben was beginning to see the picture.

"Pimental's behavior is largely ignored because the rest of the state doesn't care about Querida. We don't really produce anything and the landscape isn't exactly inspiring. The police chief also seems to live far beyond the salary of a small-town cop. There's so much going on in city hall, I wouldn't know who'd be safe to report it to if I *did* have an airtight case."

"Wow. I have a friend fighting eviction—"

"Teresa McGinnis. Cyrus Tyree seems determined to get her out of there," Fennerty conceded.

"It doesn't seem like the house is prime property."

"I don't get that, either. His father left it to him, along with a few other properties in Querida and Manzanita. I think he treats those the same way—never fixes anything and is always chasing the rent."

"I understand Corie Ochoa went to the deputy mayor for help," Ben added.

Will laughed. "Yeah, that was rich. He tried to get her to *pay* him to help and she beaned him with her purse. Didn't take that very well. Just not a nice man."

"I understand. And…one more thing."

"Sure."

"Did you report on the theft of Tyree's wife's jewelry?"

"I did. It happened in Corpus Christi, but he's well-known around here."

"TV news reported that Tyree had surveillance cameras."

"Yes. Want to see for yourself what they got?"

Ben suppressed any reaction, hardly believing his luck.

Will let Ben in behind the counter, walked around his desk and invited Ben to take the chair beside it. He stabbed in a few commands to his laptop and turned the screen toward Ben.

"Since it's from a private security system I had to get permission, but Tyree seemed happy enough to give it to me. It's clear he was robbed."

Ben's stomach sank. "By whom?" he asked innocently.

The copy of the film began to play. "That part's not so clear. It's impossible to identify anyone."

Ben watched shadows moving among the bushes in the dark. The makes and models of the vehicles were impossible to determine, and license plates weren't visible. That was a major relief.

He turned the screen back. "Do you suspect anyone?"

"No. Every other person in Querida and Corpus Christi dislikes Tyree. And his wife has serious pretensions, so any number of people would be happy to see either or both of them taken down."

"Thanks." Ben stood and shook his hand. "I appreciate your help, Will."

Ben went to Wolf's Hardware to buy three strings of one hundred-foot lights, per Teresa's instructions, several boxes of plain ornaments and a box of bubble lights, thinking the children would enjoy seeing those at work. He also bought an inflatable Santa Claus and Mrs. Santa for the front lawn. If Teresa was horrified by it, he'd just take it home with him—whenever he went home.

As Ben headed out of town for Teresa's, he noticed Corie pulling into a parking spot near the restaurant, ready to begin her shift. He punched his horn and she waved.

A SPICY AROMA tantalized him when Soren opened the door at his knock—along with two of the Santiago brothers and all of the Stripe Sisters. "We're having spaghetti for dinner, and you're invited."

"What did you buy?" Bianca stood on tiptoe to see the contents of the bag he carried. He lowered it to the coffee table so they could look inside.

"What's this?" Carlos took out the flat inflatables and unfolded them. "Look! Santa. And Mrs. Santa. And they're big!"

The other kids abandoned the bag for the big, red-suited Claus couple. Santa had a giant sack and the missus held a teddy bear and a candy cane.

"For the lawn?" Soren asked.

Ben nodded. "If we have a bicycle pump or something for blowing up an air mattress, we can inflate them tonight or tomorrow and put them out. But we should probably ask Teresa first."

The Stripe Sisters went into the kitchen to do just that.

Teresa came to the kitchen doorway, wooden spoon in hand. Soren and Carlos held up the figures. She smiled broadly. "You're a child-spoiler, Ben Palmer," she said. "Can you stay for dinner?"

The atmosphere was different without Corie. Not that she was ever particularly happy to see him, but he was discovering that he wanted to see her. He had thought about going to the Grill for dinner.

But the children jumped up and down at the invitation. Rosie, who was setting the table, told him Teresa made the best spaghetti. "You have to eat some salad with it, but the spaghetti's really good. We have garlic bread, too."

Ben felt himself relenting. He'd been loved his entire life, and he'd always dealt well with his friends' children and those he came across in his work, but he'd never experienced this almost-adoration before. He put it down to these children living in a household run by women. He was a new and different experience for them.

"Please," Teresa added. "I'd like to repay you at least a little for all you've done for us today."

"I'd love to," he said. "Thank you."

An argument followed among the children about where he would sit. Teresa settled it by placing him between Rosie and Soren, who were already bickering. "We have a dinner guest," she said, focusing a pointed gaze on each child. "Soren, please pass him the garlic toast."

As Ben accepted the deliciously garlic-scented platter, he took a minute to appreciate how different the moment was from where he'd normally have been just a week ago—thanks to Corie.

AFTER DINNER, BEN helped Teresa rummage through the shed for her bicycle pump. The children were gathered around the television with Soren in charge.

Teresa finally found it under a three-legged chair lying on its side. The box that held the pump was ancient.

Teresa laughed. "I was a cycling freak in my twenties, so this is pretty old. I hope it still works."

"The principle is pretty basic." Ben carried

the pump out to the front yard where they'd left the inflatables.

Teresa peered at the children through the front window from the veranda, and then joined him on the lawn. "The kids are glued to *Nickelodeon*, so we should be good for a little while."

Ben inserted the pump pin into the port in the large Santa Claus figure while Teresa unfolded it to allow the air to fill it. They weren't sure the pump was working at first, but soon the inflatable began to very slowly take shape.

"Corie's going to love this," Teresa said. "When she first came to live with me, we had inflatable reindeer on the roof. She was almost thirteen. She pretended to be embarrassed by them but she used to go out and look at them all the time. I don't think there'd been much fun in her life before she came here."

He nodded as he pumped. "She told me her stepmother was nasty."

"You don't know the half of it," Teresa said gravely. "When Corie was born, her father had been her birth mother's drug dealer."

"Yeah. Jack told me a little about him."

"A nice enough man, I guess, but with terrible taste in women. When he left Corie's mother, he spent time in Mexico then in Texas, and married Juanita, who had two daughters of her own."

"Right. I heard about the Easter dresses they got but Corie didn't."

"When Corie's father died, Juanita gave up all pretense of caring about Corie." Teresa looked into Jack's eyes, her own dark with angry pain. "Are you ready for this?"

"You mean that her stepmother sold her to her friend?" Ben stopped pumping. "Yeah. She told us about it when Jack came to find her."

"And you want to know what Corie was worth?"

He didn't, but he had to. "What?"

"One hundred and fifty dollars and a seven-year-old microwave."

For a long moment he had simply no words. Well, he did, but none that could be said out loud in front of Teresa. "And no one went to jail?" he finally asked.

"A lot of things happen in this area that people know about but no one wants to report because they're illegals and can't take the chance. Others don't want to get involved. Sometimes good deeds bite you back."

He started pumping again because he had to do something or explode. He thought about his carefree childhood and how, all that time, Corie had had to deal with people who hadn't cared about her and sold her like garage-sale goods. How did someone recover from that? It made the foster home stories sound almost cheerful.

Teresa stopped him from pumping. "Okay. You can't look like that next time you see her or she'll know I told you."

"Right."

"No pity."

"Of course not."

"But tolerance of her self-sufficiency would be nice."

Yes. He could certainly see where that came from.

CORIE FILLED SALT shakers while Polly followed her with sugar. It was almost closing time during a quiet shift and they'd done all the housekeeping chores that made the often busy breakfast shift more serene.

The aroma of Hector's to-die-for fajita casserole, which had been the special tonight, lingered among the freshly set tables and the empty chairs. Beyond the window where she stood, she could see two streetlights and the lights left on at night in the buildings across the street. Craning her neck a little brought the bed-and-breakfast into view. Ben's rental was parked in front. A tingle ran along her spine.

She told herself firmly that it wasn't excitement. It was interest, at the most. But interest didn't tingle; what she felt *was* excitement.

Okay, she was *excited* that Ben Palmer was only a block away. What was to become of her?

She remembered him confronting Gil Bigelow. He'd been calm, but he'd given the impression that nothing in this world could move him from his protective stance in front of her, Teresa and the children.

She didn't remember anyone ever protecting her from anything before—except for her brother, Jack, and she'd been four at the time. That was a long twenty-three years ago.

It was odd how vulnerable Ben's protection made her feel—how *soft*—and unsettling to the woman who'd learned to depend on herself.

Ben had told her to her face in the past that he didn't like her, didn't trust her, and yet… She wiped off the few grains of salt she'd spilled and moved on to the next table. She had to keep reminding herself that Ben had defended Teresa and the kids, not her.

"Want me to finish?" Polly asked. She set her container of sugar on the table with a thud. The small funnel that simplified pouring went down beside it. "You don't seem focused." She put a companionable arm around Corie's shoulders. "You having trouble with the brother who isn't your brother but your boyfriend?"

Forced out of her thoughts by the sincerity of her friend's concern, Corie bumped her teasingly with her elbow and picked up the salt container to move on to the next table. "I'm just...tired. And he's not my boyfriend."

Polly followed her. "Are you sad because he's going home?"

"I'm not sad, because he's not my boyfriend. And he's not going home."

"He's staying? With you?"

Giving her a mildly impatient look, Corie picked up the shaker. "No, he's not staying with me. He has a room at the B and B. He's staying to help Teresa."

Polly frowned at that. "You mean, help her with the children?"

"No." Corie had told Polly and Hector about Teresa's problems with Tyree. "The police chief tried to evict her this morning." She couldn't help the smile that formed at the memory of

Bigelow's shocked expression when Ben informed him that he was wrong. "Ben stopped him in his tracks. He knew all about the process and it turns out Bigelow couldn't evict her at all. Teresa's safe for another couple of months.

"It was great to see Bigelow so rattled. He arrived with a swagger and left with a definite slump to his shoulders."

Polly smiled then said with concern, "I hope Ben's careful. Those guys are vindictive."

"Yeah. But he can be tough, too."

"He looked like he likes you. Maybe even more than *likes*. And he picked you up here last night."

"That was just because I'd lost my car keys."

Polly shook her head and went back to sugar duty. "You just don't want to admit that someone cares about you. Someone male. You don't want to have to bother with that, do you?"

*"Bother?"* Corie wasn't sure what Polly was talking about.

"You know, act like a woman acts when a man has feelings for her. You don't have to act weak, or let him win at poker, or anything, but you have to be…receptive. Willing to learn more about him, let him learn about you. You have to stop hiding who you really are."

Offended, Corie put a hand to her hip. "I'm not hiding anything." She stabbed a finger at her own chest. "This is me."

"No, it's not. When Teresa or the kids, or Hector or me needs you, you're the kindest, most right-out-there friend in the world. But when you're dealing with anybody else, particularly a man, you become a five-foot-one-inch thistle."

"One and half inch."

Hector wandered out of the kitchen to survey the empty restaurant and then lock the door and turn off the neon open sign. He looked from one to the other. "What're you fighting about?"

"We're not fighting," Corie denied, turning her attention back to her work. "Polly's just trying to tell me that—" she spread both arms in exasperation "—this isn't the real me. But it is."

Hector looked puzzled. He picked up the shaker she'd just filled and held it up to her. "Then the real you just put salt in the pepper shaker."

CORIE AND POLLY left the Grill together, Hector locking the door behind them. Polly squeezed Corie's arm on the dark, quiet sidewalk. "Try to relax, Corie," she said quietly. "I think he's staying because Teresa and the kids are important to *you*."

Corie wanted to tell her she was crazy, but it was late and she was tired. She gave her a quick hug. "Good night, Pol. I'm going straight to bed. The kids are going to be wild tomorrow while we finish decorating the tree."

"Good luck. Glad it isn't me." Polly headed up the street to her little VW bug.

The night was absolutely silent, except for the sound of the rope on the American flag in the park in the next block hitting the flagpole. She drove home, putting thoughts of Ben out of her mind. She had been fine on her own all this time and she would be fine in the future. Corie pulled up in front of her house and turned off the headlights. Lights were on in the house across the street, but every other house around her was dark. She started up the narrow path to her front door and heard the deep bark of the neighbor's vigilant Lab. He sounded more agitated than usual.

She stopped, a weird fluctuation in the air catching her by surprise. It wasn't exactly a sense of being watched, it was—

The front door exploded outward and something flew at her with such force it knocked her down. She lay there stunned as the missile fell on her then righted itself and tried to stand. For a nonsensical moment she was reminded of her experience with the Christmas tree and Ben Palmer.

Her heart thumping, her brain finally responding to the threat, she grabbed at the body lifting off her, caught a piece of fabric and heard a tearing sound as the person gained footing and ran. She lay quietly for a minute, letting her heart settle down, wondering idly if she had footprints on her face.

"Corie!" Ben knelt beside her and helped her to a sitting position. "Are you okay? What happened?"

She pointed into the darkness. "A man. He went that way."

Ben looked in that direction and listened for a minute. Except for the agitated dog, there was no sound. "He's long gone. Did you see his face?"

"No." She grunted and held on to his arm as he hauled her to her feet. "But he was in my house."

"Can you walk?"

"Yeah."

He wrapped an arm around her and led her past the broken door and inside. She flipped on a light. Her sofa cushions were on the floor, the rocker was turned over and her pictures were askew on the wall. The only thing still in place was her small flat-screen TV.

She resisted Ben's encouragement to sit and walked through to the kitchen. She breathed a sigh of relief that her computer sat on the table where she'd left it.

Ben followed her, dialing his cell phone. "Hopefully there's someone at the police department besides Bigelow?"

"Chris Norton is on the night shift." She smiled grimly. "We had English Lit together senior year. He was a nice guy. Couldn't get through *Macbeth* but I lent him my notes."

He narrowed his eyes at her. That had been a strange aside, considering her house had been broken into, but she wasn't thinking clearly.

"Something else you should know, though."

"Yeah?"

"He's dating Bigelow's daughter."

"You've got to be kidding. Geez. Well, that doesn't mean he's like him. What's in your hand?"

She'd been holding the scrap of fabric so tightly, she no longer felt it. "I tore this off the guy," she said as she opened her fingers.

Ben reached for the swatch of blue cloth, the shape suggesting it was a shirt pocket. It was chambray; probably from a work shirt.

"Put it in a plastic zip bag," he directed, turning his attention to the phone. "Hi. I'm reporting a break-in on Hidalgo Road."

CHRIS NORTON COMMISERATED with Corie fifteen minutes later as he inspected the splintered door frame. "I'm sorry you were frightened."

"I'm not frightened," she denied, lying just a little. "I'm just angry—and a little...creeped out. Chris, this is Ben Palmer, a friend. Ben, Chris Norton."

The men shook hands, seeming to measure each other. "You're the cop from Oregon," Chris said.

Ben nodded. "I'm from a small town, too. I know word gets around. Other break-ins in this area?"

"Not recently." Chris looked around the living room then went into the kitchen. "Anything stolen?"

Corie followed him. "I don't think so. My TV's still here and my computer is where I left it. Why would someone just throw stuff around but not take anything?"

"Maybe he was looking for something. Drugs. Cash."

"I don't have anything. Oh! Cash! I haven't even checked the bedroom yet."

Chris gestured her to lead the way. "Let's go look."

She headed down the hallway, the two men following. She reached her room ahead of them, pushed the door open and hit the light switch.

And stopped dead in her tracks.

Corie swallowed a gasp of shock and horror before the men could hear it. On her pink-eyelet pillowcase, a diamond necklace sparkled beneath the overhead light as only real diamonds could.

It was Tyree's wife's necklace. Ben had taken it from her at his parents' house in Beggar's Bay and mailed it back to Tyree with the rest of the jewelry. A sixteen-inch strand with simple, graduated stones. She'd thought it the most beautiful of the necklaces.

There was a policeman steps behind her and the man who believed she still had possession of Tyree's jewelry.

The men came through the door. Willing her heart to start beating again, she pointed to the wardrobe closet. "I keep the cash in there," she said, "in the upper right pocket of the shoe holder."

As soon as their backs were turned, she took the crocheted throw from the foot of her bed and tossed it over the necklace.

She watched anxiously as Chris dug into the pocket and turned to her with a few twenties splayed in his hand.

She blew out a noisy breath. The men took it for relief—and it was—but not for the reason they thought.

Corie and Ben followed Chris to the front door. He studied the splintered wood of the frame and the side of the door where a crowbar had broken the lock. "It's odd that he broke in through the front rather than the back, where he would be less visible."

That was easy to explain. "There's a big, noisy dog tied in the backyard next door that barks at everything. The intruder might have attracted more attention back there."

"You going to be okay here tonight?" Chris asked.

"I'll take care of the door," Ben said.

Chris smiled sympathetically at Corie. "I'll see what I can do, but it's a national statistic that only about thirteen percent of home robberies are solved."

She took that with more grace than she felt. She had to get him out. There was a diamond necklace on her pillow!

"Thanks for coming, Chris." She opened the damaged door wider.

"Don't forget the fabric you tore off the guy when he knocked you down," Ben said, going back to the kitchen to retrieve it. He handed the plastic bag to Chris.

"Looks like it's from a work shirt." Chris held it up. "Probably a million of them around here." He grinned at Corie. "I'll put a BOLO out for a guy in a work shirt with nowhere to put his cell phone. I'll be in touch."

Corie waved him off then turned to Ben to thank him for his help and to encourage him to leave. But he'd taken out a pocketknife and was cutting away at the splintered wood so that the door could be closed.

"Don't worry about that, Ben," she said a little brightly. "Thanks for helping. I think I'll still be able to hook the chain."

"Maybe, but the door won't be closed tightly and someone could reach in and unlatch it."

"But I…"

He had gone into the living room, retrieved the scuffed maple coffee table and was putting it on its side to block the door. His eyes met hers. "I'm staying," he said. "I'm not leaving you in a house you can't secure."

No. He couldn't stay. He'd find the necklace and then he'd never believe she hadn't somehow intercepted the box of jewelry.

"That's not necessary. I'm perfectly—"

"I'm staying," he repeated. "Why don't you relax and try to get some sleep? But could you toss me a blanket and a pillow?"

She hesitated, searching her brain frantically for some way to get him to leave, when he added, "But not the pillow the necklace is on. It's a little pink for me."

# CHAPTER SIX

CORIE TURNED BACK to Ben. He watched her, hands in his pockets.

"You saw?" she asked, caught between confusion and irritation. He had a gift for making everything harder for her than it had to be.

"I did. Kudos, though, for quick thinking."

"I have no idea how it got there."

"Really." The note of disbelief in his voice was clear. "I'll just bunk on the floor like I did the last time. I'll replace your door in the morning."

She walked toward him, anger simmering. "Are you some kind of Jekyll-and-Hyde split personality sent to torment me? Sweet and charming one minute and disdainful and distrustful the next?" She poked a finger into his chest but regretted it when she withdrew it and felt as though it was crinkled. "I did not keep or intercept Mrs. Tyree's jewelry. I do not know where the necklace on my pillow came from!"

She folded her arms, finding a comforting release in yelling at him. "How do I know it wasn't *you* who put the necklace on my pillow and ran out of the house, knocked me down and then pretended to just arrive and help me up, being all sweet and kind and... He was about your height, your weight. How do I know you didn't have Grady mail the junk jewelry and you kept the good stuff for yourself? Huh? How do I know?"

He seemed unaffected by her tirade. "Because I'm telling you I didn't."

"Yeah, well I've been telling you I didn't take the jewelry for two days and you don't believe me. Why should I believe you? Maybe you didn't come for the truth as you claim. Maybe you came to plant the necklace on me and set me up to take the blame for the theft. What do you have to say about that?"

He indicated the green Henley he wore. "You'll notice I'm not missing a blue pocket. And...you did steal the jewelry originally. You *should* take the blame."

The fire went out of her argument with that obvious detail. Before she indulged an impulse to punch him, she walked past him into the kitchen with no real plan on what she intended to do there. She finally just sank onto a chair at the table. Her head was throbbing.

He followed her and went to the half-full coffeepot, the warmer plate long since turned off.

"Do you mind if I microwave a cup of this?"

"No," she said flatly. "Cups are over the sink."

"Want some?"

"No, thank you."

She put her head in her hands and heard him open the cupboard, pour cold coffee and then open and close the microwave. It began to whir.

"So, it seems you weren't robbed at all," he said, pulling out the chair opposite her. "You were *given* something. The necklace."

"I don't understand."

"Maybe somebody tossed things around a little so you'd call the police right away, then while they were looking around, they'd find the necklace. In your possession."

She looked up in bewilderment. "You think?"

The timer dinged. He retrieved his cup and came back. "I'm not sure. But I think this suggests someone knows you took the jewelry in the first place."

Something else occurred to her. "And doesn't this prove that I *didn't* keep the jewelry or somehow intercept it?"

He thought about that and finally nodded. "I believe it does. And, so, to relieve temptation, why don't you give me the necklace to hold?"

Thinking that hurting him would be so satisfying, she barely suppressed the impulse and stood.

"If you saw me cover the necklace, why didn't you just tell Chris it was there?"

"Because Jack risked everything to keep you out of jail. I'm not going to be the one to put you in."

With an audible growl, she left the kitchen and returned as far as the living room with a pillow and a blanket. Not the pink pillow. Then she marched into the kitchen and slapped the necklace on the table in front of him. She'd put it in a gauzy little bag that had once held potpourri.

"Now do you trust me?" she demanded.

He met her molten gaze. "Do you trust me?"

She considered lying but simply didn't have the energy. "I hate to admit that I do," she replied wearily. "I dislike you with a purple passion, but I trust you. We're due back at Teresa's early in the morning. You'd better get some sleep, too."

"Right. Corie?"

She turned in the act of walking away. "Yeah?"

"I saw Tyree's security tape today. That's what I came to tell you."

Interest stirred despite her fury with him. "How'd you do that?"

"Local newspaper. You can't see anything definitive. I'm pretty sure we're all in the clear."

"Great." She heaved a sigh. "Yet someone knows I did it."

"Yeah. But the police don't, so we'll just figure out who it is and beat them at their own game."

"How?"

"I don't know yet. Get some sleep. We'll work it out tomorrow. Kids are in school, so it should be quieter at Teresa's, easier to get things done."

"Sorry. Monday and Tuesday are teacher in-service days. The kids will all be there."

He ran a hand down his face. "Fine. It's all good. We'll figure this out."

She walked off to bed, hoping that he had an idea how they'd accomplish that, because she sure didn't.

CORIE AWOKE TO the aroma of…pancakes? She sniffed the air and caught the subtle sweetness of maple. It took her a moment to remember what had happened last night. Ben was here. The necklace. She'd been mired in fear and depression.

But the sunny morning and the smell of pancakes made her feel as though she'd blundered into a parallel universe. One where she felt just a little more cheerful. And where Ben could cook?

Famished, she pulled on jeans and a pink T-shirt and padded barefoot out to the living room. She stopped with a gasp at the sight of two young men in Wolf's Hardware coveralls installing a new door—a pretty one with a stained-glass fan window at the top. She went on into the kitchen.

Ben wandered around the small room, his cell phone in one hand, the other carrying plates stacked with utensils and napkins. He placed the pile on the table.

He jutted his chin at her in greeting and pointed to the plates as he walked away, telling her, she concluded, to set the table. Bossy, she thought, even with gestures.

"Yeah," he was saying to whoever was on the other end of the call. "I imagine ten yards will do it. I need an uncompressed depth of twelve inches. You're sure pea gravel is better than bark chips?"

Corie looked up from arranging the plates to raise an eyebrow in question. He reached to the counter and handed her a butter tub. "Ah… I don't know. Hold on. Corie, are there copperhead snakes around here?"

She was stunned by the question. "Um, I've never seen one, but I understand this can be their habitat."

"Maybe," he said into the phone. "Okay, well, we don't want snakes hiding in it… Yeah, right. Pea gravel can't catch fire or cause splinters." He listened for a minute then frowned. "So, what *do* you do if a kid gets pea gravel stuck up his nose? No—no recycled rubber. Smells awful and if it starts to burn it'd be hard to stop… Yeah. Okay, pea gravel, it is."

He listened awhile longer, handed Corie a bottle of syrup, then asked the person at the other end, "When can you deliver? Good… the equipment's coming next Monday. That'll be perfect. We'll have the base down before it arrives… Okay. Yeah." He read out a credit card number, the expiration date and the security code. "Great. Thanks."

When he hung up the phone Corie didn't

know which question to attack first. Since she was hungry, she went with food. "You made pancakes?" she asked. "I thought Sarah took care of you and Jack when your folks were away because neither of you has any kitchen skills."

He poured a cup of coffee and handed it to her. "I can make coffee. Though I have a Keurig at home. But, no, I did not make pancakes. Hector's wife did and delivered them."

"What? How did she have time to do that?"

"Apparently her oldest boy, Emilio, is driving now," he said, clearly pleased to have knowledge she didn't. "I called to see if she could make breakfast for us and told her I'd pick it up. Emilio happened to be there and she had him deliver. He's out and around picking up Christmas decorations for the café. She was happy to help."

He heaped pancakes onto her plate.

"Why on earth do you need ten yards of pea gravel?" she asked.

"To build a playground." He went to the refrigerator for milk.

She stared at him in stupefaction. "For…?" He couldn't mean…

He put the milk in the middle of the table, sat opposite her and gave her a look of exasperation. "For Pimental and Bigelow, to give them something to do so they'll leave you alone."

She rolled her eyes at him.

"Well, silly question, Corie. For the kids, who else? The climate's so warm here, they'll be able to use the play equipment most of the time. And Teresa told me yesterday that she didn't want the kids to worry about anything. She just wanted them to go to school and come home and have fun."

With her fork in one hand and her knife in the other, she continued to stare. This wasn't the behavior of the Ben she knew as judgmental and unsympathetic. Last night had confirmed her Jekyll-and-Hyde theory. He'd helped her when he'd found her on the ground, but he still didn't believe she was no longer a thief.

Despite her ambivalence about him, a swell of emotion filled her at the thought of a playground in Teresa's backyard. She had to look away. "How long are you staying?" she asked finally, making a production of buttering her pancakes.

"The way you're racking up impossible questions for me, I'd say the full month of my leave. At least. Until I find out who broke in, what's going on with the necklace and what to do about Pimental, Bigelow and Tyree. So I may as well be useful while my brain's working on the problem. We get the tree finished today, I'll mow the back lawn tomorrow, they're delivering the gravel the day after and the stuff comes next Monday."

"Did you talk to Teresa about the play set?"

"While you were still sleeping."

She couldn't stop staring at him. "What kind of stuff is coming next Monday?"

He took the butter from her and passed the syrup, then pulled his computer closer, hit a command and turned it toward her. "The builder is a friend of my father's and is giving it to me for a deal." He hit another key and a picture of an over-the-top play set appeared onscreen. He leaned toward her, obviously happy with the plan he'd chosen. "It has a big clubhouse thing on top with a lookout balcony, ladders, a ten-foot wave slide, monkey bars, a rock-climbing wall, lots of swings and a two-person glider." All that was visible in the amazing pictures.

She was both thrilled and worried over what the children could do with all those moving parts. "How high is the rock wall?"

"Only five feet. No taller than you." He grinned as he delivered the little dig.

"I'm five one and a half," she corrected, straightening her shoulders as though that would somehow prove it.

"Yeah, yeah. Did I mention there's a full-size picnic table on the lower level?"

Excitement was edging out her concerns. "I see it. Wow. Does it come assembled?"

"Yeah, right." He dismissed that notion with a look. "No, it does not."

"How long will that take to put together? It's huge."

"Chuck says two moderately skilled people can do it in about thirty-six hours."

"Are you moderately skilled at carpentry?"

"A little better than moderately. I worked summers with my dad when I was in high school and college."

"But you're only one person."

"Elizabeth Corazon," he said, shaking his head at her. "Do you mean you wouldn't help me?"

"I'm happy to make some time to help you but, frankly, I am *less* than moderately skilled."

"I'll take whatever help I can get. My Christmas present to the kids." He said it so easily, as though it wasn't a big deal. But she knew what it would mean to the children and it turned her heart to mush.

"What," she made herself ask, "if Teresa and the children do have to leave the house? You'll have spent all that money and done all that work for nothing."

"No. I'm going to see that she gets that house without constant threats of eviction. On the remote chance that I fail—" he arched an eyebrow in a gesture she guessed was meant to mock his own lack of modesty "—the kids will have six or seven weeks of playing on good solid equipment that'll give them hours of fun, burn off some of that steam, make them forget that their families are split up and their lives are in suspension. I don't consider that 'for nothing.'"

She couldn't help it. She reached out to put her hand over his. He looked into her eyes, clearly surprised by the gesture. His thumb covered hers. "They'll be very happy," she said. Because the words came out a little choked, she withdrew her hand and concentrated on her pancakes.

## CHAPTER SEVEN

IT TOOK MOST of the day to finish decorating the tree. Ben strung the lights on the top half and stood by while Soren and then Carlos climbed the ladder to add the strings of gold-beaded garland Corie had bought. They filled out the tree with the plain, ball ornaments Ben had picked.

Teresa held a papier-mâché angel with painted blue eyes and a sweet smile. It wore a glittery-gold gown and carried a star.

"I want to put the angel on the tree," Rosie said eagerly, reaching for it.

The youngest Santiago brother pushed her out of the way. "I want it!"

Because Teresa held the angel and Corie was on top of the smaller ladder at the back of the tree, adjusting a swag of garland that had slipped, Ben put himself between the children.

"The littlest kid is supposed to do it," Carlos said. "In our house, it was always Tonio. But here, it would be Roberto."

"That wouldn't work." Soren shook his head. "He's too little. It has to be the next youngest. Bianca. Right, Teresa?"

Tonio was now in tears and Rosie's pout threatened retribution. This reminded Ben a lot of domestic issues in his police work. Solutions to problems seldom satisfied all concerned.

Teresa smiled sympathetically at the warring factions. "You know how it is in this house. We do our best to make everyone happy, but when we can't, we try to do what's right. In this case, Carlos is correct. The youngest child puts the angel on top of the tree, but Roberto can't do it, so Bianca will."

Tonio wept but continued to hold on to Ben's hand. Rosie, however, yanked her hand away, crossed her arms and sank into a nuclear glower.

Bianca jumped up and down, realizing she had a special honor.

Teresa handed her the angel. She accepted it with reverence.

"Can you get her up there safely, Ben?" Teresa asked.

"Sure." He lifted the child onto his hip, told her to hold tightly to his neck and then climbed the ladder. When he was high enough that Bianca could reach, he stood her on a rung and held her tightly as she leaned over to place the angel on the top.

"It's crooked!" several voices shouted from below.

Ben anchored Bianca in one hand and stretched an arm out to straighten the angel. Everyone cheered.

When Ben and Bianca were halfway down the ladder, Teresa reached up to take Bianca from him. "Okay. One more cocoa break," Teresa said, shepherding the children toward the kitchen, "then we'll turn the lights on and see how it looks."

Backing down the ladder, Ben caught sight of Corie's face through the lacy pattern of branches.

She seemed less tense than she had last night. He could see that in the soft lines of her half smile. The children always seemed to ease her mood, even when they were being difficult. Tucked behind the green branches, beaded garland and glass ornaments picking up light from the window, she looked like an exotic gift.

A gift for him? He entertained the thought for a minute, until Corie realized he was watching her. She gave the garland one last adjustment and climbed down the ladder to join the others in the kitchen.

A gift for him... Interesting thought. The cop and the thief. Dangerous...but interesting.

He stepped onto the floor and stood back to check the position of the angel for himself, only to realize that Rosie still stood glaring at the tree, arms folded in disgust. Tears rolled down her cheeks. He couldn't help but empathize.

His parents had never given in to every whim or thwarted desire he and Jack had, but they'd been compassionate when it came to hurt feelings.

He knelt on one knee in front of her. "What if we all go to McAllen tomorrow and everybody buys a special ornament they really like? Then you can put it as high on the tree as you like. Except not higher than the angel. She has to be at the top."

Rosie considered; her dark eyes serious. Her answer would have sounded like a non sequitur if he hadn't known her story.

"My dad's coming." Her voice was tight, tear-filled.

"That's what I hear," he replied. And she'd get to put up the angel on *his* tree.

She looked straight at Ben. He looked back—

and refused to let her see any doubt on his part. Christmas was about believing.

"So…when he comes," she said, wiping at her damp cheeks with the back of her hand, "I can take my purple chain *and* my ornament?"

"Absolutely."

"Can I get an ornament that's an angel?"

"Why not?"

"Okay."

"Okay." He stood and caught her hand and they headed for the kitchen.

"WHAT'S GOING ON?" Grady Nelson asked. Grady, Ben's partner on the force, had called to tell him about their mutual friend Mario's purchase of a second auto repair shop up the coast from Beggar's Bay in Seaside, Oregon. "We're getting together to celebrate. When are you coming back?"

"Hard to say." Ben had left with just a bare-bones explanation to the captain and Grady. "I took a month's leave."

"You're going to spend an entire month in Querida, Texas, with a woman you don't like? I thought you'd have made her spill her guts and be on your way home by now, those jewels returned to their rightful owner."

"It's trickier than I thought."

"Why? You said she was a thief who was going to mean trouble for all of you."

"Yeah. Now I'm not sure of anything."

"Wow." There was a pause. "I'm looking up to see if pigs are flying."

"Very funny. Please tell Mario I'm happy for him. What's new with you?"

"Nothing."

After years of sharing the same squad car, hours of routine police work broken by critical situations where their lives were endangered, he and Grady knew each other well. Ben heard the undercurrent in his friend's voice.

"Something happen on the job?" he asked.

"No. Unless it's the fact you're taking your sweet time in Texas while I'm paired up with an old guy who does nothing but run license plates."

Ben smiled to himself. Cops who were more interested in traffic issues tied up the radio and took valuable time from other police work.

"Your mom's okay?"

"Yeah. She won big at bingo. Took me to dinner."

He was getting the picture. "Then it must be Celeste."

Celeste was a tall, beautiful redhead Grady had met while visiting his sister in Seattle.

She'd sounded high-maintenance to Ben, but Grady had fallen instantly in love and spent every spare moment of the past year and a half driving to Seattle to see her. He'd even planned a couple of weeks off this month to spend time with her family. He intended to propose over the holidays.

"Yeah. She's got an engagement ring," Grady said. Then added darkly, "Not mine."

Again Ben could empathize. Before Jack fell in love with Sarah Reed, Ben had loved her and asked her to marry him. She'd said no.

"Sorry, Grady. You know when I say I know how you feel, I really do."

"Yeah. Thanks." A gusty sigh came over the line. "So here I am with two weeks' vacation and nowhere to go. Mom wants me to drive her and my aunts to Reno."

Ben tried to be supportive. "Reno sounds like fun."

"Maybe, but with my mother and my aunts?"

Ben had met them once. They were loud and fun-loving, wore yoga pants and tennis shoes and loved Josh Groban.

"No, maybe not." Ben felt inspiration fall on his head. "Want to come to Texas?"

"Texas."

"Yeah. I'm putting up a playground at the

foster home where Corie grew up. The ground cover's coming day after tomorrow, and the equipment's arriving Monday. When does your vacation start?"

"I've got day shift Saturday then I'm done."

"Perfect. Come on out whenever you're ready. You can stay at the B and B. I'll set it up for you."

"Where are *you* staying?"

"I'm planning to stay at Corie's. On the living-room floor," he added when the line went quiet.

"You're planning? You're not sure?"

"Her house was broken into last night. It's part of the long story. I'll explain when you get here. We could use another cop."

"Why?"

"Again. Long story. We can put up the play set in a couple of days, where it might take me a week or better by myself. And while you're here, you can help me map out a business plan for my company."

"All right. I guess I'm in. I may drive Mom and the *girls* to Reno and fly out from there. They can drive themselves home."

"Good. Let me know when and where to pick you up."

"I'll rent a car. Give me the B and B address and I'll put it in my GPS. See you maybe Tuesday?"

"Perfect. I'll email you the address."

Happy with the way that turned out, grateful to have help with the playground and the goings-on in Querida, Ben joined the others, who were now gathered around the tree. Teresa turned off the lights and Corie closed the curtains. The children chattered excitedly. Bianca and Tonio, competition over putting up the angel forgotten, jumped up and down in their excitement. Roberto, in Rosie's arms, just stared.

Teresa gave Ben the okay and he plugged in the lights. Flashes of red, green, yellow and blue winked down the tree from the angel to the heavier ornaments at the bottom. Glass, sequins, beading and gold garland picked up the light, spreading its glow.

A collective "Ooh!" rose from the group, Ben included. It was a glorious tree. Corie stood with her hands together, her eyes shining just like the children's. Rosie, with Roberto, moved closer. "It's beautiful, Corie," she said.

Corie heaved a sigh. Teresa had told Ben this was just what Corie had wanted for the children—a happy Christmas to help them deal with the separation from their families. If the perfect tree could do that, this had to be the one.

BEN CAUGHT CORIE'S arm just as she opened the door of her truck to go to work. "Come on," he said. "We'll take my car. I'll drive you to work and then I'll come by at nine for dinner and we'll go home."

Something in the way he said that made her ask, "Home?"

"Your home," he replied as though there should be no question. "I'm staying with you. Jack would expect it."

She opened her mouth to argue and decided against it. She both loved and hated the idea. Even when she was furious with him, his presence made her feel safe. But she'd always relied on herself to feel safe, and this new dependence on him was troubling.

"Okay. Thank you." She tossed her keys into her purse and started toward his SUV.

"Wait!" he said, putting a hand to his heart. He fell back against the side of her truck as though he needed support. "You're not going to fight me? I... I..." Dramatically he raised his hand to his head. "I feel...weak."

"Sure you do. All two hundred pounds of

muscle and bark." She hooked her arm in his and pulled him toward his rental. "Just don't get overconfident. You can protect my person, but don't think you can tell me what to do otherwise."

He beeped her door open and held it while she slipped inside. "I'm afraid a bodyguard is in full control of all situations. Not my fault. It's the way the system is set up."

"Please. There is no *system* and you're not a bodyguard. You're my...brother. Sort of. You're doing this out of family loyalty, so all situations are not under your control."

He grinned at her as he got in behind the wheel. "So, you're thinking of yourself as part of the family."

"That's not what I meant."

"That's what you said."

"I said *you're* doing it out of family loyalty."

"If you understand my feelings then you must respect them. Like a family member would."

She puffed her cheeks and blew air. "I'm going to be late. Please drive."

"Wow." He started the car, checked his mirror and pulled onto the road. "This is a banner day. Not only did you resist an argument with me but I won one with you."

"You didn't win. I just stopped fighting."

"I believe that's a default victory for me."

To his complete disbelief she laughed and punched his arm. "Drive, Palmer!" she said.

He enjoyed the win. A punch from her was like a kiss from any other woman.

# CHAPTER EIGHT

BEN MOWED TERESA'S backyard with a rickety hand mower.

He was focused on avoiding the toes of the children dancing around the lawn as he pushed his way toward the old chain-link fence. They knew he was mowing the grass to prepare for the delivery tomorrow of the pea gravel for the playground.

He'd downloaded a picture of the equipment and placed his laptop in the middle of the table when they'd had their morning snack. The expressions on their faces had been worth every muscle that would ache tomorrow from pushing this rusty thing.

After lunch he, Corie and Teresa were taking the children shopping for their own special ornament. Their excitement level was tasking his efforts to finish the yard.

Teresa finally called them to get cleaned up for the trip to the mall in nearby McAllen. They ran in, shouting and screaming.

Soren came up beside him. "How come you're doing all this?" he asked, taking long steps to keep up with Ben.

"Because I want you guys to have a playground."

Soren laughed. "Yeah, sure. Why?"

"Because I like you and I think you'd have a lot of fun with it."

"You like us?"

"Yeah."

"All of us?"

"Sure."

Ben turned the mower at the fence to complete the last pass back to the house. Soren turned with him. "What about the ornaments?"

"What do you mean?"

"How come you're buying them for us?"

"Because everybody should have a special ornament that's just theirs. It's wonderful to share things, but something that you've chosen because it's exactly what you want and represents something special to you is a great thing. It would never mean quite the same thing to anybody else."

Soren nodded as though that made sense. "My mom had this ornament with an old-fashioned lady that wore a fuzzy thing girls put their hands in in the winter. You know, in the old days."

Ben tried to imagine what that was. "Ah, not sure what you mean."

Corie came out, apparently looking for Soren. "There you are," she said, crossing the yard toward them. She put an arm around the boy's shoulders. "Come on. You have to look clean and civilized to go to town."

"We're trying to think of a word," Ben said.

Soren told her about his mother's ornament and the fuzzy thing. "It's like mittens, only there's just one, and a hand goes in each side."

"Oh." Her expression brightened. "A muff. From Victorian times."

"That's it! I liked that ornament a lot. But I don't know what happened to it. I didn't get to go home again after my dad died. Some lady brought Teresa some of his stuff. That red sweatshirt she gave you." He sighed. "Makes me think about him."

"Maybe we can find something else you'll like today."

"Cool." He ran off to the house.

Corie sniffed the air. "Does anything smell better than cut grass?" She looked at him. "Except, maybe, for Oregon." She closed her eyes. "I remember standing on the bay and smelling the river and the ocean beyond, and that wind that smells as though it passed though fields of herbs and flowers on the way."

It surprised him a little that she remembered Oregon so poetically. She'd been personable and polite with his family through Thanksgiving and Jack and Sarah's wedding, but he'd gotten the impression she'd much rather have been somewhere else.

The morning air swept a whiff of something wonderful from her direction.

"Your hair smells wonderful," he said. It was straight and thick, a sheet of obsidian under the sun. "Cherry and something?" he suggested as he pushed the mower the last few yards.

She smiled. He was happy to see that. She'd been quiet after dinner last night and most of the morning. It was strange to be uncomfortable together when they were used to telling each other what they thought—and in no uncertain terms.

"You have an excellent nose. It's cherry blossom and ginseng."

He stopped and leaned an elbow on the mower.

She tossed her head, sunlight rippling through

the black sea of her hair. "Did I thank you for putting in the new door?" she asked.

He thought. "No, I don't believe you did."

"Well, thank you. It's a beautiful door. I love the fan window. Pretty fancy. And," she added with an intake of breath, as though what she said next would be difficult. "Thank you for staying with me."

He seemed surprised by that but simply nodded. "You're welcome. I didn't want you to be afraid."

"I am sometimes."

"You know I won't let anything happen to you," he assured her.

She frowned at nothing in particular then looked up at him, gauging, he guessed, his ability to understand. "I'm not physically afraid. I just hate it when I'm not sure what to do next." She put a hand over his, still resting on the handle of the mower. Hers was soft and warm. He had to talk himself out of using it to pull her into his arms. "For so long, I was afraid that I'd never see Jack or Cassie again. Then Jack found me…" She shrugged in a gesture of helplessness. "And he's so…much, you know. He lived with our mother the longest and dealt with all that awful stuff, but look at the wonderful man he's become."

Ben pushed the mower toward the little shed in the corner. "I know what you mean." He grinned. "That always annoyed me about him. He had every *dis*advantage, and still knew how to make it all come out right."

"Because he gives openly."

"I think so. And he's fearless. I think it's the fear that holds us back."

"Us?" She slid the bolt on the shed's lock and pulled the door open for him. "Are you afraid of something?"

He replaced the mower next to a collection of gardening tools and then closed and bolted the door. Corie walked along beside him toward the house. He liked the way having her next to him felt.

"I am. I've had every advantage, have a relatively good brain and strong body, did well in the police academy and like the work. I've had a few confrontations with perps, done a few takedowns, so I thought I was pretty tough. But I was shot a couple of weeks ago in a simple traffic stop."

"The scar on your shoulder?"

"Yes. It hurt like the very devil and for a minute I couldn't pull myself together to take action. I was scared. And that scared me even more. It was tough to realize I wasn't the paragon of manhood I thought I was."

She stopped walking to shake her head at him and smile. "Of course you are. You'd have to be stupid to *not* feel fear when you were shot."

All right. He could live for some time on that declaration. She seemed so sincere that he was speechless for a minute. He folded his arms and looked down at her. Why he'd ever admitted to her that he'd been afraid was beyond him.

"So you think I'm a paragon of manhood?" he coaxed, a light edge to his voice.

She rolled her eyes. "I thought we were being serious. I shared my fears and you shared yours. Don't withdraw like that."

Surprised by her tone he cleared his throat and put his hands in his pockets. He'd been chastised, but it meant their relationship had reached a deeper level than he'd realized.

"I'm sorry," he said. "I was scared and I didn't like it."

"Fear is an honest emotion."

"Then you shouldn't worry that *you* feel it. In a way, you've been through even more than Jack—at least in your family life. My parents love him as though they'd given birth to him and you went to that woman who sold you for an old microwave. I'd have a hard time getting over that."

She looked into his eyes, hers clouded with old memories. And then her expression cleared and a fragile sparkle of humor filled her eyes. "I have had a hard time. I just didn't realize until you came to brighten my life with your accusations of criminal behavior and general bad temper—" she arched an eyebrow "—that I've suppressed a lot of stuff. Or maybe I'm running away from it. Not sure which." She grew serious again. "I'm just beginning to understand that I have to deal with all my history if I'm ever going to be able to really be Jack's sister."

"You came through a terrible childhood with generosity intact. You're helping Teresa care for these children. You *are* Jack's sister."

Teresa appeared on the back porch, shading her eyes from the sun. "Are you two coming? If I'm the only one driving, I'm going to have to tie a couple of the kids to the hood."

The children spilled out of the house behind her, laughing at that suggestion.

"YOU HAVE SOREN, Carlos and Rigo," Teresa told Ben. She stood in the doorway of Forever Christmas Eve at the La Plaza Mall in McAllen to prevent the children from going inside until she'd delivered her final instructions. "Corie, you have Rosie, Lupe, Karina and Bianca." She looked into the children's eager faces. "Are you all listening to me?"

"Yes," they chorused, though they fidgeted, eager to get inside.

"All right. I want everyone's hands in their pockets. If you see an ornament you'd like to look at, you ask the adult with you to pick it up for you. We'll help you. Look around before you decide so that you're sure the ornament you pick is the one you want. Okay?"

A round of vigorous nodding.

Ben quickly lost his self-confidence. It hadn't occurred to him that the three boys would go in three different directions and each would call his name five or six times in sixty seconds. He did his best to keep track of them, but helping one necessitated taking his eyes off the other two. He knew that couldn't be good, but all he could think to do was to caution Rigo and Soren to wait patiently while he helped Carlos with a baseball-playing Santa.

"My dad played baseball when he was a teenager," the boy said, turning the ornament carefully in his hand. It showed Santa at bat, his bag of toys on the ground near home plate. "But he hurt his shoulder and couldn't play anymore."

"That's too bad."

"Yeah. I bet he'd like this." He pointed to the small button on Santa's back. "That means music, doesn't it?"

"Go ahead and push it."

A slightly tinny version of "Take Me Out to the Ballgame" played. Carlos laughed and handed it to Ben. "I want that one."

"Okay. You hold on to it carefully. Let's see what the other guys are doing."

Rigo was torn between an ice-skating penguin and a moose with a Christmas wreath hooked on one of its antlers. One boy with an ornament and another down to two choices. Ben was feeling relieved, thinking he might do a creditable job at this chaperone thing, after all. Until Rigo saw that Carlos's Santa played music and changed his mind.

Carlos took him to the musical ornaments and Rigo reconsidered. Ben looked around in sudden concern, realizing Soren wasn't in sight.

Reminding Rigo to call him if he found something he wanted to look at more closely, Ben went to the end of their aisle and turned to check all the others. He saw Corie valiantly hovering over the excited little girls as they examined angel ornaments. She glanced up to wave at him before Karina claimed her attention.

In the next aisle Teresa rolled a protesting Roberto back and forth in a stroller while the children she kept tabs on sat on the floor looking at each other's choices. Tonio handed his to Teresa and pointed to a Power Rangers display on the top shelf.

No Soren.

A resounding crash momentarily silenced the children. Ben closed his eyes for an instant; certain he knew who had caused what sounded like the shattering of glass and the drunken notes of a broken music box.

He heard Teresa's quiet but heartfelt, "Oh, no!" and saw Corie's head pop around the aisle. Ben headed in the direction of the crash along with a clerk. Standing in the middle of the farthest aisle behind a low, decorative picket fence intended to protect the delicate merchandise, Soren looked down at a cherry-wood music box, split open on the floor. The fractured tune continued to play. Soren glanced up at Ben, his eyes filled with guilt and embarrassment.

"You were supposed to call Ben if you wanted to look at something," Rosie said in her superior, conscience-of-the-world mode. Teresa, Corie and the rest of the children had converged on the scene.

Soren was too upset to defend himself. "I'm sorry," he said quickly, his voice strained. "I... I..."

"He couldn't call Ben," Carlos intervened. "It was supposed to be a present *for* him."

"For me?" Ben was completely taken aback.

Soren's face crumpled. "Yeah," he said.

Teresa began to dig in her purse. She glanced apologetically at the clerk, who was doing her best to keep smiling. "We'll pay for it, of course..."

The clerk picked up the broken box, holding the split wood together and examining the damage. "Maybe I can fix it..."

"We'll be getting more things," Ben said to her, putting a hand to Soren's shoulder and pulling the boy toward him. "Just add it to our bill." He turned to Teresa. "All right if we guys take a bathroom break? We'll be right back."

"Go ahead," she said.

Carlos put his Santa ornament on the counter and gathered his brothers to follow Ben and Soren.

Ben spotted the restroom sign and Soren ran ahead. Carlos fell into step beside Ben and his brothers. "Don't be mad," he implored on behalf of his friend. "Soren had his own money and everything. He showed me the box when you were helping Rigo."

"I didn't notice."

"Yeah. He wanted it to be a surprise. He likes you." Carlos grinned up at him. "He really misses his dad. We miss ours, too, but ours is still alive and he's gonna come back. Soren's is gone forever."

"Thanks for telling me." Ben put an arm around Carlos's shoulder, touched to the core by what these children had to bear. And that Soren wanted to buy him a present. "He's lucky to have a good friend like you."

"I'm hungry," Carlos said, putting an end to the heavy conversation.

No one said another word about the broken valet box. After the bathroom stop, it took another hour to finalize ornament choices. Corie pointed out a Victorian couple wearing skates to Soren. The woman was wearing a muff. He smiled. "I like that," he said.

Roberto had a death grip on a plush Santa doll. All the Santiago boys had made their selections. The Flores girls had chosen fairies and princesses. Rosie held a red-robed angel.

Corie showed her the cone under the angel's robe that made it suitable for the top of a tree. "She's beautiful," Corie said. "But she's a tree topper."

"I know. It's gonna go on our tree when my dad picks me up."

Corie opened her mouth to suggest a more conventional ornament, sure that when they got it home and found it hard to hang in the middle of the tree, Rosie would be upset.

"Ben said it was okay," Rosie told her. She seemed to think that should be the end of the discussion.

"All right."

While the clerk wrapped everything in tissue, the children wandered away to look at the mechanical elves in the store window. Corie and Teresa followed. Ben waited to pay and realized, when the clerk wrapped the broken box, that Soren remained at his side.

"I'm sorry I broke it," the boy said. "I should have been more careful."

"It's okay. My dad's a carpenter and I grew

up learning how to fix things. I can make it good as new."

"But the music thingy is broken."

Ben smiled down at him. "I'll just sing when I open it. What did it play?"

Soren's frown turned to a fragile smile. "That Christmas song about the bird in the tree and the turtles. I don't know what it's called."

Ben thought hard. "You mean the partridge in the pear tree and two turtle doves?"

"That's it! There's a lot of tricky stuff in it."

"Yeah. It's a great song."

"After you fix the box, you have to give it back to me so I can wrap it."

"Deal."

When everything had been wrapped and placed in individual bags with handles, the clerk reached for the credit card Ben held out to her.

"Wait." Soren put a fistful of crumpled bills on the counter. "I want to pay for the box."

The clerk looked at Ben. Knowing it was important to Soren—and humbled by that knowledge—he nodded. She took the crumpled money, removed the price of the box from the bill and rang in the purchase separately.

Once the transactions were complete, the children returned to the counter to take their bags. They glowed with the excitement of possession. Ben felt as though he'd secured world peace or something equally monumental.

"Shall I go put all the bags in the car," Corie asked, "so nothing gets lost or forgotten?"

The children resisted for a moment before handing over their purchases. Corie took off with the armload.

Ben pointed to the sandwich shop at the end of the mall. "Meet us at Burger Boy," he called after her.

The boys, instructed not to run, marched ahead as fast as they could, while the Flores sisters skipped along hand in hand. Rosie followed sedately, left out. If she minded, she didn't show it. Ben's heart broke a little.

"*Is* Rosie's dad coming back?" Ben asked Teresa as she pushed Roberto's stroller.

"He called to say he got a job driving a cab," Teresa said. "He's saving his money."

"To come and get her?" Ben didn't like the sound of this guy.

"I hope so. When I asked him, we were disconnected. Not sure if it was iffy phone service or iffy parenting. But sometimes people come through when you least expect them to."

As a cop, he knew they just as often didn't. But he was going to think positively for Rosie's sake.

# CHAPTER NINE

"I'M COOKING," BEN announced that evening at Corie's. "PB and J or peanut butter on toast."

Corie groaned emphatically. "Nothing for me." After stuffing herself at lunch with chili-cheese fries, then helping Teresa and the children bake Christmas cookies, she was sure she wouldn't be hungry until January.

He stood in the middle of her kitchen in T-shirt and jeans. She stared at him in amused disbelief. "You had a double burger, fries *and* onion rings at the mall and then you sampled the kids' Christmas cookies all afternoon."

"What's your point?"

"You should be stuffed."

"I mowed a lawn. I wrangled wild children. I've had to deal with you all day. I've worked it off."

"Ha, ha. You're lucky I always try to be *less* argumentative around the children. But, no thanks to dinner. And peanut butter's hardly dinner, anyway."

"Well." He put the jar of peanut butter and a loaf of bread on the table and turned to take a plate from the cupboard. "We Cordon Bleu-deprived types do what we have to do." He smiled charmingly at her. "Unless you'd like to make me a fried-egg sandwich?"

She smiled, tempted. She'd love to linger with him in her cozy lamp-lit living room, talking about all the fun the children had had today—and her, too. But she didn't know what her next step was so retreat seemed simpler. "No. I'm going to bed early and read. Good night." She walked away.

"Some friend you are," he grumbled good-naturedly. "Good night."

She closed her bedroom door behind her, turned on the bedside lamp and reached under her pillow for her sleep shirt. Only then did she notice the small gift bag in the middle of her bed. It was decorated with a polar bear on skates and had a matching gift card attached. It read, "Something special just for you. Ben"

Pulling a thick wad of tissue out of the bag, she unwrapped it to reveal a large, sparkly star with several smaller stars dangling from it. The brilliance of it made her smile. When she pressed the button in the center, it played "O, Little Town of Bethlehem."

She smiled to herself, remembering that Ben had left their noisy group at lunch, excusing himself to get batteries for his flashlight. He must have bought the ornament and put it on her bed when she'd run out to her truck to get her forgotten cell phone.

Guilt assailed her. She should go back out there and make him a fried-egg sandwich. But thinking this nice, inexplicable truce between them could last any longer than his visit to Querida was a pipe dream.

She did yank open her door. "Ben?" she shouted.

"Yeah?" he called back from the kitchen.

"Thank you for the ornament!"

"You're welcome!"

"And…thanks for this afternoon. The kids had a great time."

"Sure."

"And, Ben?"

"Yeah?"

"I did, too."

"Good."

"Good night."

"Good night."

She closed her door and turned back to the dresser, thinking that had been an unsatisfying conversation. She'd thanked him, but talking to him without looking into his face diminished the challenge and the pleasure. She hadn't gotten to see his taunting expression, the exasperated roll of his eyes, the often cryptic twist of his lips.

Sighing, she reached for the book on top of her dresser and turned toward the bed. She was interrupted by a knock on the door. She backtracked to open it wide, happy the conversation wasn't terminated.

"Yes?" she asked.

Without answering her, he wrapped an arm around her waist and pulled her to him. He looked down into her face, all that the earlier contact had lacked because he hadn't been within sight, now filling her with all his nearness had come to mean. His eyes were bright with passion, his arm firmly possessive, the free hand that brushed the hair out of her eyes warm and slightly rough with calluses.

He kissed her long and lingeringly. Yes, she thought absently as her senses were bombarded with so many impressions she couldn't untangle them. It was better to deal with him face-to-face.

The overall impact of his mouth on hers was both liberating and deliciously confining, filled with tension and still euphoric, a little alarming in its intensity and yet leaving her wanting more. Yes, she thought again, her breath coming in gasps as he raised his head. It was even better to have him within reach.

He studied her one last minute, that storm that was part clarity, part confusion, still in his eyes. He finally dropped his hands and took a step back, as though making himself create distance between them. "Good night, Corie," he said and walked away.

"Good night, Ben," she whispered after him. She closed the door.

BEN SAT AT the kitchen table with a cup of tea and looked over the information Will Fennerty had printed out for him. The folder held news of the mayor's election almost two years ago and his choice of Roberto Pimental as deputy mayor. Several residents had written letters to the editor disputing the need for one in a town as small as theirs. Another letter cited the mayor's health and questioned why he was elected when he required another person to help him do his job. A moot point, since the election had taken place.

Ben frowned over the casual government in Querida.

There was an editorial in which Will asked

for proof of the deputy mayor's salary. A pay stub in a very reasonable amount had been provided. There was an article about Corie's arrest for assault along with a photo of the deputy mayor with a cut lip and a gash above his right eye.

The reporter repeated Corie's claim that Pimental had tried to force sexual favors from her for his assistance in helping Teresa fight eviction. He also repeated Pimental's denial and insistence that *she* had offered *him* sexual favors. Pimental had decided not to press charges and denied having seen the delivery person who claimed to have witnessed his advances.

Pimental removed parking meters in the downtown area just before last Christmas, which had resulted in a hail of letters of praise. "He's doing a fine job." The remark, from the proprietor of a downtown business, seemed based exclusively on the parking meters.

Fennerty had also included a printout from the local town government website about operational protocol relating to a deputy mayor. Several sentences were underlined. "The deputy mayor does not become mayor if a mayor resigns. The council selects a new mayor by majority vote if there is a vacancy. The deputy mayor serves only during the absence or temporary disability of the mayor."

The mayor hadn't officially resigned, according to Will's note, but an absence of more than a year and a half was considerably more than temporary. So, he really had no right to be in office?

There was an item several years old about Gil Bigelow's appointment as chief of police. A sticky note attached to the article by Will said that he'd tried to find a connection between Pimental and Bigelow but had been unable to so far. He was still investigating.

Unfortunately, Ben thought, most of the information related to what Pimental had done in public. What they needed to know was what went on behind closed doors.

And could Pimental possibly be related to the necklace that had showed up on Corie's pillow? He and Tyree were cronies, but would Tyree have told him he'd gotten the jewelry back and was defrauding the insurance company? And, if so, did either man know that Corie had taken the jewelry in the first place?

Ben closed the folder, put it in his bag and went to his makeshift bed on the floor, distracted from his concerns about Pimental by the memory of Corie's kiss. That was a more pleasant thought to sleep on.

IT WAS HARD for Ben to imagine that children would find pea gravel so exciting. Teresa had gone Christmas shopping and Corie had ordered the children, just home from school, to remain near the back door under pain of dessert deprivation for a lifetime. "And I'm not kidding!" she added forcefully when Soren and Carlos grinned.

The boys sobered instantly and watched with the other children in complete fascination as the dump truck tilted its red box and dropped a large mound of gravel. The driver moved the truck forward, then jumped out and ran to the controls at the back to increase the angle of the box so that it dumped another load right in front of the other. He repeated the process several more times until a long, four-foot hill of gravel stood in the middle of the backyard. The children shouted and applauded. The driver took a bow, handed Ben the bill, climbed back into the cab of the truck, righted the large red box and drove away.

"That's so cool," Soren said. He turned to Ben. "Can we climb on it before you spread it out?"

Corie turned to Ben. She still had a little trouble looking at him after their kiss last night, but he met her gaze evenly, as though he thought of nothing else but keeping her charges safe. He knew she wanted to tell the children they couldn't but apparently hated to deprive them of fun. "Is it safe?" she asked.

He didn't know how to answer that. He wouldn't have thought a pile of gravel could hurt anyone, but since watching these children at play, he'd learned that their creativity could make a feather and a cotton ball into dangerous threats. "I'll be right here," he promised. "Give them half an hour on it then I'll start smoothing. But we'll set a few rules."

"Fine. I'll stand by just in case."

He tried to mimic her firm expression and no-nonsense voice as he turned to the children. "You can stand on it, slide down on it, but no burrowing into it. Everybody got that?" He frowned fiercely. He could see them meeting his eyes and trying to determine just how serious he was. He didn't flinch.

"Okay," Soren finally said. "On it and down it, but not in it."

"Right."

"Got it."

The children ran toward the pile of gravel

screaming like a military force taking a hill. Later, Ben and Corie had to extend the time limit to an hour because the kids stuck meticulously to the rules and were having so much fun.

"Who'd have thought?" she asked, leaning toward him.

He caught a whiff of her cherry blossom/ ginseng shampoo.

"That the gravel would be as much fun for them as the playground equipment? Maybe you could have saved yourself a lot of money."

He smiled without taking his eyes off the kids. "Wait till the set gets here. It's pretty cool."

"Oh, no. I have to start honing my carpentry skills for Monday, right?"

"No," he replied. "My partner on the police force has a couple of weeks off and he's coming to help."

She turned to him in surprise. "He has a couple of weeks off and he's coming here to do manual labor with you?"

"The woman he loved is marrying someone else. He's happy to be able to get away. It was come here or go with his mom and her sisters to Reno."

Corie frowned. "Poor guy. Where's he going to stay?"

"I got him my old room at the B and B. You'll like him. He's a great guy. His parents taught at an American school in Europe, then his father died and his mom wanted to move back to Oregon to be near her sisters. Grady came along to spend a little time to make sure she was going to be all right. He fell in love with Beggar's Bay. He's been there five years."

"Well, I can't say I'm disappointed that I don't have to help you measure and hammer. But I will help you spread gravel. There are a couple of rakes in the shed."

"Thank you." He pointed toward the children. "You ready to break this up? You're better at laying down the law than I am. I have to *act* tough."

"But, you're a cop. Don't you *lay down the law* every day?"

"Sure, but adults are easier to intimidate."

THE PLAY SET arrived on schedule Monday morning in four giant boxes. Corie gathered with Ben, Teresa and the younger children on the back patio to watch the delivery. Corie had driven the older children to school earlier.

Ben asked the men to place the boxes near the gravel base she'd helped him prepare. His friend Grady Nelson was due to arrive tomorrow and Ben planned to go through all the pieces today to arrange them for a more efficient assembly.

"I can't believe all you've done for us."

Corie had heard Teresa say that to Ben at least half a dozen times.

Ben's reply was always the same. "I'm happy to."

"But we've completely sidetracked you," Teresa said. "You came here for a purpose, but you've spent all your time working for me and the children." She indicated the enormous boxes sitting to one side of the yard. "There's no way we can set it up without you, but once that's done, you have to concentrate on what you came to Querida for."

"I'll get to that," he said with a smiling glance of warning in Corie's direction. He went to talk to the driver, signed paperwork and handed back the clipboard.

"I think Ben came for *you*," Teresa said to Corie, giving her a maternal smile.

"He did, but not for the reason you think."

Teresa herded the little ones into the house, Corie hiking Roberto onto her hip.

"Maybe the reason's changed," Teresa said. "You have to be open to that in life. Things start out one way and, before you know it, everything's different. That can be okay. You have feelings for him, don't you?"

"I do," Corie admitted with a wide smile as Teresa took Roberto from her and put him in his playpen. "Frustration, exasperation, annoyance..."

She gathered dishes off the table to put them in the dishwasher. The arrival of the delivery trucks had interrupted her morning cleanup.

"He puts up with you, too."

"Not without a lot of flak." Teresa beckoned Bianca to the little rocker beside Roberto and put on the children's favorite morning television show. They immediately began bouncing with the music.

"Corie, your being here has been wonderful for me. Like having a daughter. And you've made things so much easier. Still, this is my life. You have to find *yours*."

"Well. You made life possible for me. If you hadn't taken me in, I don't know what would have happened to me. So I'm happy to be here."

Teresa held her hand tightly and looked her in the eye. "I want you to reconnect with your brother. You should go to Oregon when Ben goes home and make a new life there."

"Out of the question." Corie dismissed the very thought by going back to the dishwasher. She continued to load then put in soap. "I don't fit in there, Teresa."

"You'd fit in anywhere now, Corie. You just have to want to."

Life in Oregon with Ben and the Palmers. It was a nice thought but probably more in the realm of a fairy tale. For a while, at least, she had to focus on reality.

# CHAPTER TEN

THE FOLLOWING AFTERNOON Ben cut open boxes and sorted lumber. Teresa took the younger children to town to see Santa, and Corie, who should have been helping Ben, looked through the box of treasures from her adolescence.

She and Cassie had been in touch through email then, and she'd used the library's computer to read Cassie's letters and then print them out. She'd taken them with her when Juanita sent her to Marta's. They'd been in her backpack when Marta hadn't fed her for two days because she'd talked back to her and then run away to Querida.

Teresa had bought her a pretty box for her letters and the one photo her sister had sent her via snail mail.

It was a simple school photo. Cassidy had been ten years old and in the fifth grade. Corie smiled over it now. Cassidy had large teeth with a space between the front two, a wide smile unembarrassed by the gap, and blond, bushy hair. Her eyes were bright blue, almost cobalt, and her smile said she was loved.

Corie remembered how happy she'd been when Cassie had started writing to her. She'd said her father repaired corporate software and had found Corie's father, Miguel Ochoa. Then Corie's father had died and all the awful things happened when Corie turned twelve. Cassie had moved to Paris, Corie had run away from Marta and she and Cassidy lost track of one another.

Once in Querida, Corie had used Teresa's computer to email Cassie at the old address but the message had bounced back. She'd tried the snail mail address, hoping mail was still being forwarded, but her letter came back with Not At This Address stamped across the envelope.

Corie should be able to find her now. Jack had found Corie.

She read through the letter that said Cassie and her father were moving to Paris. Cassie had been both excited and afraid. "I mean," she wrote, "boys are hard enough to deal with in English!" Corie smiled at the notion that sparkling, gap-toothed Cassie had been interested in boys.

Ben walked in, snapping her out of her

trip back in time. He was sweaty and a little grubby, and went to the front window to look out, wiping his hands on a rag. Then he came to stand behind her. "I thought you said you'd help me sort lumber. What are you doing?"

"Rereading Cassie's emails," she said, holding up the photo. "This is what she looked like at ten years old. She told me they were moving to Paris, but not where, precisely."

"Did you try just putting her name in White Pages or People Search?"

"Yes, a while ago. But I got nothing."

"Her father's name was Chapman. Did you try that?"

"Yeah. Jack told me. Still nothing. Apparently he was, maybe still is, an IT person. It's possible he knows how to make himself invisible."

Ben puzzled over that. "True, but not necessarily the way to go if you're in business. Unless he works for a company and doesn't have to get his name out there in search of clients."

Corie read from Cassie's last letter. "'Dad got a job with a company that installs and repairs computers. I forget the name. It's something French and German.'"

"When we get home tonight," Ben said, "we'll download a list of all companies in

Paris that have anything to do with packaging or installing or repairing computers to see if we can come up with a name in those two languages."

A loud knock on the door made Ben straighten. Corie's heart skipped a beat.

Ben opened the door and a tall, blond man took one step into the house and shoved Ben backward. Ben grabbed him by the shirtfront.

Corie was on her feet in an instant. Bigelow had sent someone to hurt Jack for interfering with Bigelow's attempt to evict Teresa. She leaped onto the intruder's back, wrapping both arms around his neck, knowing it would give Ben the opportunity to take his best shot with his fist.

She was completely surprised when absolute silence fell over the room. The man she held didn't struggle though she gripped him tightly. Ben released the man's shirt and reached over his shoulder to lift Corie's chin with his forefinger. She looked up from her fierce hold to see Ben bite his lip.

"Corie," he said. "This is Grady."

Too shocked to do anything, she continued to grip his friend. Ben walked around behind her, put his arm between her waist and Grady's back and peeled her off.

"Grady Nelson," he said, pulling her forward to introduce her, "this is Jack's shy and retiring little sister Corie Ochoa. Corie, Grady Nelson."

Corie closed her eyes, sighed, and when loud laughter erupted, opened them again. She apologized to Grady with a wry smile. "You shoved him," she said by way of explanation as he and Ben continued to laugh. "He grabbed you. I thought you meant him harm."

"And you wanted to help him?" Grady looked from Corie to Ben. "Wow. I want a woman like that." He rubbed his neck and cleared his throat exaggeratedly. "Much as I'd love to cause trouble for Ben, I did agree to come help. Off the job, Ben and I always greet each other with hostility. It's tradition. We've been fighting over which one of us is the toughest since we were partnered up in Beggar's Bay." He smiled at her. "I promise, though, to never do anything to upset you. I have a feeling you're tougher than Ben and me put together."

Corie reached out to shake his hand. "Hi, Grady. By way of apology, I'll get you some coffee. Please sit."

He was very interesting-looking, Corie thought, surreptitiously watching him and Ben reconnect like men who'd worked together for a long time. He was a shade taller than Ben and leaner, with burnished blond hair that waved a little over his left eye. He had a couple of days' growth of beard, and very pale eyebrows over green-gold eyes.

She brought them coffee and a plate of cookies then picked up her box of treasures and left the room to see if the latest load of laundry was ready to fold.

"Wow," GRADY SAID to Ben. "So, that's Jack's little sister, though not yours. Lucky for you. She's beautiful *and* is willing to defend you like a bodyguard."

"I'm supposed to be hers." He gave Grady a brief version of Corie's dealings with Pimental, Teresa's problems with Bigelow and touched lightly on the stolen jewelry Grady had mailed for him when he'd gone to visit Celeste in Seattle.

"Tyree was on the news, claiming when he received the box, it was filled with junk jewelry. Corie thinks he hid the real jewelry and is trying to cheat the insurance company by pretending that what he got in the mail was intended to taunt him. Someone broke in here the other night while she was at work and put one of the necklaces that supposedly hadn't been returned on her pillow."

"Why?"

"Hoping she'd get caught with it, maybe."

"Where is it now?"

Ben slapped the side pocket of his jeans. "Always with me. Anyway, I've been taking her to work and picking her up. She's a little prickly and not taking the notion of protection very well."

Grady nodded. "Now I see why you thought it would be good to have another cop around. Is there no law enforcement in this county?"

"Not that's honest. At least, not that we know of. The chief's daughter's boyfriend is the cop who responded to the break-in. Seemed nice enough, but whether he's honest or not remains to be seen."

"There's always the attorney general's office."

"That's my plan if all else fails. I'm gathering information. It's just happening slowly because there's a lot going on. Ten kids live here."

"Holy—"

"Yeah. They're great, but they make it hard to finish anything. They love to be part of whatever I'm doing and they have a lot of questions." He paused to explain how Teresa's foster home worked. "She seems to think most of the parents will be by to take their kids home before the holidays. Except for Soren, whose parents are both deceased."

"That sucks."

"Yes. And I promised they'd have the play set by the end of the week. Then we can devote ourselves to Corie's problem."

"We?"

"Yeah. You'll still have more than a week's vacation by the time we're finished with the play set."

Grady made a show of indignation. "You're taking advantage of our friendship, man."

"I am. But you're lucky to have my friendship. I mean, your girl left you and your mother's gambling away your inheritance in Reno. What have you got besides me?"

Grady hung his head.

## CHAPTER ELEVEN

MOST OF THE week went by in weird harmony. Ben and Grady worked from dawn to dusk. Corie took them cold drinks and snacks. When Teresa delivered lunch, they spread out several blankets and all picnicked in the yard. Once the older children came home from school, they were kept at a safe distance to watch as Ben and Grady swung long pieces of lumber into place.

Corie was sent to Wolf's for wood clamps and an extra cordless drill and batteries, and a ratchet with socket.

At night it took several trips with a wheelbarrow to put all the fittings in the shed. They covered the assembled and loose pieces with tarpaulins and kept the floodlight on in the backyard to discourage theft.

By Friday, the project was recognizable as a very sophisticated play set. The swing beam had three positions that included a two-person glider. A solid climbing wall about five feet tall was positioned near a wave slide and both led up to a large clubhouse with a lookout balcony. It had arches at the top to prevent little heads from being bumped. There were also wooden steps rather than rungs to allow the younger children to climb up to it.

The lower deck area featured a sandbox and several seats and a picnic table.

Teresa walked around it in awe. Corie sat in the gravel, overwhelmed by the gift Ben had given them.

"This is so wonderful," Teresa said while Ben gently pushed Bianca and Tonio on the swings. "And the kids are out of school next week for the holidays, so this will be such a treat for them—*and* for me." She laughed and wrapped her arms around him. "Thank you." She blew a kiss to Grady, who waved back.

Corie felt her take on the world shift, readjust. She'd known life wasn't all bad, but her little part of it had had its challenges. Teresa had brought so much light into Corie's life, and working with the children, then with Hector and his crew, had made each day more promising than the one before. But a future with a husband and children had seemed out of the realm of possibility. Her past was so murky; she didn't think she had the right to inflict that on anyone else. And then she'd met this man who'd given her nothing but trouble.

And a playground.

And, strangely, hope.

Ben kept insisting that she had to go home with him to spend Christmas with their family, who didn't seem to notice that she didn't fit in. Not that she'd ever leave Teresa over the holidays.

When the older children came home from school, they went crazy, dropping lunch boxes and schoolbooks on the ground and running for the play set as though they'd never seen anything like it before.

Corie knew their school had a playground, but the community was not very well funded and the equipment was old. She often took the children to the park to play on the relatively newer monkey bars and big spinner but even those now seemed dated in comparison.

Soren scrambled up the rock wall like a monkey, then climbed onto the walkway, took the stairs and emerged in the clubhouse. He leaned over the railing to wave at them.

"Good grief," Teresa moaned. "We'll have to hire a nurse. Or put 9-1-1 on speed dial."

Grady joined them. "We'll have a serious talk with them about being careful," he said.

Teresa, Corie and Ben shared a knowing look. Ben laughed and leaned an elbow on Grady's shoulder. "You're such an innocent. Corie threatens them with permanent loss of dessert. That's usually the only thing that's effective."

Grady nodded, accepting his comeuppance. "Sorry. Not much experience with children. I'm still a bachelor. Intend to remain a bachelor."

Both women turned to him with interest. "Why?"

He shrugged. "Dangerous job. Can't trust women. Happy on my own."

"Oh, that's right." Corie patted his arm sympathetically. "I'm sorry about your girlfriend, but maybe it just wasn't meant to be. And you never know what's around the corner. You might meet the perfect woman tomorrow."

"Tomorrow?" Grady looked doubtful.

"Well, by Christmas for sure."


THE ADULTS SAT around the kitchen table long after the children had gone to bed and listened to Grady's stories about life in the Beggar's Bay police department. He was interrupted by a light knock on the door.

Ben went to the window first, wondering who would be stopping by at such a late hour. He saw a slight figure he didn't recognize waiting in front of the door. "It's a woman," he said.

"It's okay." Grady had followed him to the door. "Open it. I'll protect you."

Ben pulled the door open. A pretty, young woman in jeans and a denim jacket looked up at Ben in worried surprise.

"I... Where is Teresa?" Her wide, dark eyes grew a little wild.

"Catalina!" Teresa rushed past Ben and Grady as the young woman extended her arms and began to weep.

"Oh, Teresa. I saw them and I thought you had moved or something. Is he okay? I'm sorry it's so late and that I didn't call first, but I have a job now!"

"Lina, it's so good to see you."

"I'm going to keep house for an older couple in San Antonio. They travel a lot and want to have someone to look after the house when they're gone. And they don't mind that I have a child. They had their son drive me here to pick him up."

"I'm so happy for you."

Corie forced her way in to hug the woman.

"Catalina. How wonderful! You won't believe how big he's gotten."

Grady looked to Ben for an explanation. Ben shook his head to indicate he wasn't sure what was happening, except that this must be one of the children's mothers.

"You sit down," Teresa said. "I'll go get him."

"Can I come?" Catalina asked, putting a battered brown purse on the sofa. "I can't wait to see him."

Teresa put an arm around her and led her to the stairs. Corie went up with them.

"Which child?" Grady asked.

"Must be Roberto, the little guy. The other four boys are brothers."

Teresa had been right about the kids going home for Christmas—at least Roberto. Ben was surprised to find he was almost as sad as he was happy. Teresa's home was losing its youngest, the toddler everyone in the household had rocked or fed or played with.

Catalina led the way down the stairs, the sleepy toddler in her arms. He was fussy and rubbing his eyes. She crooned to him in Spanish.

Teresa and Corie followed, the other children in pajamas in step behind them. The women's smiles were strained and the children looked upset. The Flores girls held hands and the Santiago boys stood with uncharacteristic quiet as the women hugged and said their goodbyes.

Roberto started to cry, probably not recognizing his mother. He reached a little hand toward Teresa and Corie. Most of the other children struggled with tears. Only Soren and Rosie stood by in gloomy silence.

Corie carried a small tote bag that probably held Roberto's belongings. "I'll carry this out for her," she said to Teresa. "I'll be right back."

Ben felt called upon to do something but didn't know what. So he just waded into the middle of the sniffling children. The Santiago boys crowded around him as Teresa embraced the Flores girls.

Corie returned and paused in the doorway to wave into the darkness. They heard the tap of a horn as she closed the door. Ben saw her take a moment, toss her hair, before she turned to the gloomy little group.

"I know you're all sad to see Roberto leave us," she said to the children, "but this is what we do here. We take care of each other until your parents come to take you home. That's what we all want, right? For families to get back together?"

That seemed to strike a chord and the children's tears gradually stopped. Soren looked a little lost. Rosie nodded.

"His mom's going to send us pictures," Corie said, guiding the children toward the stairs. "And she's working at a big house in San Antonio. The lady she works for says we can go and visit sometime." Teresa followed and beckoned Ben to come along. He guessed that putting the children back to bed was going to be a three-person job.

IT WAS AFTER ten when Ben and Corie finally settled in her house and Grady drove to the B and B.

Corie was quiet.

"I'm sorry," he said, pouring a cup of coffee. "I know the kids going home is what you work for, but it's obviously very hard on everybody. I'm sure all the other kids were not only thinking they'd miss Roberto but wondering if they were going to have their turn soon."

"Yes. I've dealt with these reunions since I moved in with Teresa, and it never gets easier. Each child is special, and knowing they're going out of your life, probably forever, is hard to adjust to." She sat wearily at the kitchen table and leaned her chin in the palm of her hand. "I wonder what it's like to live in a family where that doesn't happen. I mean, I know Teresa's home is a different situation, but my whole childhood was one disruption after another."

She sighed deeply then dropped her hand to the table. "I apologize for whining. I just wonder what it feels like to have that stability. Teresa gave me that, in a way, except that the kids that came and went from her house were like my siblings and they were always leaving."

"I'm sure stability is the best thing in the world for a kid," Ben said, pouring her a coffee, too, and putting it on the table in front of her. Teresa had sent them home with Christmas cookies the children had made, and he put the tin in the middle of the table. "We feel safe, protected, and that makes it easier to live in this world. But Jack didn't have any of that until he was eight and moved in with my parents and me. Though he had trouble with nightmares when he came home from Afghanistan, he's the most grounded individual you'd ever want to know. You've seen him in action. He's good and loving and not afraid of anything."

He sat across the table from her. "You're so much like him and yet you had an even harder time as a child than he did." He looked into her eyes and gave her a rueful smile. "Teresa told me about your stepmother." He made a sound in his throat as though he didn't have a word for what he felt. He shook his head. "Point is..." He suddenly smiled with reluctant affection. "You have an alarming propensity to do things the hard way but somehow you remain...lovable. For a man guided by the straight and narrow that's hard to understand."

She arched an eyebrow. "You find me lovable?" *Relax*, she told herself as her heartbeat accelerated just a little. *That's not the same as saying I love you.*

He shrugged, as though unable to help himself. "I do."

"But how can you find someone lovable when you don't completely trust them?"

He took a long gulp of coffee. "I trust you. I believe you had nothing to do with Tyree's jewelry. After you stole it the first time, I mean."

"That must be why you wouldn't let me hold the necklace that was planted here."

"I'm better able to fend off muggers."

She chose a slightly crooked, creatively

blue-frosted candy cane from the tin, no longer offended by whatever suspicions he still had about her. Even she wasn't sure about herself sometimes.

"There are moments when I feel like I don't know who I am. I mean, I used to. I was that Ochoa brat. Then Jack found me, you entered my life and now..." She contemplated the cookie. "I'm the Ochoa brat with the good brothers. That's changing my identity."

"You have one brother," he corrected. "I'm family, but I'm not your brother. Let's not get that confused."

"It is confusing. There's no getting around it. The whole Palmer-Manning family is a strain to grasp."

"The rest of us are doing fine with it. You're the only one who seems to have a problem."

She was too tired now for such serious conversation, because she knew he wasn't talking about the whole family. He was talking about her and him. She pushed away from the table, taking her cup and her cookie with her.

"I'm pooped," she said. "I'm going to bed."

He prodded. "You just don't want to talk about belonging, do you?"

"No," she said frankly and started to walk

away. Then she turned to add, "Maybe later. Good night, Ben."

He toasted her with his mug. "Good night, Corie."

HE WOKE IN the middle of the night to the sounds of a motor. He rose up off the floor and, staying low, peered out the window, thinking a car had pulled up, that someone might be watching the house. But the street was empty. The sound stopped then started again and he realized it wasn't a car—and it was coming from Corie's room.

A little concerned, he went to the back of the house. Her door was closed though a slit of light was visible under it. He took advantage of a break in the sound to knock.

"Come in," she called.

He pushed the door open—and walked into what looked like a garment factory. Garments for children. Half-finished jackets in bright colors and unusual combinations of fabric were strewed all over her bed. They were cheerful jackets, and no child wearing one would ever wander off unnoticed.

She worked at a sewing machine in the corner of her room, and turned with an elbow on the back of her chair. She wore a baggy, light blue robe and an apologetic smile. "I woke you, didn't I? It's all your fault. You gave me fully leaded coffee when we came home. Since I couldn't sleep, I thought I'd do something useful."

"Cool stuff." He looked over the jackets again, most of them almost finished.

"I'm trying to get Roberto's done so I can take it to the post office tomorrow. Catalina left us their address."

He picked up a jacket with a lot of yellow. "Who's this for?"

"Bianca. She loves ducks. The front is made from a jacket she wore when the girls came to Teresa." Corie pointed to the embroidered duck. "She fell on the playground at school and tore it. But she loved the jacket so much, we couldn't throw it away. So I backed it with a strong fabric then repaired it by embroidering the daisies and the duck."

Her thoughtfulness and the simple cleverness of the design made him smile. "So, this is your gift."

She nodded, smiling, too. "Yes, for Christmas. For all of the kids."

He put the jacket down. "No, I meant this work is your gift. Your talent. This is why you went to New York."

"Oh. Yes, I guess. I'm not sure it can be considered a *gift*."

"The jackets are wonderful."

"Thanks. I kind of like them."

"Have you thought about going back to school? You know…learn more about design. Your instincts seem right on, but maybe with more education in the field, you wouldn't have to work for someone else. You could open your own place."

She made a noncommittal gesture, bobbing her head from side to side. "It's expensive. And I'd feel out of place back at school."

"Maybe that's a discomfort you're putting on yourself. You just admitted tonight that you feel like you're changing into a different version of yourself. Take a step back and get a clearer picture. Put aside all the ugly stuff, or just accept that it's part of you. Put it in the past and move ahead. Belonging isn't that hard."

"I don't think so." She was irritated at his suggestion. He wasn't surprised. So he may as well go all out.

"It's easier to find fault with the world, to let yourself feel out of place and to choose not to fit in, than to take on the challenge and live your dreams. I don't think the world's pushing you away, you're doing it to yourself. As far as the expense of school, I could help. Or, if you'd hate that, I'm sure there's financial aid available somewhere."

A lifetime of self-sufficiency gave her almost visible defensive spikes. "Not your worry, Ben."

He folded his arms, his own annoyance sparking. "Do we really have to go over the family dynamic again?"

She turned back to her sewing machine. "Please let's not."

He followed her. "Okay, if you feel out of place with the Palmers, too, then what about just accepting help from a friend? You do know how to be a friend?"

She turned off the machine and, removing the piece she'd been working on, folded it and put it aside. "As a friend, I'm sorry I woke you. Go back to sleep. I'm going to bed."

"Okay, you can dismiss me—what is this, the third time now?—but you can't make the issue go away. You can't pout and react like a cornered cat for the rest of your life. Do you really want to live Teresa's life and let your own skill and talent go to waste because this is easier?"

Her expression darkened. "Like you know all about life being hard."

"You're right. I don't. But I don't have to have experienced the same things you have to realize you're afraid to be part of a family because the first one hurt you, then the second one. You're afraid to leave here again because it didn't work the first time. This is what's worked for you, and it isn't going to sell you to somebody else or have a bad year and close up. But you can't shelter all the time. You have to get out and be you."

He smiled in the face of her closed expression. "I actually thought about going to work for the post office after I got shot, until I realized that life's going to happen to you whether or not you're equipped for it. So you have to learn to deal with it, and not just with anger but with an educated brain, heart wide open, and in the fierce hope that you'll learn to cope."

CORIE STARED AT HIM, recognizing in the depths of her being that he was absolutely right. But she was in no mood to be cheered into rising above her life, at least not now with Pimental on her case, little Roberto gone home and the question of what to do about *him*.

Apparently reading the negative in her eyes, Ben sighed and dropped his head in resignation.

"So this is the end of the discussion—again."

"Yes."

"Discussions are usually two-way, you know. You get to say what you're thinking and I get to say what's on my mind."

"Yeah. But you do that way too often. And I don't have to listen if I don't want to."

"Okay, then. Good night."

He left her room and she made herself climb into bed.

She slept a couple of hours then got up and showered. They were to meet Grady at the Grill for breakfast.

Once settled in a booth, their food delivered, Ben seemed unusually quiet. When he did say something that required her to answer, she was stiffly polite.

Grady looked from one to the other. "Everything okay with you two?" he asked. "You're acting like a married couple in a snit."

Ben ignored him. Corie spared him a smile. "We're getting a friendship divorce," she said. "Irreconcilable differences."

"Aw." He didn't seem to know whether to take her seriously or not. "You want to talk to me about it? I've had some training with domestic issues."

"Thanks, but we'll just ignore it. We should eat up. Teresa's going to need all the help she can get today. The kids are going to be wilder than usual with full access to the play set. We're going to have to be on our toes."

AND THEY WERE. The activity was incessant. The children climbed into and on top of everything all day long, Ben and Grady watching from the sidelines. Soren had to be called over as he kept pushing the limits of his impressive acrobatic skills, putting everyone in danger of cardiac arrest.

Teresa and Corie brought lunch outside because it was clear no one was willing to go in.

The children ate at the picnic table at ground level and in the clubhouse structure at the top. Ben, Grady, Teresa and Corie sat on a blanket spread over the gravel and ate baked-chicken sandwiches and homemade coleslaw.

"Coleslaw's wonderful," Ben said, examining the bite on his fork. "I like the pineapple."

"Corie made it," Teresa replied.

He nodded. "Good job," he said without looking at her.

"Thank you." Icicles clung to Corie's words.

When the children finished eating, they tossed their paper plates and plastic utensils into a large plastic bag Ben was holding before hurrying back to the play set.

Grady left to arbitrate the dispute when two of the Santiagos began to quarrel over the only unoccupied swing.

"What's going on with you and Ben?" Teresa asked Corie.

Corie recounted most of their conversation of the night before.

Teresa frowned. "He's right, you know."

Corie shook her head. "You're as aggravating as any real mother, you do realize that?"

She was unrepentant. "I try. Listen. I'm not sure exactly where your relationship stands, but if it's as serious as it appears, he has a right to tell you what he thinks."

"He certainly does that."

Teresa was silent for a moment. "You might examine just why it is that you're angry at him all the time."

"I'm not angry at him *all* the time."

"It sounds as though you are. He takes a lot from you because you're his brother's sister.

Don't blame him because you have feelings for him you don't know what to do with."

Teresa put a hand up before Corie could tell her again what those feelings were. "I know. You claim that he aggravates you, but that's because he touches something in you I don't think you ever expected to find...a heart soft with romantic inclination." She smiled into Corie's eyes. "A heart that wants to follow him, maybe? It's all right to give up control of every gentle feeling. I doubt that he'd ever use your feelings to hurt you."

Teresa stood quickly and ran to help Grady as the other two Santiago boys got involved in the tussle over the swing.

BEN PICKED UP a few napkins and utensils the children had dropped in the gravel and wandered toward the Santiago ruckus, knotting the plastic bag. Teresa, it seemed, had the problem under control, sending the older boys in three different directions and letting Tonio have first turn on the swing.

Grady snagged the bag from Ben, holding up the coffee mugs they'd brought outside that morning. "I'm taking these inside, anyway. I'll take the trash."

"Thanks. That doesn't mean you get out of helping me watch these guys."

"Of course not. When have you ever known me to shirk my responsibilities?"

"Let's see. There was the day I went into the river after that speeder who crashed into a tree then rabbited."

"You were already wet! You ran out in the rain to get our lunch while I monitored the radio."

"The radio was on your shoulder, Einstein."

"Oh, yeah." Grady grinned. "What if I promise to explain you to Corie, then can I take a few extra minutes?"

Ben looked over to their picnic blanket and saw that Corie and the blanket were gone.

"She went inside," Grady said. "I'll be back in a few."

Ben turned as Teresa approached. "I like your friend," she said. "It was nice of him to come help you."

"He's a good guy."

"Yes." Her eyes pinned him for several seconds. "You are, too. But you should go a little easy on Corie."

He let his head fall back and groaned. "I just suggested she might want to go back to school and got this chronic I-don't-fit-in mantra she uses as her excuse not to leave here."

"Ben." She said his name softly but with audible disapproval. "You will probably never experience the rejection she's known in her short lifetime. Yet, she still gives everything she has here. She walked the floors with Roberto while he was teething so I could get some sleep to deal with the other kids the next day, and she still went to work at the Grill in the afternoon. She gives her love unconditionally to every kid who comes here, knowing they're eventually going home. Do you realize how hard that is?"

"Yes," he replied with a sigh. "I saw it in all of you last night."

"Then maybe a little more patience and a little less self-righteousness, okay?"

He guessed *she'd* told *him*. "Yes, ma'am."

He looked up. Seeing Soren leaning over the clubhouse railing, he pointed him back. The boy complied.

At Corie's later that night, Ben prepared for bed. Beyond her bedroom door came the sound of her sewing machine as she hurried to finish her projects. He pulled his shirt off and went to the guest closet for the pillow and blanket and the hiking shorts he wore to bed.

He shook out the blanket near the sofa, put the pillow down at the end nearest the door and prepared to change from jeans to shorts. He patted his side pocket to assure himself the necklace was still there.

Then he did it again—because it wasn't.

He was a trained cop with nine years' experience. He wasn't one to panic. At least, not until now. Then he remembered exactly what had happened.

He'd been lying on his side in the gravel under the foot of the slide, making sure the base was firmly placed. The necklace was an uncomfortable lump and he'd removed it and placed it beside him, thinking as he did it that he had to remember to put it back.

Grady had shouted for help with a piece at the top of the clubhouse structure and he'd hurried off, forgetting the necklace.

He knew precisely where it was under the base of the slide, but he couldn't very well go back to Teresa's after midnight. All he needed was to be found prowling around in the dark with a flashlight. And a diamond necklace.

There was no point in alarming Corie. He hated the thought, but he had to wait until morning.

He finally slept, but not until after 4:00 a.m.

Tired and feeling stupid, he was grumpy when he found the cereal box empty.

CORIE, STILL MAD at him from the night before, frowned as he tossed the empty cereal box away. She pulled it out of the trash and put it in the recycle box near the back door. "Sorry about that," she said. "I didn't notice. Want me to make you some toast? You know, since you can't cook anything?"

"Funny," he said. "I'll make my own toast."

She prepared the coffeemaker and turned it on while he dropped bread in the toaster. He went to the refrigerator for butter and jam and put them on the table. When the toast popped, he put it on a plate and sat down.

"No, thanks," Corie said in a martyred tone. "I don't care for any. But it was nice of you to ask."

"You can cook," he said tersely. "Make yourself something."

He was uncharacteristically surly and she wondered for an instant what was wrong with him this morning. Then, remembering he'd accused her of being afraid of her own life, she decided she didn't care. "I'll see you at Teresa's," she said, and left him to his toast.

Half an hour later he stared at the empty spot under the base of the slide and told himself it just couldn't be. He dug both hands into the gravel, sure the necklace had somehow been covered by it, but it wasn't there. He straightened and looked around, kicking at the surrounding gravel. Nothing.

Stupid, he thought. Serious stoopid with a double *o*.

What now? He considered that one of the children might have found it, but surprise treasures were usually big news and shown off to everyone.

Corie wandered out to where he stood, her manner cool though less hostile than earlier. He groaned inwardly at the thought of how she would react to this news.

"Kids are almost done with their snacks," she said. "I wondered if you needed an omelet or a sandwich, or something. I know you heroically cooked that toast, but…"

He heaved a sigh that came from his knee-caps. "I have to tell you something."

"I know. You've been a jerk all morning. I forgive you. Let's move on." She caught his arm and tried to pull him toward the house.

He held firm and just spit it out. "I misplaced the necklace."

She was silent for an instant, the calm before Armageddon. Then she said in a Darth Vader voice, "You *lost* the necklace?"

"I said I misplaced it," he corrected.

Her voice rose a decibel. "Do you know where it is?"

"No."

"Then that's the definition of *lost*!" she screamed at him. "I'll bet they never let you near evidence on the job in Beggar's Bay if you *misplace* things."

"Corie, take it easy." He told her how he'd done it. "I doubt there's been anyone around here but you and me, Grady and Teresa and the kids. Somebody must have found it."

She looked heavenward in supplication. "Had Teresa found a thirty-thousand-dollar necklace, I'm sure she'd have mentioned it to me. Had Grady found it, he'd have told you because you told him about it. If the kids…" Her tirade was halted by the slamming of the back door and a wave from Officer Norton as he walked toward them.

Corie closed her eyes. When she opened them again, Ben got a second-degree burn. "If the police have found the necklace, I'm turning you over to Jack. See what he does to you for landing me in jail."

Ben groaned, thinking she was being over-the-top dramatic, but Jack probably would kill him if he got Corie arrested after the lengths they'd gone to trying to prevent that.

Norton looked sharp in his uniform. Ben felt like yesterday's oatmeal.

"Good," he said as he approached, "you're both here. I have a little news to share. Can we sit there?" He pointed to the picnic table.

"Of course." Ben sat beside Corie, despite her glower in his direction, and Chris Norton sat opposite them.

"I found this at the end of the walk in front of your house when I was leaving the night of the break-in," he said, holding a silver-dollar-size object toward them in the palm of his hand. It was an advertising token: "25% off your next oil change. Corbett Motors." There was also an address in Corpus Christi in minuscule type.

Corie, still under a head of steam because of Ben's mistake, said, "Ha! Corpus Christi. Tyree sent him."

"Well, it's not a straight line to that conclusion," Chris said.

Ben decided he liked the man.

"But…maybe. And something else…" He pulled a folded piece of paper out of his pocket and spread it open on the table. It was a print-out of Corbett Motors' website, featuring photos of a pretty young woman and three shop employees. Two wore coveralls and one, the parts manager, captioned "Danny," wore a chambray work shirt.

Corie poked her finger at the manager's image. "That's him."

"Did you see his face?" Chris asked.

She huffed impatiently. "All the evidence…"

"Often doesn't account for much without a witness. And it's weird that he didn't take anything and he broke in when you weren't home, so we don't know that he intended to hurt you. Otherwise he'd have hidden in the house when he heard you coming, instead of running out."

"He did still break in," Ben said.

"Right."

Then, like something out of a surreal movie, the back door opened, catching their attention. Bianca walked out—all three and a half feet of her in a red-striped shirt, shorts and scuffed tennies, her purse slung over her arm.

She waved at them and smiled, walked around the slide and dropped her purse at the foot of the ladder. She reappeared at the top, where she sat with a big smile, looking thrilled with the world, and rode down in a gleeful whoosh, the diamond necklace at her throat sparkling in the morning sun.

## CHAPTER TWELVE

"WHAT'S SHE WEARING?" Chris asked, his gaze focused on Bianca's sparkling diamonds.

Ben leaned his elbows on the table and joined his hands together against his forehead, uttering a small sound of anguish.

"The girls have all kinds of play jewelry," Corie replied, relieved that her voice sounded normal. She felt as though she'd fallen into a well. She didn't particularly want out, either.

Bianca ran toward them, ponytail bouncing. "See what I found?" she boasted, putting a little hand to the necklace.

"Wow, that's really pretty," Chris said. "Can I see?"

Bianca ran around the table to him, happy to show it off. "I found it over there." She pointed to the spot under the slide where Ben had left it.

Corie watched the officer study the necklace. A breath that seemed to have four corners to it was lodged in her chest.

"That's really pretty," he said, looking it over. Then he glanced from Corie to Ben and asked Bianca with a smile, "Would it be all right if I looked at it for a little while longer?"

Bianca pouted just a little. "It belongs to somebody, doesn't it?"

"I'm not sure," he said. "It might. But if it doesn't, I'll give it back to you. Okay?"

"Okay." Bianca went to Corie and turned her back to her, holding up her ponytail so Corie could work the clasp. Bianca placed her purse on the table and dug out the little gauze bag Corie had put the necklace in the night it had appeared on her pillow. Then she ran back to the slide as one of her sisters joined her.

Corie was grateful for the easy-come, easy-go attitude of childhood.

Teresa appeared near the back door and shouted at the children to come with her for a ride. There was a communal groan until she promised to stop for ice cream.

Norton draped the necklace across his hands. "I don't know fine jewelry, but this looks like the real thing." Again, he glanced from Corie to Ben, his blue eyes sharp, as though somehow detecting their collaboration. "Do you have any idea how this happened to be under the slide in the backyard?"

Corie glanced at Ben with apology in her eyes. She was about to confess and hated to involve him. Even though the fact that Bianca had been wearing the necklace was all his fault.

Ben put a hand to Corie's knee to stop her from speaking. He met Norton's eyes and thought he saw a good man, though he guessed the police officer was only in his middle twenties. It was worth a try.

"Office Norton," he said, "we have a lot to tell you that will probably surprise you and make you want to put both of us in jail."

Norton arched an eyebrow but waited for him to go on.

"We're going to tell you the truth, and we're not going to rabbit, but if you listen to us with an open mind, we may be able to help each other."

Looking skeptical, Norton leaned an elbow on the table. "You're an officer of the law, so you know it's illegal to bribe one, right?"

Ben grinned. "I do. This isn't a bribe but a sincere offer to help."

"To help you keep the necklace?" he asked coolly.

"No. To find out the truth about it, because I think it might involve your department, a couple of your chief's friends and, in the end, if you do nothing about it, *you*."

Norton initially looked disturbed at the suggestion that something was wrong in his department, then nodded. "You have my attention."

"Good." Ben told him about the appearance of the necklace the night they'd called him to investigate the break-in.

"But why wouldn't the Corbett Motors parts manager have taken the necklace? He was running from your house. He must have seen it."

"I'm guessing someone hired him to put it *in* my house. Cyrus Tyree or Robert Pimental."

Norton frowned. "But why *your* house?"

"So you would catch me with it when you came to investigate." She added with a sigh, "I'm sorry. I spotted it when you followed me into my bedroom, but hid it under a blanket when you turned to check for my cash."

"Okay, but why did any of those men want *you* to be found with it?"

She hesitated a beat then confessed with a certain relief. "Because I stole it in the first place."

Norton shifted on the picnic bench and crossed his forearms on the table. "I'm going to need some coffee."

Ben left Corie and Norton to talk and went to the kitchen for three cups. When he returned with the coffee Corie was telling Norton about the news story with the Mardis Gras beads, why she'd stolen the jewelry and Ben's quick trip to Querida.

"Someone's trying to get Teresa out of this house," Ben added when she'd finished. "She rented for years from Tyree's father without problem, but Cyrus Tyree seems determined to evict her. Your boss came to tell her she had five days to get out, but he seemed to have no knowledge of the law in that respect."

Norton sipped at his coffee. "He knows the law. He probably just hoped you didn't. I don't imagine he suspected he was dealing with another cop."

"He's crooked, isn't he?"

Norton sighed. "Actually, he's a good man in a lot of ways. But life's hard around here and, I haven't seen it, but I'm guessing by what I've overheard that he's helped himself a little. I think he gets bonuses for easing Tyree's way in business—relaxed regulations, quick approvals. And Pimental gets him whatever he needs from the town."

"We want to take down Tyree. Prove that he got the jewelry back and scammed the insurance company. And find out what we can on why he's so anxious to get Teresa out. And whatever we can about his other scummy deals. Will you help us?"

"I'm just a cop on the beat."

Ben denied that with a shake of his head. "You're the most effective tool in law enforcement. You hold the line between the citizen and every bad thing out there."

Norton ran a hand over his face. "You sound like a police academy poster."

"Don't you believe that?" Ben asked. "The job doesn't have much to recommend it otherwise."

Norton smiled thinly. "Yeah, I do. Bigelow and I are on different shifts, so I just keep my distance. But I love his daughter. I've been to his house for dinner. This is going to be awkward."

Ben nodded. "If you love his daughter, maybe he'll listen to you. Or her. Maybe you can turn him around before he goes down with Pimental and Tyree."

Norton looked noncommittal. "So, what's the plan?"

"Not perfectly formed yet, but we're working on it. Can you give us that latitude for a couple of days?"

Norton looked at Corie. "You swear you sent that jewelry back?"

"I do."

"All right." He handed back the necklace. "I'm in. If I end up in jail, or in a flea-bitten department in Newark, New Jersey, because no one else will hire me, you're going down with me."

She nodded. "That would only be fair."

After Norton left, Corie sat on a swing and pushed herself desultorily back and forth with a foot on the ground. Ben walked around behind her. "Want a push?"

"That's all it would take to put me over the edge," she answered over her shoulder. "Did I do the right thing by telling him the truth?"

"Absolutely. We have law enforcement working with us. How can that hurt?"

"Bigelow is also law enforcement."

"I have faith in the kid. And his love for his girl."

He pulled back on the swing and gently let

it go. Ankles crossed, Corie leaned back lazily then tucked her legs under on the return. He moved out of her way. "I'm sorry," he said as she swung past him. "This is all my fault."

She swung outward and flew higher. "It's all right," she said. "It was my fault to begin with."

He let her fly past him twice, the second time a little higher than the first. It took him that long to realize what she'd said. "Say, what?" he asked as she returned. He caught the swing to stop her and walked around to look into her face.

She shrugged, seeming calmer and strangely philosophical. "I said it's okay. I stole the jewelry in the first place, and though my intentions were noble, the means weren't particularly well thought out. I'm relieved. But Jack's going to be ticked off at us if we end up in jail."

"True. So, let's not."

She jumped off the swing. "You said you'd help me find the company Cassidy's father works for. A French name and a German name. Want to do that this afternoon while Grady's doing his Christmas shopping? I need something else to think about. Something good."

"I'm your servant, as long as my guilt lasts."

She punched his arm. "I *love* you like this!"

Jack called while Corie went to retrieve her laptop.

"Hey," Ben said cheerfully, "how was the wine country?"

"It was beautiful. Sarah's getting together with some of her former clients for lunch. Want to meet at Betty's? Ribs are today's special."

"Ah… I can't."

"You on duty?"

"No, I'm…in Texas." He was thinking about how to explain what he was doing there without freaking Jack out. Without being freaked out himself after that little scene.

"Texas! You mean Querida?"

"Yes."

"Is something wrong with Corie?" Jack's voice was quick and urgent.

"No, she's fine." Not entirely true, but that answer would serve for now. "Uh… Tyree is claiming that he got the box we sent back, but without his wife's jewelry in it." Ben told him about the television spot with the Mardi Gras beads.

"And you went to Texas thinking Corie was somehow responsible." Jack's tone was critical.

Ben ignored it. "Corie thinks the jewelry

did arrive and Tyree's defrauding the insurance company."

There was a moment of heavy silence. "What do you think?"

"She might be right," Ben said finally.

"I hear something else in your voice."

He had to tell him something that didn't involve the break-in at Corie's, the necklace and the cop who'd found them with it. "There was security footage of the night Corie broke into Tyree's." That didn't seem like such a threat anymore, all things considered.

Jack swore.

"Yeah. But I've seen it. I've made friends with the newspaper publisher and he requisitioned the tape from Tyree to cover the story. You can't identify anyone or either of our vehicles."

"You sure?"

"I'm sure."

"Don't they have labs that can enhance photos?"

"In most areas, that's just stuff you see on TV. And these are so dark, I doubt enhancement would help."

"Does Tyree know Corie was the thief?"

"I don't think so." But somebody did.

"Ben..." Jack hesitated and made a sound of helplessness.

"Look, I've got this covered," Ben said. It felt so good to know that his brother had found happiness with Sarah. "Don't worry about it. I'm just sticking around to help with Christmas. Corie bought a giant tree and they needed somebody to help put it up. Then I realized the kids needed a playground, so I gave them this cool set for Christmas. Only trouble is, it's taken a while to build it. So I called Grady to come and help."

"Grady. I thought he was going to Seattle or somewhere."

"He was, but his girlfriend got engaged to someone else. So he had some time off and nowhere to go. He was happy to get away. Just get back to work, and I'll bring Corie home for Christmas."

"She wants to come?"

"Yes."

"Are you telling me the truth?"

Ben hesitated. "Mostly."

"Ben..."

"I've got to go. Welcome home."

"You want me to come to Texas?"

"No," Ben replied a little too loudly and

then lowered his voice before Jack could hear his concern. "No. Everything's fine. I swear."

"You promise you'll call me if you need me?"

"I promise."

Another protracted silence before Jack said reluctantly, "Okay. Stay in touch."

"Will do." Ben wasn't entirely sure he'd pulled off the lies, but at least Jack didn't suspect the real truth—that Corie might be in danger, and that he was going to have to put her in his carry-on bag to get her to Beggar's Bay. Fortunately, she was small.

THE FOLLOWING WEEK the children spent mornings working on Christmas gifts for each other, some closeted in bedrooms, some working in corners of the living room, furniture pulled around them to prevent anyone from peeking. Those measures were unnecessary but a lot of fun. There were shrieks of horror when someone got too close and stealth dramatics when they had to move from one room to another.

They had the most fun making Teresa's gift. It required each child's right hand to be painted green. They then transferred their hand print onto a plain white apron Corie had made. She placed their hands pointing downward on the fabric starting with the smallest at the top, the next two underneath, then three on the next row. The last four, the largest, formed the bottom of the Christmas tree.

Ben sat at the kitchen table, working on his once-musical box from Soren. He'd applied some leftover glue from part of the play set to the pieces and affixed a clamp over the top to hold the box together as it dried.

Corie enjoyed seeing everyone happily at work, loved the sight of their giant tree and the smell of cookies baking—a new type every day. Grady had taken the Flores girls with him to buy more baking supplies. Teresa had assured him that Lupe knew the brand of flour and sugar and the type of chocolate and peanut butter chips Teresa preferred.

Apparently, Karina had spotted cards of jingle bells and reminded Lupe of last year when they'd tied them onto their shoelaces. Grady had bought a card of bells for each child in the house.

Teresa winced at the purchase, but her lack of enthusiasm for the bells was laughed down by the children, who considered Grady a hero. When they moved in a unit, they sounded like some kind of alarm system. It was impossible for them to sneak away.

In the afternoon, the children played outside. Corie loved the sight of Ben in the middle of them, pushing kids on the swings, catching the little ones at the bottom of the slide, playing spotter when they climbed the rock wall. Grady was there, too, but her eyes were on Ben.

On Wednesday afternoon Corie received a call from Jack. She was sitting at the table, helping Rosie cut out angel cookies, and excused herself as she moved into the living room for privacy.

Jack told her about the conversation he'd had with Ben.

"He seems to think we're in the clear," he said. "That nothing's visible on the surveillance tape."

"I think we are," she said. "Nothing to worry about. Ben just wants to help me prove that Tyree is defrauding the insurance company. That's why he's still here."

He was quiet for a minute. "And the fact that he seems to have grown fond of the children."

"That, too. He's been a lot of help around here. The kids love him."

"He says you're coming home with him for Christmas."

"Uh…"

"I *knew* he was lying. Corie…?"

"Jack, I think we may have found the company Cassidy's father worked for in Paris," she said, hoping to put the subject of her going to Oregon aside for now. "And maybe still does. Bourgeois-Berger. It's on Rue Malher. There's so much going on here, I haven't had a chance to check if he's still on their staff, or, if not, if they know where he went."

"Good going. Why don't you let me do that? Palmer Restorations just bid on a job renovating the library and it'll be a few days before I hear. I'm sure you have your hands full with the kids and Christmas. I love having an excuse to call you, anyway. I like to be able to turn to somebody and say, 'Excuse me. I have to call my sister." He laughed at his unashamed sentimentality. "My sister. I love that. Take care, okay. And think about coming back with Ben. We'd all love it. I'll be in touch if I find out anything about Cassie."

"Okay." She remembered Jack first coming here, remembered the shock and complete disbelief at the sight of him. "I love you, Jack."

"I love you, Corie."

She ended the call, still finding it hard to believe that they were on Cassie's trail. They'd all be together again one day—hopefully soon. She was going to have to learn to cope with feeling out of place. Maybe Ben had been right about that.

Corie went back into the kitchen, where Rosie was applying red frosting to the robe of a cooled angel cookie.

"Good job," Corie said in praise. "Do you want them all to have red robes or just that one?"

Rosie pointed the tip of her frosting brush at the angel she worked on, bells jingling as she readjusted her feet on the rung of the chair. "That one's for my dad. It's going to be just like the ornament I bought. Red with white wings and a yellow star."

Corie had been right about the angel that had been designed for the top of the tree not fitting on the boughs without toppling sideways. So she'd attached fishing line to the wings and Ben had tied it to the light fixture in the living room. It looked perfect there.

Her Christmas spirit sank a little, though she kept her smile in place. She hated the thought of Rosie's disappointment if her father didn't come for her. She'd survive, Corie was sure, but she'd have to find another family, feel out of place until she adjusted.

Corie wished she could fix that part of Rosie's life for her, but there were some things that love and determination simply couldn't change.

WITH CHRISTMAS SO NEAR, Corie worked like a demon at home to finish her gifts for the children, for Teresa and a jacket she'd started for Ben. She added the sleeves from a thick Norwegian sweater to the body of a leather jacket, using pieces of the damaged leather sleeves to put elbow pads on the arms. She thought it was looking good, and had only the sweater's turtleneck to add to the inside of the leather collar. She just wasn't sure if it would be too snug. He had quite a neck. All in all, she was happy with her creation and thought it would serve him well in the wet and windy Oregon weather. She glanced at the clock on the other side of her bed. It was almost 2:00 a.m.

She got up to stretch and survey the lineup of little jackets hanging from her curtain rod, the molding above her closet, and on the back of her door and the doorknob. She smiled at the thought that her room looked like the dressing room of some miniature light-opera army.

All she had to do was press everything tomorrow night and she was finished. Except for Ben's collar. She felt more than just a little pleased with herself.

A knock on her door surprised her out of her self-satisfaction. She'd thought Ben was asleep.

"Yes?" she asked.

"I've got a cup of decaf for you," he said. "Can I open the door?"

"Yes," she replied then remembered that his jacket lay in the middle of her bed. She grabbed it up just as he opened the door. She stuck it quickly behind her and took a step backward.

"Thank you," she said, jutting her chin toward the dresser. "Can you put it there, please? Right on that magazine is fine."

He did as she asked, all the time watching her suspiciously. "What are you hiding?" he asked.

She shook her head, refusing to tell. "After hours, this is Santa's workshop and therefore private."

"I saw everything you're doing for the kids and for Teresa. So what are you hiding?"

He was teasing her. After the past few days of Christmas goodwill, they were friends once more and she really liked that. For the holidays, at least, it was all right that they were having fun together.

She didn't know what to do about her feelings for him in the long run but, for now, they gave everything around her, everything that happened, a little glow. And in that glow, she didn't seem to remember all the things from her past that made her feel out of place. She belonged in this life. She liked it.

"It's...a surprise," she said.

He advanced on her with a curious gleam in his eye. "For me?"

She backed away. "Maybe."

"Can I see it?"

"Then it wouldn't be a surprise." She bumped into the back of her chair and had to stop. "You're worse than the children. Go away."

"But I just brought you coffee. Doesn't that deserve a reward? Come on. It's 2:00 a.m."

"Teresa tells the children that we do nice things because we want to, not because we want something in return." She firmed her expression, but this frivolous side of him was an interesting discovery.

"Well, Teresa isn't here. Can I see? Please? I was one of those kids who had a terrible time waiting for Christmas. Mom and Dad used to let me open a present every other day the last week as a sort of safety valve."

"Aren't you embarrassed to admit that? The fact that at thirty-one you're still behaving the same way?"

"No." He was firm in his lack of shame. "What is it? Is it a jacket like everyone else is getting?" He came closer. She could smell his subtle aftershave and the cedar fragrance that still clung to him after all those days of being around the play set. He smiled winningly. "Come on. Just a peek."

She rolled her eyes, more amused than impatient. "I'll tell you what. I can't let you see it, but you can feel it because I need your help to finish it."

He looked puzzled but hopeful. "Okay. How do we do that?"

"You have to go back to the foot of the bed and turn toward the mirror." She pointed to the full-length mirror on the back of her closet door. "Then close your eyes."

"You're not going to hurt me are you?" he

asked as he backed out of the narrow space her sewing machine occupied to the foot of the bed. "Because I know the old 'close your eyes and I'll give you a big surprise' joke."

"Believe me, I'm tempted," she said, still holding the jacket behind her. "But, no. Close your eyes."

He did. She asked him to extend his left arm and then slipped the sleeve of the jacket over it. Without being asked, he extended his right arm then reached backward so she could slide the other sleeve over it. Eyes still closed, he grabbed the sides and pulled the jacket into place, shrugging until it fit—perfectly.

Excited that it looked even better than she'd imagined, she stepped in front of him to zip it up. Instructing him to "Stay right there, eyes closed," she went to the sewing machine, where she'd left the turtleneck she'd cut off the sweater. She'd slit it down the front, intending to attach it to the collar.

She turned back in shock to discover him, eyes wide open, looking at his reflection.

"Ben!" she complained, smacking his arm.

He didn't seem to notice. He looked happy, amazed, delighted with his present. He stretched both arms and shrugged, assessing the garment's flexibility in the shoulder.

"Corie," he said, his voice filled with awe as he continued to look at his reflection. "It's great. Really. It's so cool. I love it."

He turned and looked about to wrap her in his arms and crush her to him, but before she could be rattled by the gesture, he put her aside and looked in the mirror again. "I can't believe how skilled you are at this, that someone in New York didn't just make you stay, give you your own studio."

She laughed, enjoying his pleasure in her work. "Thank you, but the talent out there in fashion design is beyond anything you can imagine. I'm really small potatoes. But…"

He seemed to hear something significant in her pause and turned to look at her. "But?"

She showed him the soft, woolly band of fabric. "This is going to go inside the leather collar," she said. She stood on the trunk at the foot of her bed, giving herself the height advantage so she could fit the wool around his neck without him having to bend.

He stood still and asked again, "But what?"

She liked this completely different perspective on him, his eyes slightly lower than hers so that he had to look up. His throat was warm, his chin a little stubbly. He put his hands to her waist to prevent her from falling. Her tripping pulse made her acutely aware that what was between them awaited action. "I've been thinking about going to school," she admitted, doing her best to focus on the jacket. With the collar in place, she turned him toward the mirror. "How does that feel? Is it comfortable or just in the way?"

He studied his reflection then caught hers over his shoulder and smiled warmly. "It's great, Corie."

"The collar?"

"School." He tugged up a little on the wool and turned his head one way, then the other. "So is the collar. It's very soft and it'll be nice and warm." He turned back to her, bracketed her waist in his hands and lifted her off the trunk. "You know I think you're smart and gifted just as you are. And that you'd fit in anywhere if you let yourself."

She leaned into him, allowing herself the indulgence, and wrapped her arms around him. The leather jacket made him feel like a bear. He wrapped his arms around her and tightened his hold. Neither of them said anything. The moment didn't need words.

She imagined being able to walk into his embrace whenever she wanted and let herself reel out the fantasy. A home in Oregon, his detective agency under way, online classes for her. Starting a line of clothing to test the market, then one day going national.

Children. Children who weren't just on loan, but would forever be a part of her life.

A pipe dream, but fun to indulge—at least for a minute. She finally brought her arms between them, wedged a little space and said wearily, regretfully, "I have to get some sleep. I'm glad you like the jacket." She reached up to pull the loose fabric from around his neck. He caught her free hand and brought it to his lips.

"Thank you for doing this for me."

She hitched a shoulder. "I put my ornament on the tree and look at it every day. So, you're often on my mind."

He tipped her head up. "Do you really think it's the ornament that makes you think about me?"

Before she could answer, he lowered his head toward her. She raised her mouth to his, feeling every millisecond of anticipation until their lips met. She felt the connection lock into place. The kiss told her in no uncertain terms why he was on her mind. Because they would belong to each other if she could let it happen.

He raised his head with obvious reluctance,

pulled off the jacket and handed it to her. He kissed her one more time and then left the room, closing the door behind him.

She turned off her light and, holding his jacket to her, lay on the bed, closed her eyes and gave her dreams full rein.

## CHAPTER THIRTEEN

CORIE HAD NEVER seen the Grill looking so festive. She and Polly gathered with Hector and Abelia and their children to admire their work fifteen minutes before guests were due to arrive. They decorated every year, but with more holiday parties booked this year than ever before, Hector had gone all out. Or, his wife and children had.

Wreaths had been fastened to the ceiling, fitted around the lights, with glass balls contributing sparkle. Garland, all around the room, was draped with icicles and red-pepper ornaments. Glitter-sprayed cacti decorated every table, each one on a red cloth.

Mariachis dressed in dark blue stood in a corner at the back, setting up.

The aromas of roasted corn on the cob, *carne asada, frijoles á la charra* with onions, garlic, tomatoes and jalapeño, and a spicy quinoa dish filled the room.

Hector had dimmed the lights as they always did for dinner, but tonight the place came to life like the dining room at the North Pole—if cacti grew there.

"It's perfect," Polly said. "I think the town should be very pleased with you."

"I hope so," he said, wearing a chef's coat and hat—a formality he seldom indulged. "All right. Let's everyone get ready and put our best foot—and food—forward. Think of the tips."

Within an hour, music filled the space, conversation was deafening and everything and everyone sparkled. Abelia tended a bar set up for the occasion and Corie and Polly kept the appetizer trays filled.

When it was time to sit for dinner, Pimental stood at the front of the room and made a speech of welcome. He sounded like any other public servant, proud of the town, proud of its employees, proud of their work for the community. It was too bad, Corie thought, looking over the crowd, that it wasn't sincere.

Sukie sat in a far corner at a table with other administrative assistants, who listened attentively. Her eyes kept shifting to Pimental's wife, a dark-haired, fortysomething woman in a sequined-silver dress, who occupied the chair beside him at the head table. She either didn't know, or didn't care, that he wasn't faithful. Sukie's expression was a mixture of sadness and resentment.

At a smaller table near the front, Cyrus and Delia Tyree, in elegant holiday attire, sat with Bigelow, long divorced and without a date. His daughter and Chris Norton completed the table. She wondered why the Tyrees were here when this party was for employees. They might just be guests of the deputy mayor, or maybe they paid enough property taxes on their holdings in Querida to be welcome at any town function.

Corie and Polly were busy pouring coffee and taking drink orders through dinner.

At one point Tyree leaned across the table toward Chris in animated conversation. Delia, beside him, glanced back at the head table and a look passed between her and Pimental that spoke of shared intimacies. Fortunately for them, neither Mrs. Pimental nor Sukie noticed. Man with a death wish, Corie thought, stringing three women along.

On one of her rounds with the coffeepot, Corie saw Pam Porter from the school district lean toward Pimental. In a not-so-quiet voice she said, "I'm surprised they'd have her serve us tonight when she assaulted you."

Corie stopped, coffeepot poised, recognizing the danger of the moment. It was so tempting…

Pimental dismissed any concerns with a flick of his fingertips. He smiled up at her with angelic forgiveness. "I just had to make her understand that I love my wife. She leaves me alone now."

"Actually…" Corie began on a laugh, prepared to straighten everyone out on what had really happened. But then she looked around at all the happy guests, Hector flushed with their praise as he wandered from table to table. She couldn't ruin the evening.

With a dark look at Pimental, she turned away, seemingly unable to control the pot in its sideways tilt and spilling a very small stream of hot coffee in his lap.

He gasped, quickly leaning backward and shifting in his seat. She headed to the kitchen, pretending she hadn't noticed, pleased with herself.

"Corie!" Abelia, taking more ice from the freezer, pushed her in the direction of the storage room. "Please get more swizzle sticks. I dropped a box on the floor."

"Sure." The storage room was at the back of the building. Corie went deep into the long, narrow space since beverage supplies were kept at the back. She climbed onto a step stool to reach into a top shelf. The transom window was open to let cool air into the crowded restaurant and she stopped still when she heard the sound of Tyree's voice in the gravel yard outside.

"I don't see what's so hard about it," he was saying. "I own the building and I don't want her there. Get her out."

"I uphold the law, Mr. Tyree." That was Bigelow.

There was a scornful laugh. "No, you don't. You do what Pimental tells you, and I told him I want her out."

"I meant," Bigelow said carefully, temper in his voice, "that she has a lot of friends and if we throw her out just before Christmas—children and all—we'll create a lot of bad publicity."

"It's *my* house!"

"She's renting it. That makes it her house. And they know what they're talking about. After my run-in with that cop from Oregon, I looked for loopholes, but there aren't any. You can't make her leave without following the steps."

"What's the cop doing here, anyway?"

"Came to see the Ochoa chick."

Chick? An improvement over the Ochoa *brat*—or not?

"Girlfriend?"

"I don't know. Her brother is his brother."

"So he's her brother."

"No."

There was a moment's silence while even Querida's criminal element dealt with the weird Palmer-Manning situation.

"He was there when her house was broken into, according to Chris's report. So maybe he is a boyfriend."

"Somebody broke into her house?"

"Yeah. A week or so ago."

"Cyrus. Here you are." A woman's voice. Probably Delia Tyree. "Can we go now? The only good thing about this party is Hector's food. The guests at our party are going to love it."

"You're a snob, Delia."

"Thank you, dear. One of the perks of having a rich husband. I'll be in the car."

Corie stepped off the stool and onto the counter, hiding behind a stack of boxes in case they went by the doorway to the storage room. Well, that was interesting. She could only conclude from the conversation that since Tyree hadn't known her house had been broken into, he wasn't responsible for leaving the necklace.

Remembering her errand, she reached for the swizzle sticks at the back of the shelf and hurried to the kitchen.

It was well-known that the problem with a good party was that no one ever wanted to leave. And that held true tonight. Music continued to play, guests moved the tables aside and began dancing. Hector was thrilled with the evening's success. Corie found him and Abelia dancing in the kitchen when only a few guests remained.

Well after midnight, she and Polly cleared tables and loaded the dishwasher. While it ran, Polly saw the last of the guests out and Corie collected the garbage to take out to the back.

In the cool darkness, she headed for the collection of trash cans at the corner of the building. Music from inside drifted out and the night air was filled with the aromas from dinner and the sweet sage bushes at the park. She stuffed the bags inside the trash can, humming along with the music as she replaced the lid and turned to leave. She stopped abruptly, cold fear filling her chest. She stood face-to-face with Pimental in the dim light of the alley.

She forced a serene expression. "Party's inside," she said, walking around him.

He caught her arm in a biting grip and yanked her back. "I want to talk to *you*."

"Aren't you afraid I'm going to seduce you?" she taunted then tried again to move away. His pincerlike grip held firm.

"You're going to encourage Teresa to take her little foster home elsewhere," he said. He leaned over her for effect. She smelled alcohol and an acrid cologne. "I want her out of there by the new year."

She looked into his face without flinching. She was afraid, but her anger had the upper hand. "I'm sure Bigelow told you about his efforts to deliver an eviction notice. They didn't work."

He tightened his grip. She was sure she felt her humerus crack. "Let me clarify," he said, giving her a little shake. "I have a photo of the night you broke into the Tyrees' and stole Delia's jewelry."

Everything inside her froze. He was lying. He had to be. She hadn't seen anyone else. Of course, she'd been a little busy at the time.

"Really. Why haven't you showed it to the police?"

"As a collector of information, I use it in

the ways it serves me best. You think you're so much better than me, so it's good to make you think twice about that."

"I *am* better than you!" she said with heartfelt sincerity. "I'd never use the people around me for my own advantage or hurt them so that I can feel superior."

He shook his head at her tirade. "I want Teresa's house, Corie. You're going to get it for me because the photo I have——" he paused for effect, his threatening expression turning into a lazy, ugly smile "——is of your brother disarming the alarm system."

For an instant she couldn't get a breath. She thought back frantically. She'd been the one who'd disarmed the alarm, left it dangling in the doorway, but Jack might have touched it when he'd followed her into the house. Pimental was just trying to intimidate her into doing what he wanted.

"You'll help me, won't you?"

She wouldn't help him if he was on fire and she had a hose. Unless there was a chance he could hurt Jack.

She had to gulp for air. "I'm a pretty good photographer myself," she countered with sudden inspiration. "I was taking pictures of the kids in their Halloween costumes one afternoon and got a photo of you and Delia Tyree in the trees behind the park."

Uncertainty shone in his eyes. She held his gaze, hoping to convince him of what she said. Actually, she'd seen them walking there and wondered what they were doing together. Then she'd seen that look pass between them tonight. "I'm sure Tyree would love to know that. Whatever deal you have going with him over Teresa's house might not survive that."

His voice came out dark and threatening. "Corazon Ochoa, you're going to regret the day you met me."

"That happened a long time ago, Mr. Pimental," she said. She slapped his hand away, walked around him and went back inside.

BEN GUESSED SOMETHING was wrong the moment she got into his SUV. She smiled and handed him a crispy chocolate churro left over from the party, but he caught a glimpse of concern behind the smile.

"What happened?" he asked.

"It was a wonderful party," she replied, the smile staying in place. "They even moved the tables to dance after dinner. Hector was a big hit."

"Great. But what happened to *you*?"

Her eyes widened in innocence. "What do you mean?"

Apparently this was going to take some time. He pulled away from the curb and started home. "Something's upset you."

She leaned her head back against the rest. "I'm just tired. It was a really long evening."

"Fine." Pushing her never worked, though he always seemed to forget that and do it anyway. Tonight his brain seemed to be functioning. "Tell me when you're ready."

"Nothing happened," she insisted.

"When you're ready," he said again.

WHEN JACK CALLED early the next morning, Corie knew instantly that something was wrong. "What?" she asked.

He waited a beat then said in a cheerful voice that sounded forced, "Cassie's father does work for Bourgeois-Berger."

She felt a glimmer of hope but was afraid to indulge it. "But?"

"He went to handle a problem at their office in Bangkok."

"Why do you sound worried?" she asked.

He sighed. "There was a coup there two days ago and the Paris office hasn't heard from him."

"I...uh! Seriously?"

"I wish I wasn't serious, but I am." His cheerful tone returned. "This is just the Manning Kids Curse. We've got to fight fate to be together. And that's what we're going to do. The company said they'd tell him I called as soon as they hear from him."

"I hope he's okay."

"So far, it's a bloodless coup, but martial law is imposed and the government is controlling communication and the internet. He's probably hunkering down to wait it out."

"I remember him only vaguely."

"Sure. You were just a baby. Our mother was beautiful, and charming when she wasn't using, and he fell in love. She fell off the program and he was fired for getting personal with a client. He left. Sad all around."

"Yeah. Thanks, Jack."

"Sure. I'll be in touch."

IN THE MIDDLE of the morning, Corie blindfolded Teresa so that she could try on the jacket she'd made her to be certain it fit.

Rosie and the Flores girls were gathered around, enjoying the spectacle. They oohed and aahed when Corie shook out the green double-faced jacket she'd made out of a length of designer fabric she'd bought at an estate sale in McAllen. She'd added black faux fur on the collar and cuffs and was so proud of how perfect it looked on Teresa that she could have burst. She shushed the girls with a finger to her lips.

"It's so pretty," Bianca said.

Lupe put a hand over her sister's mouth. "We don't want her to know what it looks like," she whispered.

"I just said it was pretty," Bianca protested, pulling Lupe's hand away. "Can I tell her what color it is?"

"No!" Lupe and Corie said in unison.

"If Corie made it," Teresa said, "I already know it's beautiful, but thank you, Bianca." Then she whispered in her direction, still blindfolded, "What color is it?"

Corie turned a playfully fierce look in the little girl's direction.

"I can't tell you," Bianca said dutifully.

Corie nodded her approval. She was getting good at this, she thought, seeing how well the jacket fit through the shoulders. The length of the sleeves was perfect. She'd put on toggles and buttons rather than a zipper, giving a touch of drama to the color and the texture of the fabric. The girls' little burst of cheer lightened her mood.

There was a knock at the door.

Karina ran toward it. Corie, focused on one more scan of Teresa's garment, stopped, frozen, when Karina's voice first said softly, "Mama," then louder and with great excitement, "Mama!"

Corie turned toward the door and Teresa ripped off the blindfold. Lupe and Bianca ran toward Amelia Flores, a woman not much taller than her oldest daughter, who wrapped all three girls in her arms and wept with them.

A portly man with a big smile stood beside Amelia and her girls. Joel Santiago, the Army's father. Teresa went toward him, hand extended.

He shook and then glanced around the living room. "Where are my boys?" he asked. "There's no one in the front yard."

With a look at Corie that reflected her confusion as to why Amelia and Joel were here together, Teresa hooked an arm in Joel's and led him through the kitchen to the backyard.

"I'M WILLING TO put in capital," Grady said to Ben as they replaced the lightbulb by the back door. Ben stood on the ladder and Grady held the old bulb and handed up the new one. "I don't have to. If you want to be a sole proprietor, that's fine. I'll work for you. But if you want a partner, I'm in."

They'd been talking about Ben's business plan for the investigation and security agency, while helping Teresa with small chores, and keeping an eye on the boys. Christmas was a mere six days away and the kids were particularly rowdy.

"We could call it, 'The Brilliant Grady Nelson Agency, with Ben Palmer.'"

"Funny. What about the Palmer-Nelson Agency?" Ben put in the new bulb.

"Not terribly imaginative, but I like it. Sam still wants in." Sam Wagner worked with Ben and Grady on the Beggar's Bay police force. He was in his middle forties with a knowledge that couldn't be found in books or even at the police academy. Grady handed up the light fixture.

"He'd be a real asset. I'll talk to him when I get back."

There was a moment of quiet before Grady asked, "Are you *going* back?"

"Of course. Why?" Ben started turning the screws in place with his thumb, using the screwdriver when they were secure.

"You seem pretty connected here. You know... Corie and all. The kids."

Ben put the screwdriver in his pocket and backed down the ladder. "The kids are great, but most of them will be going home by Christmas. Teresa thinks so, anyway."

The door opened cautiously and Teresa said through the narrow opening, "And Teresa was right. Can I open the door?"

"Yes." Ben moved the ladder out of the way as she walked onto the deck with a man who wasn't very tall but looked built to carry refrigerators. He ran lightly down the stairs at the same moment that children seemed to fall off the play set. Carlos leaped off the climbing wall, Rigo jumped off a swing and Miguel and Tonio, tumbling in the gravel, looked up to see what had set their brothers in motion. All shouted, "Papa!"

The five came together in the middle of the yard, the little ones climbing onto the man, Carlos and Rigo plastering themselves to him wherever they could fit.

"That's Joel Santiago," Teresa said to Ben and Grady.

"He came for them." Ben was surprised to hear his thought voiced aloud. "That's... wonderful." He hesitated when he caught a glimpse of Soren, leaning over the clubhouse railing, looking on with longing and sadness. It occurred to Ben that if Mr. Santiago had come for his boys, Soren was about to lose his best friend.

"Not only that," Teresa said, "but Amelia Flores is in the house. She and Joel arrived together. They thought it would be a wonderful surprise for the children."

"Does it mean anything that they came together?"

"I'm not sure. No one's had time to explain. They wanted to see their children first." A ragged sigh escaped her as she looked up at Soren. She made a beckoning gesture and he came down the slide.

Everyone went back inside where pandemonium reigned as Corie helped the girls run up and down the stairs with their things.

The boys raced up to pack. Joel put an arm around Amelia and she leaned into him, tears still streaming down her face. "Joel and I met in the retraining class you put us in touch with. He has hotel experience and I've cooked all my life, so a small hotel outside Fort Worth that works with the school hired us as a team."

Joel squeezed her shoulders. "We were feeling like a team, anyway, so we thought we'd get married before we head out there."

"That's seven children," Grady said, stating the obvious. "I mean, wow."

Joel shrugged. "When you have four, what's a few more?"

"How are you going to get everybody there?" Teresa asked practically.

Joel pointed out the window. "The hotel lent us their van. It seats nine. Perfect."

"That's just meant to be," Teresa said. She looked a little stunned, Ben thought, carried along on a tide she couldn't stop. She'd given so much love and care to these children, and she was losing seven at once. He noticed for the first time that she still wore the jacket Corie was making her for Christmas, and a blindfold remained loosely knotted around her neck.

He saw the same expression Teresa wore on Corie's face as she entered with the girls. She helped them make a last-minute check of their bags and then went to get the jackets she'd made and already wrapped for them. "No opening until Christmas, okay," she reminded. Then she hugged each one.

The boys trooped down, Soren helping Carlos, who carried his things and Tonio's. Soren's football was tucked under his arm. The boys all stood together in the middle of the room, the fragile emotion making them look at each other uncertainly. It was just occurring to them that they were leaving this little Christmas haven.

"Thanks for the football," Carlos said to Soren.

"Sure. I promised if your family came..." Soren swallowed and forced a smile. "I hope you really like the new place."

Corie gave the boys their packages with the same warning. "Not until Christmas, right?"

"Oh! Our ornaments!" Lupe and her sisters and the Santiago boys went to the tree. Ben and Grady helped them locate their ornaments and take them down. Corie retrieved tissue and wrapped them to put in their bags.

Lupe took a soft package wrapped in red tissue. She turned to Corie. "Can we give Teresa her present now?"

"Yes, of course."

Lupe handed the package to Teresa and all the children moved a little closer. Teresa unwrapped it and smiled widely, tears standing in her eyes. She held up the apron decorated with a bright green tree made of their handprints. Corie had appliquéd a few colored ornaments and an angel at the top.

"This couldn't be more perfect," Teresa said. The children gathered around her for a communal hug. "Thank you. I love it!" She put it on and Lupe tied it for her in the back.

Carlos turned worriedly to Teresa. "What if you guys have to move? How will I know how to find you?"

"If they do have to move," Corie said quickly, "they'll stay with me and you know where that is. And you can call me." She gave Joel her contact information.

Joel looked as emotional as the children. "I promise we will keep in touch." He took a ragged breath and hugged Teresa then Corie. "I don't know how to thank you for taking care of my boys. I'm so grateful. Until my friend told me about you, I didn't know what to do."

Teresa wiped away tears. "That's what I do. I'm so happy for all of you." She opened her arms to Amelia. "Good luck. The kids are all wonderful. Have a good life."

Ben was suddenly aware of Rosie standing beside him, her little mouth trembling. He put an arm around her, his heart breaking for her and Soren. This had been their family for months and now, without warning, they were going away.

Soren stood on his other side, stoically watching everyone climb into the van. Ben hooked an arm around the boy's shoulders and pulled him closer. He knew there was nothing he could say that would soften the moment, so he simply held on.

Everyone waved; the Flores girls and the Santiago boys hanging out the windows until the van was out of sight. Teresa put both hands over her face and Corie held her for a long moment. "This is what we do, remember," she said bracingly. "Seven children on their way back home."

Grady looked as though he, too, was about to lose it. "I need coffee," he said.

Ben turned the kids around to follow him. "I think we all need coffee. Some of us, cocoa. And maybe cookies."

"And maybe bourbon," Grady whispered as Ben joined him with the children.

FOR THE NEXT two days the house was as quiet as a library. Everything Corie and Ben had done to make a cheerful Christmas for the children now only served to amplify their absence—the giant tree, the tins filled with cookies, the decorations everywhere, Ben's wonderful play set.

Soren and Rosie used the equipment with a sort of frantic desperation, as though running from one setup to the next would help them forget that it was now just the two of them.

# CHAPTER FOURTEEN

ON SADNESS OVERLOAD, Corie began to formulate a plan. She had to think about something other than the quietness of the house. Her plan was a little dangerous but she felt a stirring of excitement at the thought.

Maybe she wasn't as ready for the new and revised Elizabeth Corazon Ochoa as she'd thought she was. Having her brother and Ben in her life did make her realize she had to approach her future differently, but she felt a certain satisfaction in the knowledge that some of her old skills could still be useful. And what Chris Norton didn't know wouldn't hurt him.

BEN TOOK EVERYONE to dinner and a movie that evening, which served as a happy distraction. But when they got home, the silence rang loudly. Soren went to bed early and Rosie stood in a window, looking out at the driveway. Ben guessed she was waiting for her father.

He found Teresa and Corie sitting at the

table in the kitchen, a piece of paper between them. If possible, their mood was even gloomier than the children's.

"Something wrong?" he asked, taking a chair. "Something *else*?"

Teresa pushed the official-looking document toward him. "I just opened this afternoon's mail."

He scanned the paper and saw that it was a signed release of some kind. Judging by the carefully worded legalese, the signatory abdicated all control over the subject, whoever it was. He kept reading, then realized with stunning pain who the subject was.

It was Rosie.

Her father had signed over his parental rights. A note was included saying that the job hadn't worked out, after all, and he thought this would be better for Rosie in the long run. He had done this with the help of an attorney, who'd advised him that since there was no other family member to assume responsibility, Teresa would be hearing from Children and Family Services right after Christmas regarding moving Rosie to a formal foster home.

Ben was at a loss for words. He turned the offending document facedown. "What'll happen to her?"

"Just what it says," Teresa replied. "She'll end up in the system."

"How does a man just sign away his daughter?" he demanded.

"Happens all the time." Teresa pushed away from the table. "So, how do we make this Christmas happy for her and Soren? What can we do to inject a little cheer into this place?"

"Short of finding Santa, himself?" Corie added, "He could find families for them..."

Families. Family. His family. Ben put a hand on Teresa's as a brilliant idea began to take shape in his mind.

"I know just the people who can provide lots of noise and good cheer," he said. "My parents, and Jack and Sarah. What do you think? I can put them up at the B and B, and send them home right after Christmas."

Teresa's face brightened. "Do you think they'd want to come?"

"I'll explain and they'll be here before you can brace yourself."

Teresa looked around at the old but well-kept kitchen. "They can stay here if you think they'll be comfortable. I've got a few empty rooms now."

"Perfect."

He turned to Corie, wondering if she would

approve. She seemed concerned at first. Then, as Teresa's enthusiasm grew, she smiled cautiously. He dialed Jack. When the call went to voice mail, he called his mother.

She was happy to hear from him and when he explained the situation, eight children gone home with their families, leaving two behind, she sounded as though she was already packing. "I'm sure Jack and Sarah will want to come. He won a big contract to restore the library today. I imagine that's why he didn't pick up. He and Sarah are celebrating. We can be on our way tomorrow. Next day at the latest. Give my love to Corie."

"I will. Love you, Mom." He ended the call and turned to Corie. "Mom sends her love."

She nodded as though she could feel it. His mother's love was a powerful force.

Teresa patted his hand. "Thank you, Ben. That's a brilliant idea. Come on, Corie. We have a lot to do to make the rooms presentable. I'm in the process of washing all the bedding, but two rooms occupied for months by children under ten will need some serious elbow grease."

THE FAMILY WAS arriving tomorrow, the twenty-third. Corie looked forward to seeing

Jack again, but was seriously worried about whether or not Pimental had that photo. She had to know for sure. Now.

After helping Teresa move furniture out into the hall, she vacuumed carpets then removed them. Rosie and Soren were in the living room, watching a Christmas movie.

"What are you doing?" Ben asked Corie, climbing over furniture to get to the bedroom doorway. She was scrubbing floors with a squeegee.

She looked at him over her shoulder, putting a hand up to prevent him from coming farther. "It's slippery. Teresa wants things to be perfect for your family."

"This is not necessary," he insisted. "Really. My mother is tidy but not compulsive."

"It's all right. These two rooms need to be cleaned, and you've done so much for us, Teresa wants to be sure your family is comfortable. And so do I."

He shook his head at her. "Again, not necessary. But, if you won't listen, what can I do to help?"

"When it's time to move the furniture back…"

"Sure. Grady and I'll do it. Just call me. We'll be sprucing up the yard."

"Thank you."

Corie went down to the kitchen half an hour later to fix lunch. She glanced out the window to see Ben and Grady pulling weeds, and Rosie and Soren sitting side by side, swinging desultorily. She looked again to make sure she wasn't seeing things. Yes. It was Soren and Rosie, having a peaceful conversation. Would they finally be friends?

Her cell phone rang while she spread sandwich fixings on the counter. She dug it out of her jeans' pocket. It was Jack.

"You, again!" she teased, happy to hear his voice. "You'd better have good news."

"I do," he said, his voice turning serious, a note of excitement in it. "But you'd better sit down."

Several ugly possibilities crossed her mind including one where their sister's father had died in the coup and no one knew where Cassidy was. Corie sat at the table. "Did something happen to Mr. Chapman?" she asked.

"No. No. A manager of the company he was working with put him up for a few days then took him to the American embassy. He got a flight out yesterday and called me as soon as he received my message." He inhaled a breath. She held hers. "You'll never believe who our sister is."

She expelled her breath. "We know who our sister is. She's Cassidy Chapman."

"Yeah, but guess who else she is?"

"What do you mean?"

"She's Cassiopeia."

When she said nothing, he added, "You know. The supermodel."

She knew who Cassiopeia was. That was why she couldn't speak.

It was impossible. The sister of the soldier with terrible nightmares and the gutter rat nobody wanted, could not be a celebrity. *Everybody Famous*, a popular television show about movie stars and other celebrities, had called her "The Stellar Beauty" several years before when she'd taken the fall fashion runways by storm, and that was how the name Cassiopeia stuck.

Corie admired Cassiopeia because the model had brought the smile back to strutting clothes. In the interest of showing off clothing without distraction, the trend had been to reduce the impression the model made, hence the distant faces, the lack of smiles. Cassie had changed all that.

For the past few years she'd been a favorite of late-night talk-show hosts and had been linked with many of Hollywood's heartthrobs.

When Corie did finally find her voice, it was to squeak, "She's a foot taller than I am!"

Jack laughed. "That's not surprising. Her father is a foot taller than yours was."

"She had a space between her teeth and out-of-control hair."

"Well, now she's probably had dental work and has the finest hair and makeup artists in the world available to her."

Corie absorbed the shock—she was good at that—but she still couldn't quite process the information. The gorgeous, blonde, blue-eyed Cassiopeia was her sister. Jack's sister. They were the Manning family.

"It seems impossible."

"I know."

"You have to be the one to call her. I'd have no idea what to say."

"Her father wants to tell her about us and let her get in touch. Seems fair. It will probably be very shocking for her. He says he tried to find you after they moved to Paris, but that was probably after your father died and everything changed again."

"Yeah." She felt a moment's grief for all that time lost then focused on the fact that Jack had found her, Corie. "Do you think she'll be happy to find *us*?"

"I guess we'll know pretty soon. Her father said she was involved in… I don't know, he wasn't very specific. Some kind of scandal, I think. He was trying hard not to say too much. Anyway, she was hiding away in some secret location. She has another cell phone only he has the number for."

"Wow."

"Hmm. Kind of cloak-and-dagger. Might take a little time to hear from her, but after twenty-three years, I'm willing to wait. How about you?"

"Yes." She wondered if Jack had spoken to Helen yet. "Has your mom talked to you about coming to Texas?"

"Yes. That was something else I wanted to see about. What can we bring? What do the kids need?"

"Nothing, Jack. Just cheerful people full of Christmas spirit who'll want to sing carols and eat cookies and just have fun."

"Okay, that's us. We'll fly out in the morning, rent a car in McAllen and be there by the middle of the afternoon."

"I can't wait to see you."

"Me, too. Just think. Any day we might hear from Cassie."

"It's hard to believe. See you soon."

Corie hit the off button, pocketed her phone and put a hand over her wildly beating heart. Her little sister, Cassie, was Cassiopeia, the runway star of Paris, London and Milan.

She caught her own reflection in the black refrigerator. Five-one and a half, jeans and a sweatshirt, feet of long black hair that hadn't been trimmed or shaped in years. Cassie was the epitome of everything Corie was not—in appearance and probably ever other way. She was scared.

# CHAPTER FIFTEEN

HOURS LATER, CORIE sat on the edge of her bed in black jeans and sweater and black boots, ready to implement the plan. She was going to break into Pimental's office. What if she got caught and Cassie called and Ben had to say she couldn't talk because she was in jail?

Okay, that wouldn't happen. She wasn't going to get caught because Pimental never stayed at his office late, she was good at skulking and Querida wasn't a progressive town with formal security systems. And Chris Norton would never understand.

The lock on the back door of city hall was a simple pin-and-tumbler thing that was easy to disrupt with a hex wrench. The city's computers probably had more security than the building did. And at midnight, the streetlights downtown went out as a cost-saving measure.

Sukie had once told her that as Pimental's executive assistant, she was so important to him that she kept the key to his office in her desk.

And he was so important that he had an entire cabinet filled with government documents that he had to keep locked at all times. Unfortunately, Sukie hadn't told her where the key was, but she had faith in her own ability to figure it out if she could just get in there. If Pimental did have a photo of Jack at Tyree's, she wagered it would be in that file.

By the time she smoothed her bed, gently pushed open her bedroom window and climbed out into the shrubbery, her phone read 12:03 a.m. She headed for town at a run, a black bag slung over her shoulder, unwilling to risk waking Ben or the rest of the neighborhood with the sound of a car engine.

BEN LAY ON his back on the floor of Corie's living room and stared sleeplessly at the ceiling. His thoughts went from poor Rosie, whose father had given her up like something he'd bought and decided he didn't want, to Soren, who didn't have anyone to take him home for Christmas, to Corie and Jack, who could be about to meet their long-lost sister for a complete reunion of the Mannings.

He was so lucky to have had loving parents, a good education, a job he liked but needed a break from and a friend to accompany him into the exploration of a new business.

He had a woman he loved but didn't always understand. She didn't seem to get him at all. She mistook his concern for a need to control. Actually he suspected she simply didn't understand how love worked. Or did, and didn't want it because it got in the way of doing what she wanted to do. And she'd seemed unusually distracted all afternoon.

They'd watched the kids together from the kitchen window while wrapping the presents Teresa had brought down from her room. Though Corie had smiled politely and answered his attempts to make conversation, her mind had clearly been elsewhere.

Back at her place, she'd gone to bed after their late dinner of fast-food takeout, claiming to have to work on Teresa's jacket. But he happened to know she'd left the jacket at Teresa's. It was possible that finding Cassie after all these years completely distracted her, but he thought something else was at work here. He could almost see the sparking of her brain in her eyes.

He suspected she was plotting something.

When he heard the subtle sound of her window being raised, he was sure of it. He got up quietly. Still wearing his T-shirt, he pulled on his jeans as he went to the window. He watched her truck, expecting her to jump into it, and almost missed her. Fortunately a neighbor's porch light caught her dark figure running up the street.

He resented the time it took to put on his shoes, but if he was going to follow her on foot, they were a necessity. He closed the door quietly behind him and ran in the direction she'd gone.

It took him until the very edge of town to get her in sight. That small, fit body moved remarkably quickly. The floodlight in front of the Grill caught her silhouette as she passed it on the other side of the street. She was heading for city hall.

He got a bad feeling about this.

CORIE UNLOCKED THE back door of city hall with her hexagonal wrench, pushing it straight into the hole in the door handle, turning it slightly back and forth until she felt the catch. A simple turn unlocked the door. She closed it quietly behind her and stopped to listen. The building was silent. Her nostrils breathed in the residual smells of cologne, perfume, wood polish and the mustiness of the old place.

She went straight to Pimental's office. Having been there before to plead Teresa's case about eviction, she knew she had to go through Sukie's office first, mercifully unlocked. She tried the adjoining door. Locked. She hadn't counted on Sukie being that efficient. Hopefully, she wasn't efficient enough to have locked her desk.

Luck was with her. There were several keys in the pencil tray. The first one Corie tried fit Pimental's door.

His office smelled of a familiar acrid cologne. A nice fragrance if it hadn't been connected to him. She dug her key chain out of her pocket, pressed the small penlight button and flashed it around the room.

A door was open into a private bathroom with a shower. She remembered the news story about the deputy mayor insisting he needed it to prepare for meetings and the arrival of guests. Several citizens had protested the cost, but the room had been built anyway.

Corie put that out of her mind and went to the file cabinet across the room. It was locked.

Going back to his desk, she discovered that it, too, was locked. Great.

When Corie had worked in New York, her boss had rented space in an old loft furnished with ancient office equipment. It had had an old desk like this one, and she remembered that important notes were kept on a pull-out board above the drawers on the left side. She tried that. The board, termed a bread board, was not connected to the desk's locking mechanism and came out easily. There were notes taped to it with what were probably important phone numbers and dates. She ran a hand along the underside and felt the thin metal shape of a key. Ha! She ripped it off and went to open the cabinet.

Shining her penlight in the top drawer, she found files for committees that worked with and for the town, suppliers and a disaster plan. Her situation did constitute a disaster, but she doubted the plan would help her.

She opened the second drawer to discover building plans, blueprints and some personnel information. She closed it and opened the third and bottom drawer, praying she would locate what she wanted.

Her heart began to beat faster when she saw the names on the files. Her own, Sukie's, Tyree's, Bigelow's. There was a file labeled Pennington Properties and another tagged Craigslist. She'd never heard of Pennington Properties and couldn't imagine what Craigslist had to do with his goings on. At the back of the file was an electronic tablet. She yanked the black bag off her shoulder and stuffed the entire contents of the bottom drawer inside.

She was about to relock the cabinet when someone grabbed her by the arm and yanked her around the desk. No! Not when she was this close! She pulled back a fist and swung with all her might.

Her assailant caught her fist in a big hand and squeezed tightly. "Corie!" It was Ben's harsh whisper. "The cleaning crew is right behind me! Come on! The bathroom."

The room was dark but Corie used her penlight to scan the area. Ben pulled her toward the shower, carefully opening the door. Voices could be heard now as the crew walked into Sukie's office.

He closed the frosted shower door after them with the barest snick of sound. He pushed her into a corner and stood in front of her. Corie noticed that her light was still on and turned it off.

The voices grew louder. The crew, apparently a couple of older men, talked about wives and children while they worked in the outer office. Music played, something was

banged around—wastebaskets, probably—
and a vacuum cleaner roared.

The subject had turned to food as the men
drew closer. Ben remained in front of Corie
as the bathroom door opened. The sounds of
a melancholy Jenni Rivera ballad drifted in
and the overhead light went on. Corie couldn't
catch her breath.

Water splashed, the toilet flushed, more
vacuuming.

"Do we have to do the shower?" a male
voice asked.

Corie screamed silently. She felt Ben's body
brace for action.

"I saw Pimental today," the second man replied. "He didn't look like he'd showered, so
I'm sure it's clean." They laughed and the light
went out as they left the bathroom.

BEN PUT A hand to the shower door and took a
moment to collect himself. He imagined this
had been good practice for his career as a detective. Still, he'd like to plan his own death-
defying investigations.

He turned to lean a shoulder against the
shower tile and whisper-shouted at Corie,
"What in the hell…?"

"I… I…" Apparently unable to explain herself, she simply held up the big black bag he'd seen flapping emptily against her back when he was chasing her. Now it appeared to be filled with something heavy. "I needed these," she finally said.

"And what is 'these'?"

"Pimental's files. Not sure yet what's in them."

"So we just risked breaking and entering because of something you're not sure is of value to us?"

She repeated that question to herself and thought it through. "Yes," she finally replied. "What I'm looking for is or isn't in here. Either way, it's important."

What?

He pushed the shower door open, pulled her out after him and stood still for a moment, listening for the sounds of the cleaners. He caught faint strains of music from across the building.

They went stealthily down the nearest stairway, then out the door into the quiet night. He took the heavy bag from her. "It never occurred to you to tell me you were going to break into city hall?"

She was already steps ahead of him and turned to give him an over-the-shoulder roll of her eyes. "Why would I? You'd have told me not to."

He started after her. "Well, that's sound reasoning."

"I had to get these files, whether or not you approved. If what I want is in there, I can destroy it. If it isn't, then he probably doesn't have it, so all is well."

Now that they were out of the building, he was beyond angry. "Isn't it time you stopped playing your life like an extreme sport?"

She stopped. "What?"

He caught up with her. "Yeah, you treat this life like those extreme skiers and rock climbers and all those people who think the thrill of the risk is everything. Have you ever considered using your head before your gut? That there are legal ways to accomplish things without resorting to crime?"

She firmed her lips and glared at him. "Breaking and entering is what I know."

"Oh, you're a lot smarter than that, but it's what you like to do. Yeah. You're afraid to leave the old you behind because the present you doesn't fit in. Using your gut is so much easier than using your head."

"It's my heart, not my gut. I don't want Jack to be hurt."

"What about me? If it was your heart," he said, poking his finger in her chest, "don't you have some responsibility to not make me insane with worry? To keep me in the loop when you're going to do something nuts like break into city hall?"

She swallowed, tears in her eyes. "I didn't want you involved."

"And, yet, here I am!"

"Because you don't know how to leave well enough alone. I want to protect Jack... and you, but this is who I am, and if you can't deal with that, then...we have nothing more to say." She walked off again.

Yeah, right. "Except that you have a bag filled with files that you've just stolen from city hall and we have to figure out how to get them back before morning."

"After we've checked them out."

He sighed. "After we've checked them out."

"All right. Then after that, we have nothing more to say to each other."

"Oh, I have a lot to say, but I'm not going to keep shouting in the middle of the street, in the middle of the night."

They didn't speak again until they were back in her kitchen. He made coffee while she pulled files out of the bag and spread them on the table. Among the folders was a tablet.

She turned it on, leaned forward when the icons appeared, but was clearly stumped by a password. She typed in something, sighed when it didn't work, tried a few more words, then put the tablet aside and began to prowl through the paper files.

He brought her a cup of coffee and sat at a right angle to her, thinking how grateful he was that he was off duty and in a state where he *wasn't* a police officer. Technically, a cop always had a responsibility to enforce the law, but he was ignoring that until he saw what she was after.

He reached for the folder with her name on it. "What are we searching for?" When Corie didn't answer, he looked up to see her pale and fear-filled face staring into his. That scared *him*. Usually, if she felt fear, she didn't betray it. So this time it must be a bigger fear than she could control. "What?" he asked.

She swallowed and it was clear she'd rather do anything than answer him. But she angled her chin and said, "We're looking for a photo of Jack taken the night you guys followed me to Tyree's. It looks like he's disabling the security system, but actually I had done that.

He probably just touched the dangling wires when he followed me into the house."

Ben told himself he was too young and too fit to have a heart attack. But his chest constricted as though he was about to. He sorted through anger, trepidation, confusion and looked for calm. "Who took the photo?"

She flipped through papers in the file without looking up at him. "Pimental," she replied.

"And how do you know that?"

"He told me."

Things were starting to come together. "When?"

She put the papers down and met his eyes with mild impatience. "The night of the town's Christmas party."

Remarkably he kept his cool. "He's the one who scared you."

"Yes."

"What did he say?"

"That if I didn't convince Teresa to move, he'd show the Corpus Christi police Jack's photo."

That made him want to hurt Pimental, but it was always good to know the truth.

"Why was he at Tyree's the night you broke in?"

"He didn't say, but I suspect he and Tyree's wife see each other on the side."

That was interesting information and possibly useful. "But Tyree was home. Why would he risk…?"

"Maybe he was just dropping her off behind the house so he wouldn't be spotted. I don't know. I just want to see if he really does have a picture of Jack. At first I thought he might be trying to frighten me, but when I thought about it, how would he know Jack had been toying with the alarm system if he hadn't been there to see it?"

All right. It was time to get serious about this. Ben pulled the tablet toward him. "Did you try Sukie's name for a password?"

"Yes."

"Do we know his birth date?"

"No. But…try 'Delia,'" Corie suggested.

He did. "Ah!" he said as he gained access. He accessed the pictures library and began opening photos. The third one was of someone working on some kind of wiring. It might or might not be a security alarm. The photo was dark, bushes and shadows impairing the view, and the subject was in profile.

Corie, who'd come to stand behind him, whispered, "Oh, no!"

Ben held the tablet up for a closer look.

"But, if you didn't know it was Jack, could you tell?"

"Who cares, Ben? Just delete it."

He reached across the table and pulled her chair over. "Sit down."

"Ben…"

He caught her wrist and tugged her into the chair. She huffed at him.

"Think about it," he said reasonably. "If we're not absolutely certain this could identify Jack, it'd be better to leave it alone."

She looked at him as though he was causing her to lose her mind. "What? No! If there's any chance…"

"Corie. I'm guessing Pimental took this photo on his phone and sent it to his tablet. We could delete this, but it would still be on his phone. And if, God forbid, anything ever came to trial, the fact that we deleted this picture confirms that someone broke into Pimental's office and stole his files. Who do you think he'll suspect?"

"But he's a criminal."

"True. And, technically, after tonight, so are we."

She looked him in the eye. "I don't care. If Jack is hurt by this, you won't have to get revenge against me because I'll never forgive *myself*."

His promise of payback if Jack was ever incriminated because of her actions seemed as if it had happened a lifetime ago in some parallel universe. Now, as he looked into her eyes, he realized how much he loved her—and that was despite how insane she made him.

"If we're smart," he said, sweeping a hand over the files on the table, "there's something here we can use against him for leverage. We just have to find it."

"Okay." She pulled the files closer and made a roughly equal distribution of the work. She heaved a sigh and sat back in her chair. "I'm sorry, Ben. I wanted to delete Jack's photo so he'd be uninvolved, but now I've just made it worse for both of you."

He hated that she looked so worried, but he couldn't let her off the hook. He was still too angry. "Do you think either of us would ever sit back and let you go to jail?" He pointed to the files. "Start searching. Make a note of whatever looks like it incriminates Pimental or Tyree. But make sure everything remains as you found it, so we can put it back and Pimental will never know you took it."

She returned to work without comment.

When they compared notes an hour later, it was clear that Pimental maintained control with blackmail. Bigelow had gone to jail for assault in a small town in Florida ten years previously. Ben guessed that must have been hidden from whatever review board had approved him for his current job. Pimental's work, probably.

Sukie seemed to have a gambling problem. Pimental was lending her money but keeping track of every dime.

Corie pushed an open file in front of Ben. "Look at this. I don't know what it means. I just know it isn't right. These equipment purchases seem excessive for our small city hall."

Ben looked over the receipts. Dozens of PCs and printers, a dozen laptops, two dozen office chairs and a lot of artwork.

Corie said, "I've never seen artwork in city hall, except for a landscape print in Sukie's office. And there are maybe six offices total in the building, most of them doing double duty for more than one department. Why all this equipment?"

As Ben frowned over the numbers, a possible connection came to him. He pulled the Craigslist file closer and studied its contents. There were several pages of items listed for sale on the website. Many of them coincided with the town's invoices, purportedly for office furniture.

"He's been buying like he's at Costco," Ben said, looking up at her, "and reselling most of it on Craigslist. The town pays for the purchases without checking numbers of items. He could have furnished a building twice this size with what he purchased. And he pockets the money from the online sales of all the extras. He and whoever else is helping him. Bigelow, maybe." He pushed a file toward her. "And I know why Tyree is so anxious to get Teresa out of that house."

"Why?" She sifted through the paperwork.

"There's correspondence from a developer in Dallas who wants property outside of town to put up a resort exclusively for team building. There are emails between Pimental and Tyree agreeing to an equitable split of the bribe from Pennington to make it happen."

She frowned. "In Querida?"

"Sure. All they need is a lot of space. It's all about employee interaction."

She continued to frown. "But…why wouldn't he just tell Teresa that? I mean, he does own the property. Why all this harassment when he could just give her legal notice to get out?

His scare tactics with her have been going on for over a year."

He nodded. "Yeah," he said. "That part doesn't make sense. But, for right now, we can get him on this theft of town funds with all these outrageous purchases."

He pulled out his phone.

"Who are you calling at this hour?" Corie glanced at the kitchen clock. "It isn't even 3:00 a.m."

"Grady," Ben replied, hitting speed dial. "He brought his computer and he keeps a portable scanner in his carry case. I— Hey, Grady...Yeah, I know. I suck...Yeah, that, too. Listen..."

Corie went to get more coffee while Ben explained to Grady what had happened that night and why he needed his computer and scanner.

"Right. Very illegal...No. I think I have it figured out. I'll take you to breakfast after. The works...Yes, I know my family's coming in today. Don't worry. I have everything under control."

Grady arrived a few minutes later, his eyes still foggy with sleep, and Corie led him to the kitchen.

"You owe me so big," he said.

"I do." Ben pushed an empty chair away from the table for Grady. "Sit," he said. Corie had already placed a cup of coffee there, along with a reindeer cookie. "Thanks for coming. We've got some good stuff here that I'd like to scan into your computer and then you can email it to me. Okay?"

"Sure." Before he sat, Ben plugged in his electronics at the counter. He opened his account and gave Ben access. "There you go. Have at it."

While Ben worked, Corie explained what they'd found—the photo of Jack and the incriminating files—and told him they intended to put everything back before city hall opened for business.

Grady nodded. "You do remember," he said to Ben, "that we work for a police department?"

"I do," Ben replied. "In another state. But our job is to protect and to serve. And my personal job is to protect my brother from being arrested when he was only trying to help his sister."

"I get that. So, we're going to take this guy down before he can arrest Jack?"

"That's the plan."

"What if you're caught putting the stuff back?"

"Won't happen."

Grady smiled at Corie. "Remember he said that so you can use it against him when the time comes."

# CHAPTER SIXTEEN

CORIE REMEMBERED GRADY'S words an hour and a half later. She and Ben were huddled together on the floor in Pimental's office, putting the files back in the bottom drawer.

They'd gained entry the same way they had earlier that morning, and Corie had used all the familiar steps to get into the office then into the file cabinet.

"I can't believe this worked," Corie whispered.

Ben closed the drawer, pushed in the lock and they turned together to hurry out through Sukie's office when the bathroom door opened and the overhead light went on, catching them in a blinding glare.

Corie felt all her bodily processes shudder to a halt. She had no sight, no breath, and she was absolutely sure her heart wasn't pumping. Her action to try to stop Jack from being involved in what she'd done had not only deepened that problem but caught Ben in its tentacles, as well.

Pimental walked out wearing a white terry-cloth robe belted at the waist. He held a gun. Instinctively, Corie moved in front of Ben.

"Relax, Mr. Pimental," she said. She hated that her voice shook. "This is all *my* fault." She pointed Ben toward the door. "Ben has nothing to do with this. He followed me here to try to stop me." Close enough to the truth. At least it had been earlier. "He's leaving, and you're welcome to call Bigelow on me. I'm sure he'd be happy to help you. Ben, get out."

Ben took hold of her arms and moved her out of his way. "You listen to me, Pimental," he said. His voice shook a little, too, but she knew it was anger. "We discovered your Craigslist scam. You've bilked the town out of hundreds of thousands of dollars. Not to mention your blackmail schemes to keep your patsies in line. We have enough on you to put you away until you're an old man. Your little power trip here is over."

"You stole those files," Pimental said, his gun still aimed at Ben's chest. "The court won't let you use anything you found because you stole it. Fruit of the poisoned tree. It's inadmissible."

"No, I'm an officer of the law. I have a right to investigate."

"This isn't your jurisdiction."

Ben waved a sheet of paper. "I have a special search warrant."

Corie had watched Ben pick up that sheet of paper. It was the to-go menu from the Grill.

Pimental looked a little off balance, unsure whether or not to believe him. Ben pushed his advantage.

"And does Tyree know that you and his wife are having an affair? You think he'll still be willing to cut you in on the Pennington Properties' deal when he finds that out?"

Pimental's eyes blazed. "My. You two have been busy." He cocked the gun. "But if you're not here to share that information…"

Corie tried to get between them again and Ben yanked her aside. "You'll notice neither one of us has a weapon. It'll be hard to prove that you felt endangered and had to shoot us in self-defense."

"I'll say you tried to take mine. I know. It's a little old and overdone, but I think in this case, it works." He leveled the gun.

DAMN IT, BEN THOUGHT. He was going to get shot again. He remembered the hot, searing pain from the last time, the jolt to the body, the terrible confusion that took hold as the brain tried to function through pain. He hated confusion. That is, he had until he'd gotten mixed up with his brother's sister who wasn't *his* sister and had to learn to deal with it.

He also hated the fear. He loved Corie so much he was willing to take a bullet for her. And he was probably about to. But what would happen to her when he went down? He had to find another way.

Then, from somewhere behind Pimental, a high, indignant voice said, "You're having an affair with *Delia Tyree*?"

Pimental's cold attitude turned to hot aggravation and he struggled to firm his stance. His fingers worked nervously on the gun. "Not now, Sukie. Stay out of the way."

The pudgy blonde walked right around him in a short, flowered robe, seemingly unaware of the weapon, and got in his face. "You were cheating on me? With a woman ten years *older* than me?" Her high, angry voice filled the office.

He shoved her aside. The crushing betrayal was evident in her face as she caught herself against his desk. Corie stopped her from run-

ning at him again. With the two women out of
the line of fire, Ben rushed Pimental.

Damn it, there it was. The explosive sound,
the searing pain in his arm, the fear that
caused him to choke on his heartbeat, the
confusion…

He heard Corie scream his name, her
voice filled with horror. There was love in
that sound. He realized he wasn't confused
at all. If he didn't stop Pimental, the man was
going to kill him and then Corie—just when
the whole Manning family was about to come
together. He couldn't let that happen to her.

Ben landed a punch to Pimental's jaw and
managed to knock the gun out of his hand.
As the deputy mayor flew backward, Corie
beaned him with a carved wooden bookend.
He slumped to his knees and Sukie finished
the job with a foot to his back as he went
down.

Corie grabbed Ben by his good arm, put
him in Pimental's chair and then called 9-1-1.

Ben stopped the call with a finger on the
buttons.

"Ben!" she said, the sound that had been
in her voice now a dark shadow in her eyes.
"You're bleeding! A lot! I have to—"

"Do you really want anyone to know you

were here?" he asked and then whispered for her ears alone, "Like Chris?"

She tossed her head and dialed again. "That hardly matters now. You *have* to go to the hospital."

Sukie came to yank the phone out of her hand. "Hello? Yes! I need an ambulance at city hall. This is Susan Sophia Cunningham. The deputy mayor just shot one of my friends. And you might want to send the county sheriff. I'm not sure who we can trust in the police department. Please hurry." She fixed Corie with a steady stare as she hung up the phone. "You let me do the talking when they arrive."

Now dressed in a white shirt and jeans, Sukie was masterful. As the emergency medical technicians worked on Ben, she showed the two county sheriff's deputies who'd accompanied them the files in the open cabinet drawer. "I've been Mr. Pimental's secretary for some time, and I've suspected some shady dealings for a while now. I brought my friends with me for support to help me reclaim the record on my gambling debts. He's been using them against me to make me conceal some of the purchases he's made with town money, then sold on Craigslist. When he walked in and saw the drawer open, he flew into a rage.

"Mr. Palmer, there, tried to defend me, and Robert shot him. I'm guessing there's things in there you all might want to see. I believe he was ordering extra office equipment and furniture and selling it online. He accepted a bribe from…" Sukie went on as the deputy took rapid notes.

"I CAN'T BELIEVE you let someone shoot you again!" Ben's mother sat behind him in Jack's rental car as they drove home from the hospital.

"Helen, I'm sure he didn't *let* himself be shot," his father said. "He was just trying to defend Corie. Very commendable, son. It would have been smarter to not let him shoot you, but, hey…"

Ben turned to Jack, who spared him a glance away from the road, doing his best not to laugh.

"I mean, last month," his mother continued, "when we got home from Arizona, and you were wearing two miles of gauze around your arm, that was one thing, but now we come all this way to spend Christmas with you, and Jack gets a call from Corie to come to the hospital instead of to Teresa's because you've been shot again! Same arm!"

"Sorry."

"I hope so. I've half a mind to take back the desk we bought you for Christmas."

He turned to look at her over his shoulder. He winced when the action hurt his injury, which had turned out to be a simple flesh wound. "You bought me a desk?" he asked in complete surprise.

"Yes. For your new office."

"That's wonderful, Mom, but I don't even have an office yet."

"Sarah and I got you a Realtor for Christmas," Jack said with another quick grin. "To help you find just the right place."

Ben laughed. "How do you buy a Realtor?"

"Technically, you don't. It's one of Mario's cousins, and we gave him a retainer against the commission we'll owe him when you decide on something. Did you and Grady hear that Mario and Margie had another girl? They named her Noelle."

"Oh, that's great." He was happy for his friend, and touched by his family's thoughtfulness. "Thanks, guys."

Ben pointed the finger on his good arm to Grady's car several lengths ahead of them, making the turn onto Rio Road. "Right up there," he said to Jack.

Jack nodded. "Yes. I've been here before, remember?"

Grady had thoughtfully volunteered to drive Corie and Sarah back to Teresa's so that Ben could visit with his parents and his brother on the way there. Ben kept telling himself that this loud group that offered both blessings and harassment was what Soren and Rosie needed to keep their minds off the absence of their friends.

TERESA AND THE children were waiting on the steps when everyone arrived. Ben's mother engulfed both children in her embrace, then took each by the hand and asked them to show her the play set Ben had built. As they led her around back, Ben heard her voice, diminishing in volume, talking about the gifts Santa had given her to deliver to them.

Both children were cynical beyond their ages, but listened with wide smiles, her good cheer contagious.

Teresa hugged Ben worriedly. "I can't believe you got shot again!" she said. She scowled at Corie. "Sweetie, this has got to stop. I appreciate how brave you are, but if you get yourself in a fix, it puts someone else in danger because he wants to help you."

"This was my idea," Ben said, feeling called upon to defend her since they wouldn't have made the return trip to city hall if it had been up to Corie. Things would not have ended well for her, he was sure, but at least they wouldn't have been there for Pimental to catch, and Ben wouldn't have been shot.

Corie glanced at him with more annoyance than gratitude for his contribution to the conversation. They hadn't been able to make up after their middle-of-the-night argument, and though she'd been upset when Pimental shot him, she hadn't had much to say since.

Jack, who'd heard the whole story while sitting in the waiting room with Corie, shook his head at his sister then his brother. "Seems they were trying to protect *me*. As though I would let them take the fall alone for anything I was involved in."

Sarah, Jack's wife, tucked her arm in his and leaned her head against his shoulder. "That's family love, Jack. You know that."

"I do. I just don't want anyone sacrificing anything for me."

"Well, then, this whole family would have to learn to stop breathing."

Teresa ushered everyone inside, looping her arm into Ben's and Jack's father's. Gary

Palmer grinned at Jack and pointed toward the car. "Would you get the bags? Ben's disabled and I have a lady on my arm."

"Why not?" Jack pretended exasperation. "What happened to feeling the love?"

"Oh, we're here for you, Jack." Sarah tightened her grip on him and Corie took his other arm and turned him toward the car. "Come on. We'll help you."

"There must be fifteen bags in the two cars."

"We'll make a few trips."

"I'll have to learn to get shot so I'm not the one who always has to carry everything. Remember when Ben came home from the hospital the *first* time he got shot, and it was pouring rain, and you ran out of the house to help him in and I had to carry…"

Sarah reached up to kiss him firmly. "Stop whining or I'll shoot you myself."

Corie admired the way Sarah dealt with her husband. But that threat wouldn't work on bullet-ridden Ben.

BEN HAD FILLED a bucket with water and was on his belly under the Christmas tree, filling a saucepan from the bucket and pouring water into the tree stand with his good arm.

Everyone else was doing their own thing before dinner, except Soren, who was stretched out a few inches away, watching Ben work.

"How come you're not talking to Corie?" he asked, holding the bucket steady as Ben dipped the saucepan in again.

"Who says I'm not talking to Corie?"

"Well, nobody *says* it, but everybody knows it. Teresa asked me if I knew what happened."

"Nothing happened."

"Is it 'cause you got shot?"

"Why would that make me not talk to her?"

"'Cause it was her fault, right? You went to rescue her and the mayor guy shot you."

"It wasn't her fault. I went to help because I wanted to."

"Then why are you mad at *her*?"

Ben poured in the water then looked at Soren. The boy's face was just inches from his. Soren had been glued to Ben's side since Ben had gotten home yesterday.

"I'm not talking to her," he explained, though he didn't quite get it himself, "but it's not because I'm mad at her. It's because sometimes... I just don't know what to say to her to make her understand what I'm thinking. Our brains don't seem to work the same way and that makes it hard to communicate."

"I know what you mean. I used to feel that way about Rosie. Until everybody else was gone and I started to understand what she was saying. It's easier to think when there's not so much noise."

"So, you like Rosie?"

Soren looked horrified for a minute. "Well, not like a girlfriend."

"Of course not."

"Like a friend. A sister. But you love Corie like a girlfriend. Couldn't you just kiss her?" Soren asked with a sly smile.

Ben frowned at him. "How would that help?"

"That's what they do on television. They play a little tonsil hockey."

Ben groaned. "Tonsil hockey is a disrespectful expression for something as nice as kissing. And they do a lot of things on television that wouldn't work in real life."

Soren rested his chin on his hands. "Then you're not getting married?"

Geez. "Why did you think that?" Ben handed him the empty saucepan.

"I don't know. Rosie thought you might."

Ben crawled out from under the tree, pulling the bucket with him. He carried it into the kitchen to empty the little bit of water in the bottom. Soren followed him to the sink and stood beside him, putting the saucepan on the counter.

"What's your life like in Oregon?"

"Kinda cool, but nothing special," he replied, wiping out the bucket. "I go to work every day. Grady's my partner. He's not married, either, so sometimes we have dinner together after work. There's a place called Betty's that everybody likes. It's a little bit like the Grill, only without Hector's delicious Mexican dishes."

"But you're not going to be a cop anymore, right? You're going to have a detective agency. You and Grady."

Ben turned to him in astonishment. "How do you know that?"

"I heard you talking. I wasn't listening in, I was just going by and…you know, you weren't whispering or anything."

"Right."

"Do you live with your mom and dad?"

"No. I have a condo that looks over the water."

"Is it big?"

"Ah, no. It's roomy enough, but it's not really big."

"How many bedrooms?"

"Two and a bonus room."

"What does that mean?"

"That I could turn it into an exercise room or a den or something, but I haven't done that yet. It's empty."

"Huh." Soren smiled. "Do you have a dog?"

"No."

"A cat?"

"No. I'm gone a lot and pets should have someone around to keep them company."

"Huh. Teresa says when I'm not being difficult, that I'm good company."

There it was. Ben had answered all his questions, thinking at first that it was simply genuine interest in his life. But now he saw that Soren was wondering if it would be possible for him to fit into that life.

Ben didn't know what to say. It crossed his mind that his communication issues with Corie might be his problem and not hers.

He liked Soren a lot, but he was a single man wanting to start a new business. A ten-year-old boy dealing with a lot of losses should have a child-psychologist for a parent, not a cop who'd broken a lot of laws and loved a woman he didn't know how to deal with. He had to divert the boy's attention.

"You want to come to the store with me?" Ben asked.

"Sure." Soren smiled. "What are we buying?"

"I have to get a present for my brother and sister-in-law."

"That Christmas store had ornaments for people who just got married. They did, right, 'cause you and Corie were in their wedding when she went to Oregon."

"Right."

"They say 'For your first Christmas together.' It was a couple kissing under the mistletoe."

"That's a brilliant idea." Ben pushed him toward the door.

"I'm also pretty smart when I'm not being difficult."

"Well, you'll have to stop being difficult."

"I've tried. It's really...difficult." Soren laughed at his own joke. Ben groaned and opened his hand over Soren's face and pushed teasingly. The boy laughed again and followed him out to the SUV.

# CHAPTER SEVENTEEN

"PUT YOUR FINGER over the ribbon." Corie held the ends of the Christmas ribbon tightly, leaving room for Rosie to put her plump index finger in the middle of the package where the ribbon crossed over itself.

"Ben and Soren went out," Rosie said, pressing down as Corie made a knot right over her finger.

"They did? Where?"

"Shopping. Guys don't usually like to go shopping, but Ben forgot to buy a present for Jack and Sarah." When Corie looked surprised at her knowledge, she shrugged. "I was wrapping Soren's present in the pantry so he wouldn't see. They were talking in the kitchen."

"I hope they're home in time for dinner. We're having meat loaf."

"I love meat loaf."

"Me, too. We'll just eat theirs if they're late."

Rosie smiled. "You'd never do that." She was quiet a minute while Corie wrapped curly ribbon around her fingers, cut the ends to make a bow, then secured it to the middle of the package.

"That's pretty," Rosie said. "Are you gonna go back to Oregon and live with your brother?"

"I'm not sure what I'm going to do," Corie admitted, putting the package aside. "My brother's very busy and his wife has a new and important job she's training for. I was thinking about going back to school online."

There was another moment of silence then Rosie said, with practiced detachment, as though they were still talking about Corie's plans, "I know my dad's not coming. I heard you and Teresa talking about how he'd signed this paper that says he's not my dad anymore."

Horrified that Rosie had overheard them, Corie wrapped her in her arms and pulled her close. She could feel pain in the child's stiff body. And somehow, almost worse than that, was the stoic acceptance.

"I think he did that," Corie said through a tight throat, "because he knows he can't take care of you and believes someone else could do a better job."

Rosie looked up at Corie. Corie read the

"Can *you* do it?" in her eyes, but, mercifully pride prevented Rosie from saying it aloud.

*You don't have your own life together,* Corie told herself. *You couldn't possibly guide anyone else's.*

Rosie straightened away from Corie and looked down at her twisting fingers. "Wouldn't it be fun if you and Ben and Soren and me were going to the movies in the car and a big storm came and blew us far away where nobody could find us? And we'd have to stay together forever?"

For a fraction of a second a deep place in Corie's heart rose to meet a thought from a far corner of her brain and she almost nodded. Then reality regained control and she smiled at Rosie. "I think you might grow up to write fairy tales, Rosie."

The thought of her and Ben, who could not agree on most things except how nice it was to hold each other, raising two children who didn't get along, either, was pure fantasy.

"Yeah," Rosie said. "We could call it... what's Ben's last name?"

Oh, dear. "Palmer."

"The Palmer Family Fairy Tale. What do you think?"

Corie nodded. "I think it would be a fine fairy tale."

Rosie sat up suddenly. "I'm going to start writing," she said, and hurried out of the room.

BEN AND SOREN were back in time for dinner, a noisy affair with as much laughter as food. Jack had brought several adventure movies and he, Grady, Sarah and Soren watched for hours. Rosie sat in a big chair writing diligently on a yellow pad with a Santa bobblehead pen Corie had given her to cheer her up. Teresa brought out drinks and cookies.

Corie pushed Teresa out of the kitchen and cleaned up, ignoring Ben, who was working at the table on Grady's computer, looking over the documents they'd scanned from Pimental's files.

"Corie!" he said.

She turned to him, forgetting that they weren't speaking to each other.

"What?" She picked up a tea towel and dried her hands as she went toward him.

"We missed something in our initial look through the files."

"What's that?"

He pointed to the screen and a document entitled simply "Tyree."

"This was in a stack of notes that had been clipped together in Tyree's file. I got most of the way through it and figured the last few pages were just more of the same incriminating stuff. I hadn't read the last few pages in the stack. It relates to Kenneth Tyree. I presume that's Cyrus's father?"

"It is. Did Pimental have something on him, too?"

"No, it's Kenneth Tyree's will. It leaves the house Teresa is living in and the property the house is on to *her* not to Cyrus."

Corie gasped and leaned closer. "Ben! Teresa owns the house? He just never told her?"

"Apparently. Looks like he left everything else to his son and the house to Teresa. Cyrus was his father's lawyer and the executor, so he just kept it all to himself and pretended he got the house, too." He scrolled down to the altered will. "This is the one he changed and filed."

"How did Pimental get that?"

Ben shrugged. "Delia?"

"That Tyree is a rat! I'm going to—"

"You don't have to do anything. This is all the proof the court needs. How long has Kenneth been gone?"

"Two years."

"I'm sure we can even get back the rent Teresa paid Cyrus for those two years." He, too, forgot they weren't speaking and smiled up at her. "He obviously wanted to sell it to Pennington. So, he had to get Teresa out without anyone knowing why. Wow. Teresa owns the house."

Gleeful, Corie wrapped her arms around Ben's neck. "She'll be so happy," she said. "Imagine never having to worry about rent!"

"True. But there'll still be taxes and insurance. I think we should keep all this to ourselves until it's declared legally hers."

"That'll be hard, but I'm sure you're right."

She just became aware that in her euphoria, she'd thrown herself into his arms. Or he'd taken her into them. She was sitting in his lap and didn't remember how it had happened. She pushed herself slowly to her feet.

"I think you're also right that it's time I set out on my own. I can do online school from anywhere."

He seemed to hesitate before saying, "Oregon's a good place. Your family's there."

For an instant she had that same heart-to-brain feeling she'd had when Rosie had shared her fantasy.

"Is that where you're opening your detective agency?"

"Yes. Jack and Sarah gave me a Realtor for Christmas to help me find the perfect spot. And Grady's in."

*Do you really love me enough to take in a couple of scrappy kids and make a family?*

When the brain-to-heart feeling became actual thought, reality set in at the absurdity of it. She and Ben didn't get along. Soren and Rosie didn't get along. Considering life together was insanity.

Not that she was unfamiliar with that state.

"Maybe my Realtor could find you a place, too," he said.

She shook her head, apparently finished with that particular discussion.

Ben had trouble refocusing. His arms still felt her in them. Her cheek still touched his.

"What do we do about the will?" she asked. The anger that had been between them was gone but a polite distance remained in place. "If we bring it up to anyone, they'll know I took the files and we made copies."

Ben thought a minute and an idea so insidious it could have come from Corie's brain was born, full-blown.

"I have a thought," he said. "Remember

when Hector was telling us that a friend of his is catering an affair the Tyrees are holding at their home in Corpus Christi, and he's been invited to help?"

She nodded.

"Do you think he could get us hired as staff?"

She blinked. "What? Why?"

"Trust me."

"Have you ever waited tables?"

"You don't wait tables at that kind of affair, do you?" He stood, warming to the idea. "You just wander through the crowd carrying trays. I can do that."

She looked worried. "You're supposed to be certified through the state's liquor control..."

He grinned. "The woman who broke into city hall is going to worry about that?"

"Maybe if I knew the plan."

He smiled wickedly. "It's beautifully simple. I'll just bet if Delia Tyree did get her jewelry back, she won't be able to resist wearing at least one piece at her big holiday party. If we can get a photo of her in it we'll have proof it was returned."

She frowned at Ben for a long moment. "You think she'd really wear something she claimed was stolen?"

"I do. But most of her guests won't know whether it was part of that lot or not."

"What if she doesn't wear any of it?"

"If we're there, maybe we'll overhear something."

She looked first pleased then reluctant. "You're starting to sound like me. I'm not sure that's good."

"Why, Elizabeth Corazon," he said with a laugh, "now you know how I feel."

That was true, she thought. Was she really starting to see the world in a different light?

"I think," he added, "Tyree's going to get caught as being part of Pimental's schemes in the next twenty-four hours or so, anyway. I doubt Pimental will protect him when he starts talking. I'll call Norton. Maybe he can get the Corpus Christi police to be there if we get anything good."

She thought about it, her dark eyes fixed on him with uncertainty.

He must be making headway, he thought, because she replied with clear trepidation.

"Okay."

"WHAT YEAR IS IT?" Jack asked Ben. They sat at the picnic table in the play set, drinking coffee and eating red-velvet cupcakes Teresa had made for Christmas. Soren and Rosie played on the slide and Helen and Gary had gone to town.

Ben frowned at him. "What are you talking about?"

"I'm asking if you know what year it is. Or who is president. Or what your date of birth is. If you want Grady, Sarah and me to go to Corpus Christi with you tonight and pretend to be catering staff, I have to conclude that you've gone over the edge. It's not that I'm surprised. I knew this day was coming. It's just that a couple of days before Christmas is lousy timing. Mom will be really upset."

Ben sighed at Sarah. "Can you shut him up?"

"Sorry. I think he was born with an Energizer battery in his vocal cords. He can harass like that for hours."

Ben turned to Corie in feigned surprise. "Huh! That gene must run in the Manning family."

She elbowed him. "I'm not sure what he wants to do, either," she told Jack and Sarah, "but I've promised to trust him, and it would be nice if I wasn't in this alone. Please."

Jack nodded. "Anything for my little sis. Okay, what do we do?"

Ben briefly outlined the plan.

Jack's narrow-eyed gaze turned to Sarah. She smiled widely. "I waited tables in college. We can do this."

"I've talked to Hector," Ben said. "He's getting us in."

"Getting us out again is what I'm worried about," Jack countered.

"Not a problem."

"Without getting shot, I mean."

"Ha, ha. Without getting shot. Unless you screw up and somehow reveal us to be construction jockeys instead of catering staff."

"If you—!"

Sarah put both hands up. "Please, stop. We're doing this for Ben and Corie after all they've done for you."

Jack sighed and finally shrugged his shoulders. Then something seemed to occur to him. "But Tyree knows Corie, right?"

"Right." Ben had been dreading telling her this but he couldn't put it off any longer. "She has to stay home."

Steam almost came out of her ears. "What? No! Ben, I will not be left out of this, out of some misguided—"

"It is not an effort to protect you." That was just a small lie. "Just think about it. Tyree knows you. And a caterer's jacket isn't going to conceal your identity. A simple wardrobe change worked for Superman, but that was a comic book. This is real life—with very important issues at stake."

She fumed. "Fine," she said eventually and left the table.

CORIE WALKED INTO the house, privately making her own plans about Tyree's party. And while she was at it, she had to talk to Teresa. She found her in the kitchen, chopping vegetables. Corie leaned on the counter beside her. "I have a question," she said. "Or, rather, a statement."

Teresa glanced her way, did a double-take and studied her closely. "You look very determined. What is it? Have you taken out a contract on Ben rather than learn to deal with him?"

Corie swatted Teresa's arm. "No. I want to talk about Rosie."

Teresa rested the knife on the counter and turned to her.

"I want to adopt her." The notion had been coming on gradually, and suddenly seemed like the only course of action.

Teresa's smile formed slowly. "I think that's

the best thing that could happen to her. And to you. But—what about going to school?"

"I can do both. I'm feeling invincible."

"No kidding?"

"No kidding. The thing is…"

"Yes?"

She winced as she asked, "That would hurt Soren, wouldn't it? I hate that."

Teresa sighed and folded her arms. "Poor guy. There's almost no way to avoid hurting him, whatever happens. But he's smart and adaptable. He's been happy here. You stayed here happily."

"I know." Corie shook her head sadly. "I don't think I could deal with two kids."

"Taking one child is big."

"And yet you do it all the time, knowing you can't keep them."

"It's what *I* do." Teresa smiled and wrapped her arms around Corie. "Rosie will be what *you* do. And she adores you. She'll be so happy." Teresa glanced out the kitchen window, distracted by the sight of Grady, Jack, Sarah and Ben. "What's going on in the backyard? Looks like a summit meeting."

Corie laughed lightly. "The less you know about that, the better. I'm going home. See you in the morning."

She heard Teresa's questioning, "Corie?" but kept going. Explaining Ben's plan for Tyree's party—and her own—would not lend Teresa comfort.

THAT EVENING, DRESSED in dark slacks and jackets bearing the gold Creative Catering logo, Ben, Grady, Jack and Sarah were put to work as part of the team in the Tyrees' white-and-chrome kitchen.

"Please keep quiet and get yourself in stakeout mode," Ben told Jack.

"Stakeout mode?"

"Yes. Just keep your eyes open. And watch Mrs. Tyree particularly. The jewelry could be earrings or a necklace or a ring. You remember the stuff we dumped out of Corie's bag that night."

"Sort of. I was busy being horrified by what she'd done."

"Yeah, well, if you were a cop, you'd get over being horrified by what people do. They're amazingly resourceful at breaking the law."

Jack was quiet for a minute. "You've fallen in love with her," he said.

Ben met his eyes. "Yes."

"She's in love with you."

"I don't know. Maybe."

"What are the two of you mad at each other about?"

Ben moved a stack of trays, preparing to lay them out. "It's just become a way of life for us. She's wild and fearless and leans toward criminal solutions to her problems." He smiled grimly. "But when I try to keep her from harm, I end up doing more shady things than the Soprano family. And I'm a cop! This can't go on."

"So, you'll figure it out. She wasn't very happy being left behind today."

"It just made sense. If Tyree recognized her, we'd be dead in the water."

Jack's smile was wry and affectionate. "Love involves a large gray area that can't be tidily labeled good or bad. You can do things for love that you can't do for the law. I know you don't like being off balance like that. But sometimes that's good. Gives you a new perspective."

Ben took another tray from him. "Very profound, Yoda. Forget about me and focus on Delia Tyree, okay?"

The words had just left his mouth when the woman in question walked into the kitchen, buxom and smiling in an elegant green-silk gown with pearl buttons down the front. She wore no jewelry that Ben could see, though her ears were covered by long, blond hair.

"Welcome to my home." She spoke in broad Southern strokes. "We're looking forward to a very special evening, so I'd appreciate it if you would all treat my guests as very special people." She waved a hand toward several of the dishes set out on a large chopping block in the middle of the room. Ben focused on her hand, but the back of it was turned away from him and he couldn't see if she was wearing that ruby ring Corie had stolen. There was no jewelry around her neck.

"The food looks wonderful, and you're a very handsome crew." Delia glanced at Grady, who was helping to make open-faced sandwiches with a group of women, and then her gaze lingered over Jack and Ben an extra moment, her smile widening before she addressed the entire staff. "So, please do your very best and Santa might give you something extra."

The promise dangled in the air and she smiled as she walked away.

"I didn't see any jewelry," Jack said quietly. "But then, maybe she isn't finished dressing."

"True."

David Walther, a tall, big man who looked more like a wrestler than a caterer, walked through the kitchen to check on their progress. He stopped beside Ben and Jack. "Everything okay, here?"

"Yes," Jack replied.

Walther studied him then Ben. He frowned from one to the other. It felt like the time Ben had been sent to work undercover in the next county to smoke out a bartender dealing drugs. A friend of Jack's had come in and blown his cover. "Hector told me you weren't very experienced, but that you had class and, as long as you didn't have to cook, you would make me look good." Walther didn't appear to be convinced that was true. "Don't make a liar out of him."

"Right."

"I need champagne glasses on those trays."

Jack punched Ben in his good arm as Walther walked away. "You're not selling the caterer's assistant thing," he accused. "You always look like a cop."

"Me? You're the one with bulging biceps and the eye of the tiger determination that says 'Army through and through.'"

"Well, pardon me for being good at what I do. What I did."

"It's all right. You can't help it. You're just a born hero."

Jack heard something in his voice that made him give Ben a closer look. "Haven't we had this out before? I'm afraid a lot. I just keep going." After a moment he added, "You're a cop. How many people with fear issues are cops?" He looked at him more closely. "You're afraid of Corie, aren't you? Of loving her. Of getting her out of her dark memories and bringing her into the fold, into our family."

Ben hated it when Jack did that—understood him better than he understood himself. "I don't seem to be getting through to her. Whatever she feels for me doesn't change anything for her."

"It will. Give it time."

"I'm running out of time. I have to get back to work, give my notice and find an office."

Walther reappeared with boxes of champagne glasses. "Speed it up, guys. Guests will be arriving in ten minutes."

Without discussion, Ben and Jack concentrated on preparing the trays.

An hour later the huge living room that spilled into a dining room and a sunroom at the back was filled to capacity with guests in glittery holiday dress. The women sparkled and laughed. The men tugged at their collars and talked college football as though it were any other occasion.

The house was lavishly decorated with fat garlands and large pots of cacti entwined with lights.

Ben felt as though he'd been a caterer's assistant most of his life. It didn't take long to become comfortable with the tray on the flat of his right hand, lifting it high over his head to work his way between the tight knots of conversation. Dosing himself with ibuprofen before he left home had been a good idea. He was feeling strong and barely noticed his injured arm.

The women smiled at him and some of the men—those for whom he'd gone into the kitchen in search of the bourbon they preferred—slipped tips into the breast pocket of his jacket. He tried to resist, sure Walther would disapprove, but had a pocket full of bills anyway.

Christmas carols provided background music but became almost inaudible as the conversation level rose and the evening wore on. He went to the kitchen to pick up a tray of chipotle shrimp and was distracted by the sight of a shapely woman in a lacy-black evening dress that skimmed her knees. She had short red hair with long bangs that fell into her eyes.

Nibbling on a shrimp, she sketched him a wave and wandered out the back of the kitchen toward the stairs.

It took him a minute to realize that he recognized the easy sway of those hips and the set of that cocky little head.

He caught up with her in three strides and grabbed her arm. Ridiculously, the first whispered words out of his mouth were, "You *cut* your *hair*?"

Corie looked up at him, almost unrecognizable under the glamorous makeup.

"No!" she whispered, looking around to make sure they were alone. "It's a wig."

She tried to pull away but he tightened his grip and led her back into the kitchen. "What are you *doing* here?"

"I noticed Delia isn't wearing any jewelry tonight. I thought I'd look upstairs to see if it's in her drawer."

"You will not."

Her eyes ignited. "Ben…"

He'd promised himself he wouldn't issue orders again…but, then, he was dealing with Corie.

"What if Tyree catches you?" He tried reason. He didn't think it would work but he tried anyway.

She arched an eyebrow. "*You* didn't recognize me and you claim to love me."

She was going to be the death of him. "I don't *claim* to love you. I *do* love you. But I'm going to murder you if you don't—!"

Walther walked into the kitchen and Corie said with a light laugh as she patted Ben's arm, "Thank you, waiter. I so appreciate your getting me the plate of shrimp. My blood sugar drops every once in a while. I shouldn't have skipped lunch today, but I was buying this dress..." She smiled at Walther as she twirled and the sequined skirt of her dress flared. Ben heard Walther's intake of breath.

"Fine crew you have, sir," she said, walking past him. "Very courteous and accommodating."

"Thank you, ma'am."

"I'll tell my host." Corie smiled charmingly at the caterer. "In fact, do you have a business card? I have an event coming up in late January."

"Of course." Walther dug into his inside pocket and handed her a card. He offered his hand. "I'm David Walther."

She shook it. "Magdalena Manning. Delighted to meet you. I'll call you soon, Mr. Walther."

Ben was going to stroke out with tension.

"Now, that's a woman," Walther said, watching her walk away.

Ben groaned silently.

*You have no idea,* he thought.

# CHAPTER EIGHTEEN

CORIE STRUCK THE mother lode. The top drawer of the right side of the French Provincial dresser in the Tyrees' master bedroom held the large velvet box Corie remembered from the last time she'd been in this room and emptied it into a small cloth bag. Several diamond pendants of various sizes, a gold pendant and a broach of clustered emerald stones. This time, she took only a photo. Well...several, to show that everything stolen had been returned.

She felt so relieved to see everything there, so vindicated. The bedroom door opened and Cyrus Tyree walked in. He stopped in his tracks just inside the door and stared at her for several seconds, his mouth open. The he closed it, and the door, angling his head as he frowned at her.

"Who are you?" he demanded, his eyes going over her in an attempt to identify her. "And what are you doing in my bedroom?"

She helped him by pulling off her wig. It still took him half a minute. She realized he'd only ever seen her in the jeans and sweatshirt she wore at Teresa's or the waitress uniform she worked in.

"The Ochoa brat!" he said in astonishment. His expression changed to one of comprehension as he pointed to the drawer. "So, it was *you* who took Delia's jewelry."

She nodded. "Here it all is, and yet you told your insurance company, and national television, that all you got in the mail were Mardi Gras beads."

He shrugged as though that was unimportant and pointed a condemning finger at her. "You *stole* from me."

"You stole two years' worth of rent from Teresa by failing to tell her that your father left the house to *her*. She's struggled to pay her rent, when you've been the worst landlord on the face of the planet. You never fixed anything and sent Bigelow to throw her out. You're worse than a thief, you're a crook! A small-time swindler!"

"You stole my wife's jewelry!"

"To sell it and pay up Teresa's rent and try to buy the house from you so we didn't have to deal with you anymore. There seemed a certain justice in buying the house from you with money from the jewels I stole from you. But it was Teresa's all along."

"What happened to that plan?"

"My brother found me after all these years. My very honest brother. He made me send the jewelry back. Honesty's not a consideration for you, though, is it? You were going to put Teresa and her kids out on the street so you and fat-cat Pimental could split the bribery money from Pennington Properties."

He shrugged that off. "I needed that money. Big business is expensive. And Delia is very high-maintenance, fashion-wise—and almost every other way." His eyes went to the camera in her hand. "I suppose you got pictures."

"I did."

He took a few steps toward her. She held her ground.

"You know I can't let you show them to anybody."

She sighed and sat on the foot of the bed. Her heart was beginning to race. He looked bigger up close and very annoyed. She'd had to laugh in the face of threats from people like him her entire life. "Well, I know you wouldn't like me to, but modern technology is an amazing aid in situations like this. I've already sent the photos to Officer Chris Norton."

His skin turned a frightening shade of tomato. He was clearly too furious to speak.

"Sukie turned everything in Pimental's bottom drawer over to the police yesterday," she said. "Didn't Pimental tell you? Oh, that's right. He's in jail. Apparently you weren't his one phone call. It's over for you, Mr. Tyree."

Tyree looked horrified by the news. She could see every deal he'd ever made with Pimental pass across his eyes as he contemplated the effect his partner in crime's arrest would have on his own life.

He sat beside her on the foot of the bed and put his head in his hands.

"I guess that puts an end to a lucrative relationship," Corie said.

He lowered his hands and nodded grimly. "Yeah. It also puts an end to his affair with my wife. There's an upside to everything."

It was Corie's turn to be surprised. "You knew?"

He gave her a superior look. "I'm not completely stupid."

"Then why didn't you try to stop it?"

"Because it didn't really matter anymore. I

no longer had to spend evenings with a woman I didn't understand. We used to be crazy about each other, but that changed a long time ago."

"That's very sad."

He sighed heavily. "Like I said, doesn't matter. So, the young woman who once hit Pimental in the face with her tip can is now a crime fighter?"

She had to smile at that. "I guess I am."

She stood and would have left the room, jewelry mystery solved, if Delia hadn't chosen that moment to walk into it.


BEN, CARRYING A tray of heirloom tomato bruschetta, signaled Jack with a tip of his head that he was going up the stairway. Jack, offering lamb meatballs as he wound his way through the crowd, mouthed, "Wait!"

Ben, however, had as much inclination at the moment to be careful as Corie did. He put the tray down in the kitchen and headed for the stairs, taking them two at a time. He'd seen Tyree go up, followed shortly after by Delia, and half expected the sound of a ruckus. But all was quiet. He hoped that meant Corie was already out of the bedroom or had managed to hide.

He didn't know which room was the master bedroom, but saw that all the bedrooms were open, showing off elegantly covered, pillow-mounded beds, except for one. That had to be it. When he heard screams coming from inside, he was sure.

He burst through the door without hesitation to find Delia Tyree locked in mortal combat with Corie on the carpet.

Cyrus Tyree tried to stop them but was upended as they rolled into him, screaming.

At that point Ben had simply had it with everybody. He hauled Corie to her feet with one hand and Delia Tyree with the other.

"The jewelry is all in the drawer," Corie said in a breathless voice, her hair in her face. "Except for the necklace we have."

Tyree smirked at her. "So you *did* keep something."

"No, I didn't. Someone sent me one of the diamond necklaces."

"What?" he demanded. "Sent it to you? I don't understand."

"Oh, Cyrus!" Delia said with a growl. She sank onto the edge of the bed. "You *never* understand. I had Danny from Corbett's put it in her home so she'd get caught with it."

"Danny?"

She shrugged, studied her nails. "He does odd jobs for me."

Tyree remained confused.

"So she'd go to *jail*."

He clearly still didn't get it.

"Because Robert hates it that she thinks she's better than he is, and he'll forever wear the scar that proves it's true."

"You did that for *Pimental*?"

"Yes, but it didn't go according to plan. Your friend Bigelow runs such a dinky police department that even though she reported the break-in, the officer who responded never noticed the necklace. So I called in an anonymous tip and apparently the dispatcher missed it."

"No, she didn't." Gil Bigelow, Chris Norton and several members of the Corpus Christi police department walked into the room.

"We got the message," Bigelow said, "but I knew you had your jewelry back so I ignored it."

Corie turned to him in surprise. "How did you know?"

"Mrs. Tyree told Mr. Pimental. He told me."

"And you let him get away with scamming the insurance company?" Corie challenged.

Bigelow made a face. "Insurance companies run their own scams."

"I took pictures of everything," Corie told Ben, pointing to the open drawer, "and I forwarded them to Chris."

Jack burst into the room, Grady right behind him. They relaxed at the sight of the Corpus Christi police.

"I told you he wouldn't need backup," Grady said to Jack.

"You did," Jack replied, "but he has a terrible propensity for getting shot. I was sure he'd need us."

Corie was explaining the Tyrees' scam to the police. It appeared that they were familiar with the case.

"You say you took pictures?" one of the officers asked. "Are you from the insurance company?"

Corie opened her mouth to explain that she'd originally stolen the jewelry and wanted to prove she'd returned it, but Chris Norton spoke first, holding up his cell phone.

"I've got the pictures right here," he said. "She told me her suspicions about the case when I investigated a break-in at her home."

He went on to tell them about the planted

necklace. "Chief Bigelow, being Mr. Tyree's friend, knew the jewelry had been returned to the Tyrees, so we teamed up with Miss Ochoa and her boyfriend to prove it."

The officer narrowed his glance. "That's a little unorthodox."

Chris shrugged. "It's Querida police work."

Corie smiled gratefully at Chris. She guessed he'd had a discussion with Bigelow because the chief seemed willing to let him talk.

Ben told the officers that the county sheriff had Pimental in custody and could fill them in on more of the activities, specifically mentioning Cyrus's father's will. One of the officers took down their contact information, explaining they'd have to answer questions.

Everything in the velvet box was poured into a plastic evidence bag. Corie gave them the necklace to add to it.

The officers led the Tyrees away, Bigelow and Norton following, though Chris turned back to give Corie a grateful smile.

Jack gathered Ben and Corie to him when they were alone. "Thank God!" he said. "What were you doing with the necklace in your purse, Corie?"

She sighed with relief. "I hoped this was

going to end tonight, and I wanted to be rid of the darn thing."

They started down the stairs. Apparently the sight of their hosts being taken away in handcuffs put a quick end to the party. Guests left in a stream while Walther looked on in confused surprise. Sarah stood beside him, apparently explaining why the four of them had hired on.

"I hope he got payment in advance," Jack whispered to Ben.

"Yeah." Ben grinned. "He still owes us for tonight."

"I DON'T SUPPOSE you want me to drive?" Ben asked Corie as they approached her truck. Jack had taken Sarah and Grady in his rental. "I mean, it's late and you have had a rough evening."

She astonished him by walking around to the passenger side. "I am really tired. Do you mind? I'm sure you're tired, too."

"I don't mind at all."

Corie leaned her head back and closed her eyes as her old truck rumbled along the highway. She was happy, for once in her life, to let someone else be in charge. She was exhausted and she was dealing with the overwhelming realization that she wanted Rosie's fairy tale. Ben and her forever. Soren and Rosie as their children. And more children. She had her own fairy tale.

She rolled her head sideways on the headrest and opened her eyes to look at Ben's profile. He was unusually quiet; his mouth and chin set in hard lines. It was entirely possible she'd ignored him one too many times. He had made it clear he'd like her to stop scaring him to death.

He'd been right. She did treat her life like an extreme sport. How else could she come to terms with it? It had never been like anyone else's life with a shared history, common qualities and similar expectations.

So, what else was there to do but fly in the face of all the cautions and run ahead, flat out, toward…what? She'd never really examined that part. But now it was time. What was she running toward? That was easy. Love. She was madly, deeply in love with Ben. This life was finally going to lead somewhere.

The question was: Did Ben still love her? He'd said he did the other day, but since then she'd ignored his advice and done what she did best—whatever she wanted. Maybe it was time to stop that.

"Do you realize what we've accomplished?" she asked lazily. "We put Pimental away, proved that Tyree did get the jewelry back, and got Teresa her house and property. Our lives are our own again."

BEN THOUGHT ABOUT her question before he answered, considering her words. "Our lives are our own again." *Our own*. That didn't necessarily mean "My life is yours and your life is mine." He'd have liked it better if she'd put it that way. She probably meant "Your life is yours to go home to Oregon, and my life is mine to do whatever I want with like I've always done."

She behaved like a loner only half the time now, so her statement could be open to further interpretation. She'd told him she loved him, though she never thought twice about dismissing his thoughts on anything.

Something had changed her lately. She seemed much less the reckless kid and simply a headstrong woman. Until tonight, when she'd terrified him with her plan to photograph Delia's jewelry to prove she'd gotten it back.

"I know," he said, taking the light and lazy

tone in which she'd asked the question. "We're like a pair of crime fighters ready to retire."

"Castle and Beckett?"

"Boris and Natasha."

She laughed and punched his arm. "Funny, but they were really bad guys. I'm sticking with Castle and Beckett. They're not ready to retire but the principle is the same."

There was a protracted silence.

"Have you heard anything from Cassie yet?" Ben asked.

"No. It's possible whatever scandal she was dealing with is more important at the moment than Jack and I are."

She'd said that easily enough but he'd detected underlying disappointment in her voice.

"Maybe her father hasn't been able to reach her."

"Maybe."

He put a hand out to pat her knee affectionately. "I'm sorry. Wanting to see her must be making you crazy. Not that you're ever completely sane."

"It's okay," she said. "For most of my life, I thought I'd never see either of my siblings again. But now I have Jack and...one day we'll all be together."

"I believe that."

CASSIE TRIED ANOTHER tack to gauge his thoughts. "I've been talking to Teresa about Rosie."

He hesitated a beat. "Yeah?"

"Yes. I'm adopting her."

He looked away from the road for an instant, his eyes catching light from the traffic, their expression indeterminate.

"That's a big step."

"Well, she has this fantasy…"

Before she could tell him about it he said, "It's pretty clear she thinks of you as belonging to her. Or that she wants to belong to you."

She sighed. "I know. I sort of get her, where not a lot of people do. And it breaks my heart that she knows her father just signed off on her. I mean, if he'd do that, it's probably for the best, but it's time for me to step up. Teresa would keep her, of course, the same as Soren, but I think Rosie needs someone's individual attention. She needs a family—even if it's just me."

"So—will you stay here?"

"I'm not sure. I have the job here, which is a definite plus if I'm going to support a child. And Rosie would still be able to see Soren. They act like they hate each other, but that's just kind of a sibling-like thing. Right now, with all the other children gone home, they're anchoring each other. And I can take my on-line classes at night from anywhere."

"Well, if you stay, that might be a problem," he said, focused on the road but looking relaxed.

"What do you mean?"

"I've pretty much decided to take Soren home with *me*."

"No!"

He shot her a quick glance. "You don't think it would work?"

"It would be perfect. I just didn't know you were thinking about it."

His smile faded. "But, if you stay here, he won't be around to help ground Rosie. He'll be in Beggar's Bay with me."

She sighed. "I'll just have to help her see how good that will be for him. She'll be fine. I'll…be fine."

So, SHE WAS STAYING. That pretty much put paid to the question of whether or not she needed him. He watched the road, grateful for the straight stretch home. His brain was thinking about the popular theory that if you loved someone and their hopes and dreams were different than yours, the thing to do to prove *your* love was to let them go.

That went against everything he felt.

He found the lighted parking lot of a small supermarket and pulled off the road.

"What's the matter?" she asked, her tone concerned. "Are you feeling sick?"

He parked under a light, turned off the truck and faced her. "I am," he said. "Sick of this waltzing around between us, sick of not saying what's on my mind, sick of hoping that if I just don't push, you'll come around."

"Come around?"

"Understand what I feel," he clarified, "not just what you want."

She waited for him to continue.

He groaned. "Would you please do me the courtesy of acting like you know what I'm talking about? I love you, you love me. How are we going to make this work?"

She looked a little off balance. He liked that.

"I thought it sort of was working, isn't it?"

"No, it's not!" he declared. "You scare me to death all the time with your free-for-all approach to everything. We argue about it. You even made a concession to being a law-abiding citizen when you told Chris Norton everything, but then you broke into city hall, you came to Tyree's party in disguise, marched up to his bedroom and confronted him—"

"I didn't confront him. He just happened to walk in."

"Well, what did you think would happen when you walked into his bedroom!"

"You're yelling."

"Oh, good. I'm glad you can hear me because that'd be a first."

WHEN JUANITA USED to yell at her, Corie grew calm and quiet. It used to drive her stepmother crazy. It had become her go-to defense in life.

"Ben," she said reasonably, "you seem to think that because you've told me something, I should do it, or if you've warned me against something, I shouldn't do it. That's a little Neanderthal."

He put a hand to his eyes and just held it there for a minute. When he dropped it, his voice was calm. "I don't think that, Corie. But I do believe that when you love someone, you have a responsibility to try to keep yourself safe. If *you* need *me*, I'm here. If I need *you*, you're stealing jewelry, breaking into buildings or cornering criminals..."

She rolled her eyes at that exaggeration.

"Okay, I'm here now," she said, crossing her hands on her lap. "A captive audience. What do you need from me?"

That hand went to his eyes again. "Love," he replied finally. "Loyalty, dedication, passion. Forever."

Put into such clear words, it was unsettling. She opened her mouth and stammered over a reply. She finally said in a frail voice, "That's a lot to give away."

"Damn right," he said. His voice boomed in the small space. "Except that you don't really…give it away. You offer it, it comes back to you, it's nurtured, it grows, it fills the space and pretty soon…it's everything. It's love."

"I love you," she said, putting a hand to his arm. "It just doesn't sound like what I have to give is what you want."

"What do you think I want?"

"Someone who thinks and acts like you do."

"Corie, I don't. I want someone who listens to what I think and respects it, and acts in a way that I can live with. I would do that for you."

She wasn't sure she saw the difference.

When she struggled to stifle a yawn, he conceded. "Maybe we should talk in the morning. When we're not so tired."

"Good idea," she said. He turned the key, backed out of the parking spot and headed for the highway.

She fell asleep on the way home, her hand still on his arm.

# CHAPTER NINETEEN

CORIE LEANED BACK in her chair at Teresa's kitchen table. Everyone but Rosie had gone to a sale at Wolf's Hardware. The house was quiet. She'd researched art schools all morning and concluded that one of the Art Institutes programs would best suit her situation. The tuition was a little steep, but if Jack was still willing to offer help, she'd be happy to accept it, provided he agreed to a repayment plan.

Rosie sat across the table from her, painting frosting onto star-shaped cookies. "Everybody keeps eating cookies," she said. "I didn't think grown-ups liked cookies as much as kids do."

Corie laughed and closed her laptop. "Well, this particular bunch of grown-ups is a lot like little kids. They still like to do fun things and eat sugary stuff. Are you all finished writing your fairy tale?"

Rosie held up the frosted paintbrush while she thought. "Almost done. It's under my pillow."

"Why under your pillow?"

"So the fairy-tale fairy will find it and make it come true."

"Um, I'm not sure there is a fairy-tale fairy." She watched Rosie suspiciously. The child was usually the last one to fall for fanciful benefactors.

"There has to be." Rosie seemed sure of it. "Or else why would they call them *fairy* tales?"

Hmm. Fair point. Rosie seemed without the reserve that usually defined her behavior— particularly since she'd found out about her father. There was an acceptance about her that was both laudable and very sad.

"I have something to ask you," Corie said, pushing her computer aside.

Rosie continued to paint, carefully covering every point on the star. "Yeah?"

"Would you like to come stay with me after Christmas?"

Rosie's head came up, her eyes enormous. Tendrils of hair lay against her forehead and cheeks as she finally set the brush down to concentrate, as an adult would do.

"When would I have to come back?"

"You wouldn't. You'd live with me. Always."

Rosie stared at Corie. Her face crumpled.

Corie put her arms out, inviting her close. She'd seen the little girl cry in sadness before, and in anger, but never in happiness. At least, she hoped it was happiness.

"You mean, in your little house?"

"Yes, probably, to start. Then we might go away somewhere new. What do you think?"

Rosie held her tightly then leaned back to look into her eyes. "What about Soren?"

"Soren's going to stay with Teresa."

"But…he doesn't have a mom and dad, either."

"I know. But he's happy here."

Rosie stayed in Corie's arms for a moment, the sweet sugar-cookie smell surrounding both of them. She sighed and hugged Corie again. "No, thank you," she said and went back to her decorating.

"Okay." Shocked, Corie got up from the table and went to do dishes, trying not to feel bad about herself. She was 0 for 2 so far in the love department. She couldn't snag a husband *or* a daughter.

EVERYONE RETURNED TO Teresa's around lunchtime with three pizzas and several bottles of soda. Teresa sent Ben to the pantry for paper plates and cups. Soren followed him in to show him where they were kept.

"So." Ben reached up to the top shelf and handed down a pack of napkins. "Do you think you'd like to live in a condo, even if there isn't a dog?"

Soren's eyes grew wide as saucers. "Me?"

Ben reached up for plates. "Well, there's only me and you here and I already live in the condo."

"Live with you, you mean?" Soren took a few steps closer, his face pale, clearly needing confirmation.

"Yes," Ben said, the plates in one hand, the other settling on Soren's head. "Two guys together through thick and thin."

A smile broke and there was elation in Soren's face. Then a shadow clouded his eyes. "No Rosie?"

"Ah, no." He didn't want to say too much on the chance Corie hadn't spoken to her yet.

For a minute the boy looked as though he'd been punched. He gave Ben a frail smile, that pallor deepening. "Thanks, but... I can't."

"Why not?"

Soren shrugged. "'Cause. But..." His voice cracked. "That's a really nice thing to think about."

Completely confused, Ben said, "You mean, you're going to think about coming with me?"

Soren's smile quivered. "No. I'm just gonna remember that you asked me."

He walked out of the pantry with the napkins while Ben remained with the plates and a stomach that felt the way Soren looked. Did that mean he didn't want to leave without Rosie? Whom he constantly harassed or was infuriated with?

Well, that confirmed it. Ben must be pretty unlovable if a woman who knew he adored her couldn't love him back—at least, not in the way he needed—and a homeless kid who seemed to like to be around him didn't want to be adopted by him.

Wow. Big-time loser.

LUNCH WAS QUIETER than usual, the children silent. Helen handed each of them a gift she'd bought at Wolf's. Their faces brightened a little then broke into smiles when the torn paper and open boxes revealed snake lights. Soren's was a serious light with a bendable stem that could be wrapped around a neck for hands-free work. Rosie's was pink, the bulb head shaped like a puppy.

Corie smiled at Helen. Every family needed a child-spoiler and Jack's mother was quite the professional.

Over lunch the men talked about the power tools they lusted after but didn't really need. "I'm not in business anymore," Gary said, "and Jack's got all my old tools and some great new stuff."

"I did like that drill and impact driver," Jack said, looking nonchalant. "And it came with free batteries for a year. Hint, hint."

"I liked the thermal-ionic hair dryer, myself," Sarah said, leaning into Jack. "Hint, hint."

"Thermal-ionic?" He looked skeptical. "What does that do?"

"The box says it produces millions of negative ions to make hair healthier and shinier."

"If you were any more beautiful," Jack said, leaning in to plant a kiss on her lips, "I'd go insane."

A communal "Awww!" rose from around the table.

The doorbell pealed. Grady, at the end of the table, pushed Ben down into his chair when he tried to stand. "I'll get it. Takes forever for food to reach my end of the table, anyway. It keeps stopping at Jack."

There was a quiet moment while Corie poured more soda and distributed extra napkins. Everyone heard the front door open then Grady's shocked, "Cassiopeia!"

Jack was out of his chair like a shot, Corie following him, her heart in her throat. She heard a soft, breathless woman's voice say, "Cassidy, actually. Used to be Manning, then... Chapman. I'm sorry I arrived without warning."

Corie and Jack reached the living room, unnoticed by the visitor, just in time to see her rip off a pair of sunglasses with a shaky hand and wrap her arms around Grady's neck. "Jack! I can't believe it! Jack?" Then the young woman collapsed against Grady, completely limp.

"Whoa!" Grady exclaimed, catching her and lifting her in his arms.

"The sofa," Jack directed, standing by to help as Grady placed her among the cushions. Jack bellowed toward the kitchen, "Sarah!"

Corie took the throw off the back of the sofa and covered her. She pulled off Cassie's Manolo Blahnik shoes and held them against her, appreciating the artistry that had gone into them and respecting the price tag. And the fact that they belonged to her *sister*!

Sarah came running and knelt beside Jack at Cassie's head. "What happened? Is this Cassie?"

"Yes," Jack said. "She just collapsed."

Sarah took Cassie's wrist with her index and second fingers on her pulse. "Strong," she said after a minute, putting Cassie's arm at her waist. She pointed to Corie. "Pillows under her feet," she directed.

Corie complied.

"Maybe she's just hungry. You know, models eat next to nothing. Did she fly in?"

Grady went to the porch where Cassie had dropped her bag and purse and brought them inside. "Tags on her luggage," he reported. "From Dublin to New York to McAllen."

"Air travel," Jack said. "She's probably starving."

"I'll warm up some soup."

Corie looked up to see that everyone who had been in the kitchen was now clustered around the sofa. Helen, who had spoken, hurried off, Teresa beside her.

"She's so pretty," Rosie said, coming closer. "She's your sister?"

"Yes," Corie replied. "And Jack's."

The little girl put an arm around Corie's neck. "That's nice. She's not gonna die, is she?"

"No." Corie pulled her closer. "I think she just fainted."

Sarah gently shook Cassie's shoulder, saying her name. She patted her cheek lightly then shook her again.

Cassie moaned, rolled her head fretfully, and opened her eyes. Long, dark lashes fluttered and bright blue eyes turned to Sarah. A frown pleated her forehead.

"You're not Corie."

Sarah patted her hand. "No, I'm Sarah. I'm your sister-in-law. Jack's wife. Here's Jack."

Sarah vacated her place on the edge of the sofa for Jack and shepherded everyone else back to the kitchen.

"Hey, Cassie," Jack said, squatting beside her.

She smiled at him. "Hi," she whispered. "What happened?"

"You collapsed at the door in Grady's arms. We thought maybe you were tired or hungry."

She laughed lightly. "Both. Poor man. I threw my arms around him, thinking he was you, and then I fainted?"

This time Jack laughed. "That's probably the best thing that's ever happened to him.

They'll be talking about it at the station for years."

"The station?"

"Grady and I are cops." He pulled Corie closer. "And look who else is here."

Cassie raised her head and Jack stood to help her sit up. He and Corie sat on either side of her. "Corie!" she said. "I can't believe it! I thought you were both lost to me forever."

"So did I." Corie held her tightly, feeling ribs under her fingertips. "But Jack was determined to reunite us. And here we are."

Cassie freed Corie and turned to Jack. He opened his arms and held his youngest sister while she sobbed.

Corie saw through tear-filled eyes that he wept, too.

"I'm sorry I couldn't call," she said, still holding loosely to Jack and reaching for Corie's hand. "But I've been dodging reporters and…a few other people. Once my father got the news to me, I headed for the airport. I flew to New York in a baseball cap and sunglasses…" She added in an aside, "That was fun to pull off in December. Dad arranged for a helicopter to pick me up and take me to McAllen. I took a cab from there. I can't tell you how good it is to see you."

"You don't have to," Corie said. "We feel the same way. Jack's mom is making you soup. Can you stand?"

Jack helped her to her feet and held on until she felt steady. "I *am* hungry. I boarded the plane without eating and there just wasn't time between flights. I got peanuts on the plane from Dublin, but the military helicopter had nothing. I could eat a mastodon!"

Corie laughed, thinking she looked like a goddess and talked like anybody's best friend. "And keep that body? I don't think so. Come on. Everybody's dying to meet you."

Jack made introductions. When he got to Ben he said, without thinking how it would sound to her, "This is my brother, Ben. Ben, this is my sister Cassidy."

Cassidy looked puzzled. "Your brother?"

"Right. Gary and Helen adopted me. You were probably too small to remember them, but Jack and I were in grade school together and best friends. They took us in the night our mother went to jail. Ben is their natural son."

"Ah. Okay, I've got it. Nice to meet you, Ben."

"And you." Ben gave her a quick hug. Corie noticed that even in bare feet, Cassidy was almost as tall as he was.

They all pushed their chairs together to make room for an extra straight-backed chair Teresa brought in from her office.

Helen put a bowl of soup in front of Cassie. "It's chicken noodle—3the kids love it. Hope that's all right."

"It's wonderful," she said, smiling around the table. "It's so nice to meet you all. You won't mind if I just dig in? I'm starved."

There was general approval then everyone busied themselves with more pizza while asking her questions about her trip.

She answered between spoonfuls of soup, and when she was finished, asked for a piece of pizza.

Corie looked on, thinking that Cassiopeia looked like a long-stemmed rose in a vase of daisies and ferns. She had everyone's rapt attention. They asked shameless questions about her life as a model and a celebrity. Grady even wanted to know about Fabiana Capri, a dark-haired beauty now dating a football player.

"She's as beautiful in person," Cassie replied, "as she is in the eight or nine advertising campaigns she's involved in. She's in great demand. I believe this year she has the cover for the swimsuit edition of *Sports Illustrated*."

A roar rose among the men.

"Are you in it, too?" Sarah asked. "Didn't you do last year's?"

She glanced away for a moment, as if considering what to say and Corie wondered what was behind that.

"No. I'm on a break for a couple of months." She smiled. "Nothing serious, but I'm hiding out for a little while. The press is driving me crazy. Thankfully, I think I got here without anyone on my trail."

"Well, that's good," Jack said, pouring her more soda. "Because we want you all to ourselves for a while."

CASSIDY NAPPED THAT afternoon in Teresa's bed in preparation for Christmas Eve while Corie volunteered herself and Ben to clean up.

"I thought women always cleaned up at family dinners so they could bond over doing dishes," Ben said.

His mother, already at work wiping off the table, snapped him with a towel. "I taught you better than that."

Corie took the towel from Helen. "Thanks," she said. "I've wanted to smack him so many times. You go sit down. Ben and I can manage."

"Of course you can," Jack said, pulling out the extra chair and rearranging the others. "We used paper plates and cups. He always gets the easy jobs."

Corie pushed him toward the door. "Nobody asked you, Jack."

"I'm just sayin'. When it comes to the messy stuff after Christmas dinner, like mashed potatoes and gravy and candied yams and cranberry, it's not going to be my turn on dishes."

Ben rolled his eyes. "You did the same thing when we were kids. I always got spaghetti night and you did ham-and-baked-potato dinners."

Gary caught Jack's arm and pulled him toward the dining room. "Can't you tell they want to talk privately? What's wrong with you?"

"ROSIE DOESN'T WANT to come with me," Corie said, dropping a stack of cups into the plastic bag Ben held for her.

He found that hard to believe. "How come?"

"She didn't say, but it seems to have something to do with Soren. I think she thought I should take him, too."

Ben groaned. "If it makes you feel any better, I was also rejected."

She looked at him in surprise. "You mean Soren said no?"

"Yeah. He asked if Rosie would come, too, and I said no because I knew you were going to talk to her. Then…he said no. I got the impression he really wanted to, but something held him back. I'm wondering if he and Rosie made a deal or something. One kid gets parents, he makes them take the other one, too."

Corie pulled out a chair and sat. She looked depressed. "I don't know what I'd do with a ten-year-old boy. I mean, he's a love in so many ways, but he's strong-willed and needs someone who'd be better at channeling that will in the right direction."

Ben nodded. He sat, too. "What would I do with a little girl who's a cup-half-empty kind of kid? I wouldn't begin to know how to deal with her."

"Actually," Corie said, "she's not quite the cynic she appears to be. She's been working on this fairy tale in which you and I and she and Soren are driving somewhere in your car. A storm comes up and blows us far away where there are no other people. And we stay together as a family. She keeps it under her pillow so that the fairy-tale fairy will grant her wish."

He did his best not to look shocked—not only because Rosie entertained such ideas, but that Corie had told him about it while looking him in the eye, her manner very matter-of-fact.

He dodged. "I've never heard of the fairy-tale fairy."

"There isn't one that I'm aware of, but who'd have thought there'd be a fairy assigned to the collection of teeth? Fairies are a fuzzy area in child mythology."

"True." He looked down, cleared his throat and then looked up at her. "So, how do you feel about that scenario—minus the storm, of course? Would you be able to leave here?"

"I would," she said without even stopping to think about it. "But I'm worried about getting kids involved in something that might not work."

What? "Why wouldn't it work?"

"Because... I grew up to trust myself, to do what I thought I could—or should. But you're always mad at me for it. Like yesterday."

He studied the pugnacious expression on her face. She wanted him to reassure her that he wouldn't question her, that he'd keep his opinions to himself and let her do as she pleased. After the difficult morning, he was disappointed and even a little angry. "Then why are we even having this discussion?" he asked. "If you make no concessions to living like a woman instead of a wild runaway with her hair on fire, then I give nothing, either. The children would be miserable if you and I got together for their sakes and hated it."

He took a deep breath then stood. "Let's face it. It's just not going to be one of those happily-ever-after Christmases. Although you did get your sister back. That's pretty big. I'm happy for you."

Cassie came down the stairs as he spoke, a silky, lavender robe billowing around her. Even tired, she was gorgeous.

"Hi, guys," she said, walking into the kitchen. "Am I in time to help clean up?" She took the bag from Ben before he could reply. "I'll do this. You guys go into the living room and relax. Shoo!"

Corie gave him a look of such…he had to analyze what it was and decided *sorrow* best described it. So…she did love him, but she wasn't giving up anything to keep him?

That wasn't going to work.

"Cassie and I'll finish," Corie said, her voice raspy. "We'll bring coffee out in a little while."

He hesitated.
"Go," she said.
So, he did.

# CHAPTER TWENTY

CORIE AND CASSIDY sat on the love seat watching the children open presents, Jack perched on the back behind them.

"I feel so awful that I don't have gifts for anyone," Cassidy said. "One extra day and I could have done some shopping, but there just wasn't time."

"The fact that you're here is gift enough for us," Jack said. "Why don't you come home to Oregon with the family and me? Corie's going to come so we can all be together to see in the new year."

"I am?" Corie asked.

"You are. I spent all this time getting us together and I'll be darned if we're going to part already. Cassie said she's taking a couple of months off, and you could use a little time, too, couldn't you?"

"I…" She began to decline the invitation.

"Good," he said. "I'll make a few more reser—"

"No," she said forcefully, turning to smile at him. "It'd be lovely, but I don't want to leave Teresa alone."

"Teresa's thinking about going with friends to New York until after the new year."

Corie could have fallen over. That was the first she'd heard of it. "What about Soren and Rosie?"

He frowned. "She seemed to think they were looked after. She told me you were taking Rosie and Ben was adopting Soren."

She stood in distress. "Rosie doesn't want to come with me and Soren doesn't want to go with Ben."

Jack slipped off the love seat and turned to lean both hands on the back, frowning. "Why not? He's crazy about Ben."

"I don't know. I think the kids made a deal or something."

"It was a pinky swear," Cassidy said, turning toward Corie, her bright blue eyes serious.

Corie gasped. "How do *you* know?"

"Soren told me," she said. "He helped me take the garbage out to the shed. They made a deal that they'd only go with either of you as long as you took both of them, and then they'd work on getting you guys together so they'd have two parents. This is family building at its most sophisticated." She spread her hands as though it was obvious. "It's the only way the Palmer Family Fairy Tale is going to work."

"The Palmer Fam—" Corie gasped again. "You've been here all of eight or nine hours and you know more about the kids than I do?"

"What can I say? Little girls love models, and little boys will spill their guts to a sympathetic woman who will listen."

"*I* listened," Corie complained.

"But you're part of the secret, so Soren couldn't tell you." Cassie hunched her shoulders in a gesture of excitement. "So, you and Ben, huh?"

Corie fell against the back of the love seat. "No. I don't think so."

"Why not?"

"It *is* her and Ben," Jack corrected, "but he's too in charge and she's afraid someone else's self-confidence will compromise hers. So they're going to be two lonely people, with a couple of lonely children left in their wake."

Corie put an elbow on the side of the love seat to look into Jack's eyes. "Soren's been with Teresa for a year and a half. She and his father were friends. He'll be fine. And maybe Rosie will get lucky and find wonderful foster parents. Everyone will be fine. I will be fine by myself and so will Ben."

Jack closed his eyes, summoning patience. "Is that all you want out of life? To be *fine*? Don't you want to be fantastic? Don't you want to flourish? For your life to be so filled with love that people will have to cross the street when you walk by to make room?" He tugged at her hair. "You're not going to get that by yourself."

Corie growled and turned to Cassie. "Love converts are so obnoxious. He found Sarah—stole her from Ben, actually—and now he thinks he knows everything."

"I think he's right in this case."

"You do realize—" Corie leaned toward her in mock threat "—that I'm the *older* sister? I'm supposed to give you advice."

Cassie laughed. "And I'll be happy to take advantage of that at birthday time. For now, though, I think you should fix whatever the problem is with you and Ben."

Their attention was reclaimed by Rosie, who had just opened the jacket Corie had made her and put it on. Corie had appliquéd an angel on either side of the front closure. Rosie beamed with delight and threw her arms around Corie.

"I love it! I love it!" Then she straightened, her smile quivering. "I'll send you a picture every time I wear it."

Corie's throat burned.

Across the room Grady, Teresa and all the Palmers were helping Soren with the biggest box of Legos that Corie had ever seen. Ben, uncharacteristically quiet, sorted pieces.

As though he sensed her attention he looked up and, like the words of the old song, their eyes met across the crowded room.

BEN SWORE HE heard the clang of their gazes meeting. She had that independent set to her head and shoulders, that out-of-my-way attitude that defined her. He knew there was softness in her, but she seemed to have hidden it away these past few days.

He wasn't entirely surprised. Just…sad that they couldn't connect in a way that made both of them happy. He was willing to compromise on a few things, but not everything.

He felt bad, too, about the children. He'd told Teresa that he'd keep in touch and if Soren changed his mind, he'd come back for him immediately. Teresa said she had a similar agreement with Corie regarding Rosie.

It was cool, though, to see all the Manning

siblings together on that love seat, to think of everything Jack and Corie had braved to be brother and sister, and to find Cassie, who seemed to be just a sweet woman without Jack's and Corie's demons.

Corie had her siblings now. Maybe she simply didn't need him anymore. He'd have to rethink his feelings on that "if you love something, let it go" theory.

He'd learned a lot in Querida, he realized. All the brave children had taught him a lesson in believing, and even those whose dreams hadn't come true, had taught him that sometimes the best you could do was endure and wait for better times.

Teresa's generosity was a lesson in itself. And… Corie. She'd been an education in accepting that there were some things in life you just couldn't have, no matter how badly you wanted them.

He smiled across the room at her, hoping what he felt for her showed in his face and told her what he couldn't say.

Needing to get away, he gathered up some of the gift wrap littering the floor and wadded it in his hands to throw away in the kitchen.

"Quite a Christmas Eve, huh?" Corie's voice

made him turn. Her hands were full of crumpled wrap. She must have had the same idea.

"Yes," he said, holding the garbage bag open. "I doubt any of us will ever forget it."

"Did I tell you I picked out my classes?"

"No. I'm glad you're doing that. Someday, when Cassidy is modeling your designs, I can say I knew you when."

"Yes," she said, "you did." She seemed uncomfortable. He hated that. He liked to think that his presence provided comfort for her, security. She smiled suddenly. "We're having ham for Christmas dinner," she said, "so Jack's on dishes tomorrow."

"Good," he said. "I'm probably going to be gone, anyway. I have an afternoon flight back to Salem, so I have to get to McAllen early."

"Oh?" She made a small distressed sound.

He found that a little encouraging but not enough.

"You're not going with everybody else?"

He shrugged. "No. I did what I came to do. You're free of Pimental. We proved Tyree scammed the insurance company. Bigelow seems to be turning around, though he may have to answer for a few things. Teresa has her house. Speaking of which, I think it's safe to tell her about it. It'll be a great Christmas present for her."

Her expression brightened just a little. "Great. we'll tell her together."

"No…"

He pulled away, but she caught his arm. "Please, Ben."

"Are you two in here making out when you should be helping me pour champagne?" Teresa teased them over her shoulder as she gathered glasses, then looked into their faces and turned. "What?"

Corie opened her mouth to reply, but her lips trembled. "You tell her," she whispered to Ben.

He patted her shoulder consolingly, feeling a little choked up himself. "This house and property are now yours, Teresa," he said. "It'll take a couple of weeks until you get the legal paperwork, but it's yours."

Teresa stared, alternately smiling and frowning, wanting to believe, but seemingly afraid. "I don't understand."

Corie found her voice. "Kenneth left it to you in his will, but Cyrus altered it to make it look like he inherited everything. We found the paperwork the night we had the altercation with Pimental."

"No more threats of eviction." Ben put an arm around her shoulders. "Though you'll have to fix maintenance issues yourself now. But that should be easy when you get the two years of rent back from Cyrus."

Tears filled Teresa's eyes as she wrapped her arms around Ben, then reached out to draw Corie in. "I can't believe it. It's a miracle."

Ben committed the moment to memory. "It is. It's the season."

Teresa pulled herself together and pointed Ben toward the refrigerator. "Would you get the champagne. I was going to toast the Manning family reunion, and now there's more to be happy about. Corie, can you bring the glasses?"

Ben poured champagne, Corie distributed glasses, and Teresa offered a toast to the Mannings. "I'm giving you Corie on loan," she said, raising her glass to the Palmers. "I'm not giving up my claim on her as her foster mother, but I'm happy to share her." Then she told them about the house and there were cheers and raised glasses again.

While everyone congratulated Teresa, Ben went back to the kitchen. Corie followed him.

"I've been thinking that Cassie will want to stay with you tonight," he said. "I'll bunk with Grady at the B and B. I'll get my things out of your place tonight so that I don't have to disturb you tomorrow."

She looked as though she hated the idea. She dropped her lashes and firmed her lips. When she looked up again, she smiled politely. "That's fine."

"Good." He gave her a quick hug, inhaling that cherry scent of her shampoo, memorizing how small she felt in his arms but how big in spirit she really was. "Grady and I'll be on our way, then. I'll leave my key on your kitchen counter."

"Okay. Good luck, Ben."

"To you, too, Corie."

"I LIKE YOUR SISTERS," Grady said to Ben as they packed up Ben's belongings in Corie's quiet little house. "You know, the sisters that are your brother's sisters but not *your* sisters."

"That joke's getting old." Ben handed Grady his computer case then shouldered his bag. Geez. Now he had two pseudosisters.

He looked around to make sure he hadn't forgotten anything and almost lost it. He remembered the night he'd given Corie the ornament and she'd looked so vulnerable in her appreciation that he'd kissed her, and the night he'd found her sewing. If he closed his eyes, he could still feel her in his arms, the silken strands of her hair in his fingers.

"I'm sorry it didn't work out with you and Corie." Grady watched him worriedly. "She's quite a woman. They're quite a family, actually."

"Yeah," Ben agreed. "I'm glad they have each other."

*Who do I have?* Ben asked himself before the needy, pathetic nature of the question hit him.

"Cheer up. You've got me," Grady said, as though he'd listened in on Ben's thoughts. "I bet you could have her, though, if you told her you love her and promise not to spend your life bossing her around."

Ben turned to his friend in disappointment. "Hey. Doesn't she owe me a little peace of mind? I cheer her self-sufficiency but you can't have a marriage if *everybody's* independent."

"You also can't have a marriage if you let her stay here while you go home."

"I'm not *letting* her stay here. She wants to stay here."

"I don't think she really does."

"How do you know that?"

"I don't absolutely, but she showed me Rosie's fairy tale. Have you read it?"

"No. No one's showed it to *me*."

"Well, I brought it with me. We ready? Let's go back to the B and B."

BEN SAT ON the foot of Grady's bed and read Rosie's fairy tale, noting the title, "The Palmer Family Fairy Tale." His throat closed and his eyes burned.

Corie and Ben were friends.

Rosie and Soren were friends.

Because everybody was friends together, they went to the store for ice cream in Ben's car.

Then a big black cloud came with wind and rain.

Ben's car got sucked up by the wind and he drove across the sky.

They saw chickens and cows but no other people.

Then the storm stopped and Ben's car fell into a tree.

Corie and Ben and Rosie and Soren climbed down the tree but didn't see any other people. They didn't know where they were, just that they were all alone.

So, Corie and Ben got married and made Soren and Rosie their children. And they lived happily ever after.

Ben cleared his throat, touched by the outrageousness of Rosie's thoughts. "How did they get married if there were no other people?"

Grady rolled his eyes. "It's a fairy tale, Palmer. Wake up. All of life is a fairy tale. Or a horror story. Depends on your perspective."

Ben looked at him in surprise. "You're very philosophical all of a sudden."

Grady grinned. "I just met a supermodel. And she fell into my arms. That'll change any man's life."

Ben placed the two sheets of wide-lined paper covered in child's script on the desk and sat in the chair.

"At first, Corie was lost and alone and I was helpful. Now she's got Jack and Cassie and she doesn't need me anymore."

"Oh, come on! Are you sure you're not just worried that you don't know where you fit into that equation? You need her to prove how much she wants you by giving up the woman she's always been?"

Ben got up from the chair, stood uncertainly in the middle of the room, and frowned at Grady. "I thought you were on my side."

"I am. I want you to have her."

"On her terms?"

"Who gives a flying fig about terms? You can work those out as you go."

Ben groaned over his friend's ridiculous notion. "I'll sleep in my car."

"We took *my* car. Yours is still at Teresa's. And your terms would be that when you get annoyed, you leave?"

"Then I'll sleep in *your* car."

Grady tossed him his keys. "You're being juvenile, but go ahead."

OKAY, THIS HAD to be close to rock bottom, Ben thought—Christmas Eve spent in a rental car. He was comfortable for about a minute. Because his legs were too long to stretch out, either in the front seat or the back, he finally moved to the middle of the back and stuck his legs between the two front seats.

That was okay for ten minutes or so.

He got out of the car and sat on the hood and leaned back. The air was cool and sweet, the inky sky filled with a million stars. He remembered that the very close conjunction of Jupiter, Saturn and Mars was believed to be the Star of Bethlehem. Christmas Eve on the hood of a car. Better than inside the car.

He started to count the stars so he didn't have to think about whether or not Grady was right.

CASSIE SAT CROSS-LEGGED on Corie's bed in a pair of pink silk pajamas, brushing her rippling, light blond hair. "Why won't you come to Oregon with us?" she asked. "I'm looking forward to seeing Beggar's Bay and where the guys grew up."

Corie sat on the foot of the bed in her purple sleep shirt, entwining her black hair into a bun. "I went to Jack's wedding when he first found me. It's a wonderful place." She sighed and dropped her hands into her lap. "But I've seen it."

Cassie leaned forward to touch a hand to Corie's knee. "Why don't you just let yourself love Ben? I know your life's been hard and I feel so guilty that mine's been so good. But..."

Corie shook her head. "Guilty? If your life had been awful it wouldn't have made mine any less awful. I'm happy that you've been happy."

"Are you afraid that you won't know what to do with a good life? That you won't know how to be happy?" Cassie smiled. "Because I think Ben could teach you how in a minute."

Corie fell back against the bedspread. "He's already done that. The trouble is that I feel myself slipping away when I'm with him."

"You mean your unhappy self? Because you could do without her."

Corie rolled her eyes at her sister. "I mean my self-sufficient self. I don't want to give her up. What if I need her again?"

"You mean what if your relationship fails?"

"Well…yeah."

Cassie swatted Corie's bare knee. "You're just afraid to put your heart out there. Ben's a doll and you know that. He'll try to boss you around because he wants to protect you, but is that really such a bad thing? Just tell him what you want and listen to what he wants. It's that simple."

Corie looked into Cassie's eyes and saw a shadow there. "How do you know that?"

"Everybody knows that. Do you really want to let him go without finding out what could happen if you told him you love him and want to be with him?"

THIS WAS CRAZY, Corie thought as she drove in the dark, jeans pulled on under her sleep shirt. But by the time she reached the B and B, it seemed less crazy and more…critical to the rest of her life. Her heart was pounding and her breath was coming in short puffs, as though she was doing Lamaze. The birth of a relationship, she thought a little wildly.

She pulled up beside Grady's rental car, leaped out of her truck and ran to the door of the B and B. She put a hand to the knob then pulled it back, wondering what she would say.

"Ben..." She practiced quietly. "I love you and I want to marry you." No. That might frighten him.

"Ben," she tried again, "what do you see in the future for us?" Gross. Completely unimpassioned.

"Hi, Ben. I, uh, have gotten so used to having you in my life that the thought of you being half a continent away just..." What? She groped for the right description of how she felt. A terrible sadness came over her. "Breaks my heart," she said. "Makes my whole world like nighttime." She looked up at the starry sky. "And not a night like tonight, but a night that's stormy and...scary."

Okay. That wasn't bad.

"I don't care that you're bossy. Well, I do, but I can live with it if you promise you'll listen to what I want, try to understand how I feel. You're usually good at that. And I'll try to be less..."

She heard a sound behind her and turned

with a gasp of alarm to see a figure leap off the hood of Grady's car.

"It's me, Corie." Ben's quiet, rumbly voice came out of the darkness, soothing her fear, quickening her heartbeat. "I've been right here while you were talking to the door."

She put her arms out in the dark. They went unerringly around his waist as he pulled her close.

"Oh, Corie," he said, crushing her to him.

She felt the tension in his hands, his heart beating under his shirt, matching the rapid pace of hers.

"I love you so much. I'll do anything you want, except stand by silently while you do things that scare me."

She held tightly to him, feeling her life fit into his. This was where she was supposed to be. The kid who'd had such a hard time finding her niche, belonged here, in Ben Palmer's arms.

"I'll try hard not to do that. I don't have so much to prove anymore. The Manning kids are back together and you love me. Right?"

"Right."

"And speaking of kids..." she said with the barest hesitation. "Are you up to starting our lives together with *two* children?"

"I am." He didn't hesitate. "And if we're all going back to Oregon tomorrow, we'll have to explain it to Teresa, then to them, so we can all go together."

She uttered a sad little gasp for the woman who'd been like a mother to her. What would Teresa do with an empty house?

Ben read her mind. "Maybe Teresa will want to come with us for a visit."

Corie hugged him a little harder for understanding what she felt. "I'll ask her. Jack said she was going to New York with friends for the new year. Funny that she didn't tell me."

"Well, we can extend the invitation. Want to get married New Year's Day? Just the family and us?"

She hesitated, expecting panic to set in, fear to paralyze her. Instead she felt elation, a sense of security, of rightness. She reached up to loop her arms around his neck. "I'd love that. This is my fairy tale come true as well as Rosie's, you know."

"Really." He cupped her head in his hand and leaned down to kiss her. "For me, it's reality come true. More than I ever dreamed for myself."

He held her close and they simply stood together under the starry sky as fairy tale and reality merged into one longed-for miracle.

EVERYONE WAS DELIGHTED by Corie and Ben's engagement. Teresa had made caramel nut rolls for Christmas morning breakfast and Jack and Sarah, Cassie, Grady, Gary and Helen, Ben and Corie, and Teresa talked about what a wonderful Christmas it was.

"Were you really planning to go to New York for New Year's?" Corie asked. "Because you can go. We haven't told the kids yet, but I presume they're going to want to come with us."

Teresa smiled wryly. "That was the plan, but there's been a sudden change."

"What's that?"

"You'll see very soon."

Ben pushed his chair in and caught Corie's hand. He looked out the kitchen window. "Soren and Rosie are just sitting on the swings, talking. Looks like the right time."

Corie couldn't believe how nervous she felt. "What if they've changed their minds," she asked, walking beside him across the yard, "and don't want us?"

He squeezed her hand. "Come on. Who wouldn't want us? We're charming and have it all together. Well, you have some of it together and I had some of it, so..."

He stopped because both children stood slowly off the swings, a sudden, breathless quality in the air around them. They looked at each other, then at Ben and Corie approaching. The longing in their eyes was almost painful to see.

"What happened?" Soren asked, trying to appear cool, unaware that his face had already revealed everything.

"I asked Corie to marry me," Ben replied, "and she said yes."

"Wow." Rosie took her hand and frowned at her bare finger. "You're supposed to give her a ring," she chided Ben.

"Yeah. But it all happened kind of quickly, so there wasn't time. We'll get one in Oregon."

Rosie blinked, uncertainty in her eyes. "Are you going with everybody else tomorrow?"

"Yes." Corie put a hand to Rosie's head and tugged her closer. "You want to come and help me pick it out?"

"You mean...in Oregon?"

"Yes."

Rosie executed a small leap then replied, "Sure."

Soren looked stricken. Ben put an arm around his shoulders. "You want to come along?"

"Yeah." His grin was blinding. "But...how'll we get back?"

"Do you want to *come* back?"

Soren looked afraid to ask, afraid this couldn't be true.

Corie knew how he felt.

"We'd like you and Rosie to stay with us," Ben said, putting an arm around Corie. "It isn't quite as exciting as Rosie's fairy tale about being picked up in a storm, but we want the four of us to be a family. The Palmer family. What do you think?"

Soren pressed his face into Ben's chest and Rosie wrapped her arms around Corie's waist and squealed. "I can't believe it! I don't have to go into the system. Everybody hates the system." She looked up at Ben and Corie. "What is the system, anyway?"

"You don't have to worry about it," Ben said, turning them all back to the house.

Soren dragged the back of his hand across his eyes and held on to Ben. The boy who'd been without a father for so long apparently feeling secure again.

"We should get you guys packed so we'll all be ready to go tomorrow. Okay?" Ben asked.

The children ran ahead of him, Soren shoving Rosie, who yelled in complaint then chased after him.

"I think their peaceful collusion is over," Corie said.

Ben pulled her closer. "That's okay. Ours is going to last forever."

She pinched his waist. "No, it won't. Oh, it'll last, but it won't always be peaceful."

"I'm a cop. I keep the peace."

IN THE HOUSE everyone had left the table, and Teresa stood in the living room with a young woman and two blonde little girls about four and six. Corie shooed Soren and Rosie upstairs to start packing.

As Corie and Ben got closer, Ben realized that Teresa had two new residents. The little girls were beautiful and looked frightened.

"Guys, come and meet Katie and Joanna," Teresa said. "Girls, this is Corie. She used to live here."

Corie squatted to look into their eyes. "You're going to love it here. When you put your things away—" there were tall paper bags at their feet "—I'll show you this cool play set we have in the backyard."

BEN TURNED AT the sound of a commotion behind him. Soren and Rosie were dragging Teresa's ladder toward the tree.

"Hey, hey," he said, intercepting them. "What are you doing?"

"We want to get our ornaments and our chains down." Rosie pointed to her angel tree-topper ornament hanging from the dining room light. "You said we could take them home with us. And we're going home, right?"

Ben had the best feeling. "Right," he said.

Corie came to throw her arms around him. "So am I," she whispered then kissed his ear.

# EPILOGUE

GRADY HATED THE thought of going home. He loved home, but this Christmas, with the Palmers in Texas of all places, had been one of the best in his memory.

Everybody was packed and ready to go, except for Teresa, who was staying with the new children. She'd made caramel nut rolls again this morning as a last hurrah before they all piled into cars to go to the airport in McAllen.

A lot of this trip had felt surreal, most of all the arrival of the supermodel who had thrown her arms around his neck then fainted in his arms. He could live on that memory for a long time. He realized a relationship with such a woman would never work for him. She was too beautiful, too famous, too…too everything. He was suspicious of anything that was too good to be true. Like Celeste. Taking that chance once had been enough.

Everyone sat around the table, having a last cup of coffee for the road, but he was in the living room, rooting through his luggage for his plane ticket.

"Grady!"

He looked up at the sound of his name. Cassidy, peering through the curtains, beckoned him. He still couldn't get used to the sound of his name on the lips of a supermodel.

He went to join her. She grabbed his arm and tugged him out of sight of the window, pulling back the curtain. He looked in astonishment at a caravan of cars and vans with high-tech surveillance equipment on the roofs and the call letters of television stations emblazoned on the sides. Men and women began to ooze out.

"Can you take me to the airport?" she asked urgently, her eyes like a lake in a storm. "Please? You can come with me. You won't have to ride folded up in coach."

"Uh…"

"If we slip out the back I can have a helicopter waiting for us in McAllen. Please, Grady? If I'm photographed now, I'm dead."

Jack wandered out of the kitchen, frowned at what appeared to be their urgent conversation and then noticed the traffic in front of the house. "What's going on?"

"The press found me," Cassidy explained

briefly. "Grady's going to take me out the back and we're going to Oregon by helicopter. Will you cover for me?"

"Uh…of course. Go. I'll keep the reporters busy to buy you some time."

"You're a prince, Jack!" She kissed him quickly and picked her bag out of the lineup of luggage near the stairs, ready for everyone to leave later in the afternoon.

Grady closed his bag, shouldered it and followed her pleading look to the kitchen.

"Jack will explain," she said as she walked around the table to the door. Grady just followed. "I love you all. Thanks for everything, Teresa, and I'll see the rest of you in Oregon."

She blew a kiss. Grady waved into their looks of confusion and led the way to his car.

"Shall I put you in the trunk?" he teased softly as he stowed their bags in it without making any noise.

"My legs are too long," she whispered back. "Do you have a blanket in the car?"

"This is a rental. Are you cold?"

"No. I was going to hide under it. You don't know much about escaping the press, do you?"

He smiled wryly. "Doesn't come up very often in my life. You can have my jacket. It was in the thirties when I left Oregon."

"Perfect." She climbed into the back. He tossed a leather jacket over the seat. As he drove south, he saw the caravan pulling away from the curb van by van and heading north. Jack was as good as his word.

"Yech!" Cassidy exclaimed from under the jacket. "There's a smashed candy bar in your inside pocket!"

"Sorry. But, then, I don't faint from hunger into strangers' arms, either. And stay out of my pockets."

Grady drove like a madman, glancing in the rearview mirror. He had a question of his own.

"When you said, 'If they photograph me now, I'm dead,' did you mean literally?"

\* \* \* \* \*

# LARGER-PRINT BOOKS!

**GET 2 FREE
LARGER-PRINT NOVELS
PLUS 2 FREE
MYSTERY GIFTS**

*Love Inspired*®

## Larger-print novels are now available...

ULP15

# LARGER-PRINT BOOKS!

**GET 2 FREE
LARGER-PRINT NOVELS
PLUS 2 FREE
MYSTERY GIFTS**

*Love Inspired.*
## SUSPENSE
RIVETING INSPIRATIONAL ROMANCE

*Larger-print novels are now available...*

**YES!** Please send me **The Montana Mavericks Collection** in Larger Print. This collection begins with 3 FREE books and 2 FREE gifts (gifts valued at approx. $20.00 retail) in the first shipment, along with the other first 4 books from the collection! If I do not cancel, I will receive 8 monthly shipments until I have the entire 51-book Montana Mavericks collection. I will receive 2 or 3 FREE books in each shipment and I will pay just $4.99 US/ $5.89 CDN for each of the other four books in each shipment, plus $2.99 for shipping and handling per shipment.*If I decide to keep the entire collection, I'll have paid for only 32 books, because 19 books are FREE! I understand that accepting the 3 free books and gifts places me under no obligation to buy anything. I can always return a shipment and cancel at any time. My free books and gifts are mine to keep no matter what I decide.

263 HCN 2404   463 HCN 2404

| Name | (PLEASE PRINT) | |
|---|---|---|
| Address | | Apt. # |
| City | State/Prov. | Zip/Postal Code |

Signature (if under 18, a parent or guardian must sign)

## Mail to the **Reader Service:**
**IN U.S.A.:** P.O. Box 1867, Buffalo, NY 14240-1867
**IN CANADA:** P.O. Box 609, Fort Erie, Ontario L2A 5X3

# LARGER-PRINT BOOKS!
## GET 2 FREE LARGER-PRINT NOVELS PLUS
## 2 FREE GIFTS!

**HARLEQUIN®**

*super romance®*

## More Story...More Romance